JUST CAN'T LET GO

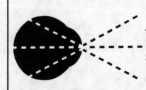

This Large Print Book carries the
Seal of Approval of N.A.V.H.

THE CRYSTAL SERIES, BOOK 2

JUST CAN'T LET GO

MARY B. MORRISON

THORNDIKE PRESS
A part of Gale, Cengage Learning

GALE
CENGAGE Learning·

Farmington Hills, Mich • San Francisco • New York • Waterville, Maine
Meriden, Conn • Mason, Ohio • Chicago

GALE
CENGAGE Learning®

Copyright © 2016 by Mary B. Morrison.
The Crystal Series #2.
Thorndike Press, a part of Gale, Cengage Learning.

LIBRARY OF CONGRESS CATALOGING-IN-PUBLICATION DATA

Names: Morrison, Mary B., author.
Title: Just can't let go / by Mary B. Morrison.
Other titles: Just can not let go
Description: Large print edition. | Waterville, Maine : Thorndike Press, 2016. |
   Series: The crystal series ; #2 | Series: Thorndike Press large print
   African-American
Identifiers: LCCN 2016032762 | ISBN 9781410494337 (hardcover) | ISBN 1410494330
   (hardcover)
Subjects: LCSH: African Americans—Fiction. | Large type books.
Classification: LCC PS3563.O87477 J87 2016 | DDC 813/.54—dc23
LC record available at https://lccn.loc.gov/2016032762

Published in 2016 by arrangement with Dafina Books, an imprint of
Kensington Publishing Corp.

Printed in Mexico
1 2 3 4 5 6 7 20 19 18 17 16

*John Ferguson, rest in peace
brother-in-law
Elester Noel and Joseph Henry Morrison,
my guardian angels*

ACKNOWLEDGMENTS

Praising the Creator for keeping me mentally, spiritually, physically, and financially sound. The life I've been blessed to live for well over a decade, I do not take for granted.

Celebrating sixteen years in the literary industry with Kensington Publishing Corporation is truly a blessing. Steve and Adam Zacharius, you continue to own and operate a publishing empire that proves more successful each day with innovative and cuttingedge ideas. With you, I'm more than an author, I'm family.

I couldn't be happier for my editor and friend, Selena James, on birthing a beautiful baby boy into this world. Congratulations, mommy, also on your engagement.

I've adopted over a thousand (aspiring and published) writers into my circle. April 2015, I started a Facebook group to inspire my fans, family, and friends to write. The name of my group is Mary B. Morrison's

Write a Book in 90 Days Challenge.

Many of you have a story to tell. Some don't know where to start. Others have a difficult time committing to the process. Encouraging you to do something you're passionate about is one of my ways to give back. By the time this book is in print, some of you will also be published authors. I'm looking forward to becoming your fan!

Always cheering the loudest for my son, Jesse Byrd, Jr.; his first novel, *Oiseau: The King Catcher,* was published in 2015. His content is for ages twelve and over. I've said it before and I'll say it again, "God gave me the right child." I continue to pray all great things for Jesse and his beautiful fiancée, Emaan Abbass.

I have amazing siblings: Wayne Morrison, Andrea Morrison, Derrick Morrison, Regina Morrison, Margie Rickerson, and Debra Noel, I love you guys. My in-laws Angela Lewis-Morrison, Dannette Morrison, Roland Johnson, and Desi Rickerson are the best. I appreciate all that each of you has added to our family over the years.

My unmarried husband and true friend, Richard C. Montgomery, with an upstanding man like you in my life, I may never say, "I do."

A special shout-out goes to Kenneth

Todd, Bill Voget, Clarence Randall, and Edward and Tasha Allen. Also to Felicia Polk, Robin Green, Vyllorya A. Evans, Myra Evans, Marilyn Edge, and Patrease Watson for surprising the hell out of me when you guys walked into my dressing room for the production of my stage play, *Single Husbands.* I was moved to tears. I will never forget that moment. Margie Maisonett, the wine basket was right on time, lady. Taliseia and Gregory Charles, one of my favorite couples.

These standouts made *Single Husbands* stage play a huge success: my entire cast, Christal Jordan, owner of Enchanted PR, Kass Ishmel and Briana Dixon of Enchanted PR, my best friend since third grade, Vanessa Ibanitoru, my nephew and personal assistant, Roland Morrison, promoter, Jeremy 'JD' Hill, radio personalities Missy E. Partydoll and Joyce Litel, and photographers AJ Alexander and Jack Manning.

There are so many people I need to express my gratitude to. If your hands and/or heart touch my production, I am eternally grateful.

Kendall Minter, no entertainment lawyer reps like you and I'm blessed to be your client. You've supported me on levels that I can never repay you for. Congratulations on the release of your book, *Understanding and Negotiating 360 Ancillary Rights Deals.*

What's life without social media, baby (pumping both palms toward the sky)! I can never have enough Facebook fans, Twitter, Tumblr, and Instagram followers, and Mc-Donogh 35 Senior High alumni supporters, but I can say, "I love you for supporting me!"

Wishing each of my readers peace and prosperity in abundance. *#Educate #Elevate* Visit me online at www.MaryMorrison .com. Sign up and invite your folks to do the same for my HoneyBuzz newsletter. Join my fan page on Facebook at TheReal MaryB; follow me on Twitter at @maryb morrison and Instagram at @maryhoneyb morrison.

Everything a man does is for sex . . . and more sex.

PROLOGUE: DEVEREAUX

"No! Stop! Stop! Stop! Please! Stop!"

For every "stop" I banged on the script in front of me. I stretched my arms toward heaven, then whispered, "Lord Jesus, please don't let me fling these papers in her face." My fingers curled to fists; my right leg trembled. Refraining from calling her a bitch, I shouted in her direction, "Who in the hell are you?!"

The actress seated across the table from me was not the same woman I'd hired.

Her audition for the role of Ebony Waterhouse was spectacular. Her performance for the pilot was worthy of an Emmy nomination. My prediction upon executing her contract was she'd get better with each taping of my next ten episodes. But she hadn't improved over time. The talent of the person I'd chosen to star as the lead in my new show had disappeared, and the person I was looking at now made an early cancellation seem imminent.

The only thing that kept me from hurling these lines in her direction was a lawsuit. "I swear to you. I'll rewrite this script and kill your ass off in the first episode if I have to." With each word, I pounded my fist on the table. "Do you hear me?" Coffee splattered onto the pages right before several sheets slid to the floor. The actress sprang to her feet.

Pointing at her, I yelled, "Sit! Your ass down!"

Moving in slow motion, her rear end descended until it touched the edge of the leather cushion. She scooted back and leaned forward.

My assistant picked up my mug, raced to craft service's corner of the room, returned with a fistful of napkins, cleaned up the spill, placed a fresh script in front of me, then gathered the pages near my feet.

Exhaling hot air from my mouth, I softly said, "Thanks, Tiera."

"You're welcome, Ms. Crystal." Hesitantly, she asked, "Would you like a fresh cup of coffee?"

"Not now." I held my aching head in my palms, then grunted, "Ugh!"

Tiera sat in the seat next to me. Rolled her chair closer to mine.

Staring at the stranger facing me, I noticed that her high vanilla cheekbones didn't flush to any shade of red. She didn't move. Those big, bright hazel-gray cat-like eyes narrowed to a slither, but she didn't blink. She acted as though she were immortal.

Is this bitch challenging me? If my office wasn't on the second floor, I'd . . . I heaved.

Her fabulous twenty-two-inch wavy blond human hair lace front wig draped her toasted tanned shoulders. She'd literally transformed herself into a million-dollar mannequin.

The black lace halter jumpsuit — suctioned to every curve of her upper body — barely covered her areolas. The pants hem flared above her red Manolo shoes. The Cartier diamond pendant and the six earrings (three two-carat studs in each ear) didn't impress me. All that bling, dazzling in the sunlight that beamed through the glass, added heat to my flaring nostrils.

Silence made me want to pick her ass up, put her in the window, and leave her on display. She wasn't supermodel runway chic when she auditioned, but the new look could significantly increase my ratings. Sexy as she was, this wasn't a goddamn game.

I massaged my shoulder.

The problem was apparent. She was

15

flashy, but she wasn't refined. Hunger didn't loom in her eyes. The taste of a standing ovation from people around the world wasn't on the tip of her tongue. It was on mine and I'd die before I'd swallow.

"West-Léon, out! I have to find someone who really wants to costar with you."

Handsome strolled alongside the conference table. His masculine, chiseled, mouth-watering body inspired me to flip his real name, Leon West, to something more suitable by hyphenating his first with his last and enunciating it with a French accent.

Each of my lead girls had two guys. Ebony would eventually have three. The third, the heartthrob of them all, the one who was sure to make millions of panties wet and some boxer briefs too. I wasn't revealing him until the finale.

Standing in the doorway, West-Léon said, "She's nervous, Devereaux. She'll be okay." Then he exited the room.

For her sake, I hoped West-Léon was right. Now that I'd gotten my big break as creator and executive producer for my television series, *Sophisticated Side Chicks ATL,* she was reading for the first episode like she had a fart lodged in her brain. I had no idea whom I'd really put on payroll.

Disgusted with her staring at me, I pushed

my chair back and stood. "Answer me, Goldie!"

She sat up, adjusted her breasts.

Boom, boom. Boom, boom. Boom, boom.

The blunt force of my pulse thumping nonstop against my temples gave me an instant migraine. I removed my glasses, pressed my thumbs into the sides of my forehead, and then took a deep breath. Slowly, I made my way to her, pulled out the chair with her seated in it.

"Get up," I told her.

Quietly, she elevated herself on her six-inch heels and faced me. I moved so close I felt the rise and fall of her breasts against my collarbone.

Inching back, I lowered my voice. Calmly, I asked again, "Who are you?"

Tears clouded her eyes as her lips tightened.

"Save it for the camera. Answer me."

A few days ago, I'd sat one-on-one with her as I'd done with my entire cast. She told me she was an artist first. Professed that her passion for acting took precedence over everything in her life, except her mother and father. They were natives of and resided in Colombia.

I didn't ask her to, she *told* me, if necessary, she'd place her career before the husband who made her a United States citizen. If she'd had a child, I sensed this woman might sacrifice being a parent to make sure she shared in this grandiose moment of my becoming a trailblazer on a mission to dismiss every double standard men had created to suppress women.

She took one step back. "I'll get it together. I promise. I just need a minute."

This time I took the deepest breath I could. Slowly exhaled a fraction of an ounce of relief. I did not want to embrace her. If I did, good intentions could turn bad. My hands could wrap themselves around her long, narrow neck.

"Goldie, what's wrong? Did somebody die?" I asked, praying there was justification for her behavior.

At this very moment, the silence was deafening. Three of the producers were in the room with the three of us. They'd worked on numerous shows, had IMDB pages filled with notable credits. They'd generously invested their finances with me. The largest contributor loved my female empowerment platform, but their company insisted on remaining a silent partner. They'd come aboard like a knight in shining armor just in time to save our prime-time slot. All I'd witnessed was the miracle of their paper trail. They were relying on me, not the actress I'd hired.

I was not a violent person, but I was ready to strangle Goldie. If I failed, no one would give these two black women a second chance. Our success was dependent upon one another. Tiera, my cast, my set designers, my technical staff, my drivers, wardrobe, hair, makeup artists, and everyone receiving a 1099 were all depending on a paycheck from me.

Atlanta was swarming with talented females who would do practically anything to snatch the role of Ebony Waterhouse. I had four leading ladies. Brea, Misty, and Emerald all read well. I'd saved the best to end our week on a high note, or so I'd thought. We were set to start filming shortly, and I refused to increase my bottom line to give Goldie additional time to get her shit together. My team was not working on the weekend, and I had a fiancé to please and other shows to pen.

Her real name was Goldie Jackson. I started to shut her out for that reason alone. My fiancé, Phoenix, had pleaded for me to give his client a chance. Phoenix had reinvented himself . . . again, boasting how over three hundred film projects had roots in Atlanta last year. Starting a talent consultant firm to advise models and actors on how to break into the industry was a challenging spinoff from his former role as publicist. He had no contracts. A few people he'd taken on never paid him. He'd insisted that Goldie was his golden ticket. I tried to offer him my attorney's assistance with getting legal documents executed, but Phoenix was my proud, broke man.

Since I'd refused to let him get involved directly with my production, I had to support him. His attempt at success was lame. A visionary had a plan. A dreamer had hopes. I gave this Goldie girl a chance based on Phoenix's dream. Now I might be the one fucked.

Staring into her eyes, I said, "You are no longer Goldie Jackson. You are Ebony Waterhouse. You live, eat, breathe, sleep, and shit as Ebony Waterhouse every second of every hour of every day. Until the very last episode is in the can, you are Ebony Waterhouse.

"I want you to think like her. Walk, talk, fuck like her. Close your eyes. Listen to me. When West-Léon comes back in this room, I need you to unleash on him! You are that brilliant bitch who brings it each and every time. No regrets. No apologies. You reign supreme over *all* dicks. Men beg to be yours and you let them crawl to you on their knees. Now sit down and read your part from the top."

Ebony took a deep breath, slowly opened her eyes, and then stared at me. Based on her talent and sexual prowess, we could have the number-one show of all the networks combined. We could top *Empire.*

She stood five eight on those platform heels. Towered three inches above me in my flats. One hundred ten pounds. Tiny waist. Cute banging booty. Perky breasts. Twenty-six years young. She looked hot, but her appearance alone wasn't going to win us anything.

"Time is money, Ebony. My money. My investors' money. Right now, you are a liability. Not an asset. Is there a problem?" I asked, staring back.

Couldn't wait for this day to end so I could go home, indulge in a glass of cabernet, and get me some good Friday night loving.

I was a fiancée, mom of a two-year-old princess, the eldest daughter, and a sister to three siblings. When I wasn't on set or writing (which was almost always), my world revolved around family.

I motioned to Tiera. "Bring me my cell."

I asked Ebony, "Do I need to have my

casting agent find your replacement? If your double showed up to read for you today, get the hell out, and don't either of you come back until you find my character."

My iPhone was in my hand. I'd do it if necessary. I was willing to take a chance on replacing her. I refused to risk letting her drag both of us down.

"Can I have a ten-minute break?" she asked.

"Sure. Hell, take twenty. Thirty max! But if you don't have it together before you step in this room, don't bother coming back."

I didn't get this opportunity being empathetic, or letting anyone — especially men in the industry — walk over me. This was my first shot. I was going to make sure it wasn't my last. I started the stopwatch on my cell.

Excusing myself, I went across the hall into my private office, closed the door, and called my fiancé, Phoenix Watson, the person responsible for this madness.

"Hey, babe. How's it going?" he asked, sounding cheerful.

A portrait of Phoenix, our daughter, and me was in a frame on my desk. Hearing his voice made me smile on the inside, then told him, "Ebony, I don't know what's wrong with her. She was excellent when we filmed the pilot. You saw it. Now she's freezing up on me. I know she's your recommendation, but I might have to replace her."

"You mean, Goldie."

"Ebony Waterhouse is her name from now on. Goldie is dead to me."

He didn't respond.

"You still there?"

"Yeah, babe. Sorry 'bout that. You worry too much. I know this girl. She's your star. She'll be just fine. Maybe I can help out and take Ebony on as a full-time client. She —"

"And do what? Babysit her psycho behind?" I asked, checking the time on my cell. Five minutes and counting. If she was two seconds late getting back in the room, her services were terminated.

Business for Phoenix was getting slower. His checks were dwindling. A lot of models and actors in the ATL had agents or PR reps. They didn't want to pay a consultant to brand them. From escorting them onto the red carpet to getting them on VIP lists, the title "publicist" was one artists preferred.

Phoenix was a great father. With his part-time schedule, and help from his mom, I never had to worry about having Nya dropped off at my office or on set. I was cool with the idea of him managing talent full time in about three to five years when our daughter could communicate better. Not now. There were some things I couldn't put a price on, and not having our daughter be raised by people we didn't know was one of them.

"Dev, let me manage Goldie's, I mean Ebony's, career. I'll keep her focused. You know actors need a person to keep them from slipping up off set too. Listen, you pay Ebony. She pays me. You don't want to lose her. Realistically, you don't have time to find her replacement. This can work out for everybody, babe. Think about it."

I was thinking about the pros and the cons. It might not be a bad idea to have my man closer to me without putting him on my payroll. His mother was retired. I could pay her to care for Nya full time during the week. Plus, my silent partner made sure Ebony was earning eight hundred thousand this season. I loved Phoenix. I had to trust him and give him this chance.

"Okay," was all I said.

"Babe, that's my mom calling. Let me hit you back."

CHAPTER 1
EBONY

#TGIF #dontneedthisish #iamthatbitch
Backspace on all that except #TGIF. Tacked
on #importantdecision #SSCATL. Never
posted without ending with my hashtag
#iamebonywaterhouse.

Knowing Tiera was hawking my social
media pages, I'd revised my tweet before
posting. She'd definitely alert Devereaux
should a light enough to pass for white
ratchet enough to lead any housewives
series newcomer go #left with a well-
deserved defamatory public announcement.
I was looking #edible for *my* male followers, #glamtothenine for all *my* gurlsquad, so
I posted a selfie to Insta with #bossbitch.
Had to keep things in character until I knew
which direction I was flowing in. 467
retweets in less than sixty seconds. #cool-
beans

Devereaux could hire a zillion Ebonys, but
there was only one #GoldieJackson and she

knew it.

The humidity coated my bare shoulders with moisture while I paced back and forth on Peachtree Street in front of the building where Devereaux's office was located in midtown. To defuse my frustration, I made the sidewalk my runway. I placed my Bluetooth in my ear as I stomped fifty feet demanding my space as others stepped aside. My hair blew in the warm breeze. I rocked the best designer outer and under gear year-round. This was #mylife before #SSCATL. Shorts, skirts, halters, blazers, pants, coats, corsets. Black was my favorite color, but I wasn't a #OliviaPope bland hue type of chick. Didn't care too much for the spot her a mile away #rainbowshine either.

I held the button on my iPhone, commanded Siri to, "Call BJ."

People continuously moved out of my way. Pivoting to retrace my steps, I noticed men #hawking my ass, women admiring my diamonds. I smiled, kept strolling. Two-Faced Melted Strawberry liquefied lipstick was my usual.

Most days I had a destination when I left house number one. Sometimes it was to go to house number two. Was seldom sure where I'd end up after dark. T.I.'s Scales 925. Ritz. Taboo 2. Intercontinental. Pin

Ups. Mandarin. Lips. With my side. With my main. With my husband.

This celebrity thing was really happening overnight. What if I couldn't handle the #fame? It was ten thirty in the morning, already seventy degrees on this gorgeous summer day.

My hubby answered, "Aren't you supposed to be working? Everything okay?"

I hadn't had a requirement to report on a regular since I'd said I do. His inquiry was legit. A few people spoke to me. I nodded. Kept moving.

"I don't know if I can do this show."

"Honey, this is your fresh start. Give it a chance," Buster said. "This is the big break you've dreamt of. You're just a little nervous, that's all. You'll be fine. Big daddy has spoiled his Colombian angel, but it's time to spread your wings. I'm not going to let you fail. You need me to fly in from New York? I can make it to Atlanta by six this evening. All you have to do is say yes."

"Not yet. Maybe. I'll text you in an hour."

I tweeted, #ilovemyman #iamebonywaterhouse.

Had to keep posts general when it came to dicks. That way they all thought it was intended for them. My man was whatever guy I wanted at the time. 843 retweets and counting.

I'd done well for myself. Lied about being in law school until I snagged and married a seventy-one-year-old (well, he was sixty-nine at that time) millionaire whom I seldom saw. Tired of the young broke lames, lots of ATL females were hitching to much older men with money.

We owned a home in Long Island where he stayed. The house my ex-sugar daddy bought before I got married that I'd told Buster I'd sold was in Brookhaven a few blocks from Devereaux's. The six-thousand-square-foot home in Conyers had an indoor pool and a natural lake as our backyard. Our vacation proprieties were in Hawaii and Paris. Buster got what he wanted, a pretend husband in New York and me, his real trophy wife in Atlanta. I had no complaints. I was #wellkept.

Early in my relationship with Buster he'd told me, "If you keep your mouth shut, I'll take care of you."

That was a #donedeal.

On the real, the compensation for my role was sweet. Straight up, my lifestyle wouldn't change if I went to the garage, got in my black-on-black Benz with the tinted windows, and drove off with my personal tags that read, #AYMSSIK, which meant kiss my ass.

All females outside my ATL circle were haters. That was how I had to regard those #jealousbitches like Devereaux's sister Alexis. She was pimpin' on the peasant stroll. Policing her stripper gurl, or should I say, ex-gurl, Chanel every night at Pin Ups. Only thing Alexis and I had in common was spending other people's money.

Bills, I'd never seen one since my first date with Buster. My husband, I sexed him when he wanted, but he preferred to watch me spread for other men. Whenever we saw each other he'd play with my pussy, tits, and finger-fuck me until I came really hard. He had his life. I had mine. He didn't question me. I gave the same #respect.

I responded, "I always need you."

My husband was my biggest supporter. That was why I'd called him. My family in Colombia trashed me for being a gold digger. Now they were trying to come up on my coins. My ass was never wetter than my wallet.

"What's really bothering you, sweetheart?" he asked. "Stick with this, Goldie. Of all the professions you've pursued, this is the perfect one. You love being in front of the camera, and God knows it adores you

29

almost as much as I do. Having a career is better than any amount of money I can give you. Take advantage of this opportunity. Just remember. Whatever you do, don't mention anything about me on that show. I'll divorce you and dissolve your trust."

Public humiliation was Buster's biggest fear. He did not want to have people gossiping at his funeral.

"Don't be so defensive, baby. It's not a reality show. She's filming the show *like* it's a reality series."

"Well, make sure she doesn't write me into the script. I'm too old to leave here shamed. People will do anything for ratings. I don't want any parts of the spotlight."

Too late for the nondisclosure. Before I auditioned, I told Devereaux I was married, knowing that would allow her not to view my business relationship with Phoenix as a threat. I didn't tell her BJ's initials or his name. The rock on my finger was the real proof.

Our marriage has always been private. Buster Jackson felt the less people knew about our personal lives, the fewer problems we'd have.

Sucking in my lips, I became quiet. Stopped walking. Stared at the ground. The way Devereaux wrote the script was like she was writing my life story. Couldn't tell my man half the things in the script indirectly applied to him, to us. #Coincidental. Soon I'd have to give him a heads-up, bail on this series now, or risk getting served divorce papers.

Busta was right. I did love this role. Couldn't afford to jeopardize my financial security on either end. Just didn't know how to be that bitch Devereaux wanted without risking becoming homeless again.

In the script, I was secretly married to an Italian tycoon. I was enjoying perpetrating the single life in the United States, but I wasn't a citizen. Unbeknownst to my husband, I was the side chick to two men — one married, one engaged: West-Léon and Travis. The finale was going to shake things up when the sexiest Italian man in film landed on American soil to take me back to his home in Italy.

Phoenix Watson's name registered on my cell.

"I've got to take this call, baby."

"You're a star, Goldie. Own it, sweetheart. I want you to be happy. Call me when you're done. I'll fly in and take you to Chops for dinner tonight. I'm proud of —"

"Thanks, BJ. Gotta go."

Touching the end call/accept call image

31

on my iPhone, I didn't want Phoenix's call to go to voice mail. Obviously, Devereaux had called him since he was the one who referred me to her.

I answered, "Hey, babe. What's up?"

"I got some good news," he said.

"I wish I could say the same. You must've not spoken with Devereaux. She's pissed at me."

"Dev is going to let me manage you."

"Are you serious, nigga?!" Lowering my voice, I hissed, "I can't let you do that ish."

"You worry too much. If you fail, I fail. If you don't get back on track, Dev will never accept another one of my clients. Branding is what you need, Goldie. Dev is providing the platform for you to become a red carpet celebrity overnight. I want to make you the biggest star on television, get you major roles in films, commercial endorsements, all of that. They will beg you for appearances. I'm talking about branding you as Ebony Waterhouse. You are the woman everybody (men and women) is going to fall in love with. I'm going to manage you and that's final," Phoenix insisted.

"I don't need you. I'm good."

"Haven't I taken care of you?"

"You have."

"Well, I need you to do the same for me.

Don't you see if this works out, I'll become the go-to man for branding the potential A-list. For a measly five grand I helped you get that eight-hundred-thousand-dollar paycheck. The least you can do is help me pad my pockets."

I nodded. "Fine, Phoenix. Fine."

"Well, all right. I got this. I'm officially your manager now. Think I'll rename my company Phoenix Stars Branding and Imaging Corporation."

It wasn't the manager title I was worried about. "What if Devereaux finds out we've been fucking for years?"

"I got this. I told you Dev has daddy issues. She doesn't even know the dude. On her birth certificate her father is listed as unknown. There's no way she's going to let our daughter grow up without my being in the house. You keep making love to me and let me take care of Dev."

Shaking my head, I glanced at my phone. "Oh, shit! I gotta go. I'ma see you tonight?"

"You know it," he said. "Soon as I'm done taking care of the home front, I'll be over." I could hear in his tone that there was a smile on his face.

Oh, damn! Buster said he was flying in. "Wait, I need to go over these lines tonight. Come by tomorrow."

Joy turned to disappointment in his voice when Phoenix said, "Cool."

We never ended a conversation by saying bye. I whispered, "I love you, my babe." I contemplated going to the garage, getting in my car, going home, and leaving this opportunity behind. That was the respectable thing to do for Buster, myself, Phoenix, and Dev.

Softly, he said, "I love you, too, my babe."

With less than a minute to make the biggest decision of my career, I didn't want to be a second late if I were going back into that reading room.

CHAPTER 2
ALEXIS

The valet attendant at T.I.'s Scales 925 opened the door to the white convertible Lexus my fiancé, James Wilcox, gifted me. I stepped out modeling my five-inch red Louboutin pumps, a diamond anklet, and a silky salmon-colored dress that barely covered my bootylicious buns. The newest Michael Kors purse dangled on my forearm.

My engagement ring was where it belonged. At home. In the black box it came in. Inside my drawer. All the way to the back. For what it was worth, James could have it back and ship it to his side piece in LA. The ice my ex-girlfriend, Chanel, gave me was in my purse. Missing her, I dug into my bag, put her ring on the thin twenty-four-inch chain, then wore it around my neck. Legally I could say I do to either of them.

I wasn't here to meet James or Chanel. I needed to talk heart-to-heart with my brother.

I took my ticket, told the tall, handsome, blond-haired guy, "Thanks," and then strutted up the sidewalk and into the front entrance.

The scene was popping off, as usual.

A lot happened to me twelve weeks ago that I couldn't shake. My life was one big lie. Hell, I was so good at deceiving people I didn't know what to believe myself, especially when it came to love. Being in college was the main thing that kept me from going insane. Dreading that summer break was here. Non-fam who rubbed me wrong could get their ass kicked. Wish I'd never begged my mother to help me find my father. Biggest mistake of my life.

Taking one class would've kept me partially occupied. Too late to enroll. Shouldn't blame my fiancé, my ex-girlfriend, my mother, or my brother for my dilemma.

I stood in dining area number one; fluffed my dress. I stared at the round, pale man cracking chicken bones with his teeth. He gazed at the flat screen television in front of him. I looked around for my brother; he wasn't in this section.

The choices I'd made three months ago had gotten me in this horrible situation. I shook my hands as though they were dripping wet recalling the way I'd leaned on my brother's stovetop, let him penetrate me from behind until he came inside of me. That hadn't seemed like a bad idea at the time, when I had no idea my father was his father, too. Around that incident on a different day, one Saturday morning I'd pulled down his pants in my mom's kitchen, then sucked him off in sixty seconds. Brother or not, he was undeniably hot.

Gliding up the staircase to the second floor, I strolled to the end of this dining room. He wasn't in here. I could've texted. Would rather wait. Didn't want a disappointing, can't make it response or a request for a rain check. I'd gotten enough rejection from James lately.

I asked my brother to meet me here. Desperately, I needed someone to talk with. Someone who was just like me and wouldn't judge me. That eliminated my sisters Devereaux, Sandara, especially Mercedes. Confiding in my mom wasn't happening since her man was my newly discovered biological brother. Shit was complicated. It was best for me not to speak to my mom yet.

Skimming the crowded room buzzing with chatter, I didn't see him anywhere, but as usual, lots of eyes were on me. I went to the rooftop. A few people were doing hookah.

Inhaling the fresh air, I gazed out over midtown, then rode the elevator back to the first floor. This place, famous for its shrimp and grits, stayed open until three in the morning. Checking my cell, I saw it was 1:01 a.m. People were drinking, laughing, talking over one another.

One man held up an empty glass, then shouted to the mixologist, "Hey, buddy, put a round on my tab for me and my new friends here!"

I sighed, rolled my eyes at him. Why was he so damn loud and happy? I hated jolly attention whores.

En route to the restroom, a guy seated at the bar grabbed my hand. "Hey, baby. Let me buy you whatever you want."

From the shoes on his feet, to his jacked-up fingernails, to the gray hairs sprouting out of his wide nostrils, he couldn't afford me. If he'd looked at my face instead of gawking at my ass, he would've seen I was already annoyed. I snatched my arm away, stared down at him. "Bitch, don't you ever touch me again in your life." Scales was too upscale not to have a dress code.

He leaned back. "Bitch?" His brows grew closer together.

I didn't give a fuck what he thought; he'd

heard me correctly. He should drop the defense. He wasn't offended when he violated me. I hated the disrespectful shit men did. He didn't know me. That fool also didn't know I had my fully loaded forty in my purse, but if he touched me again, everybody up in here would find out. Some other woman might find his offering (probably a cocktail not a house) flattering. Not Alexis Crystal.

I had a fifty-thousand-dollar car outside. Registered in my name and paid for by James. The balance on my college tuition was zero thanks to James. Rent. Paid in full every month by my gurl or my guy. Now that Chanel was my ex-gurl, I'd have to be nicer to James, but I wasn't putting his ring back on 'til he ditched his side. Normally, this time of the morning I'd be at Pin Ups waiting for Chanel to finish stripping; then I'd empty her money bag into my oversized purse. Depending on how my conversation with Spencer went when he arrived, I might drop by the club on my way home.

Maybe I could convince my sister Devereaux to cast me in *Sophisticated Side Chicks ATL*. Outside of having a super-sexy hourglass frame with a big butt and huge tits, I didn't know what Devereaux saw in gold-digging Goldie Jackson. Lucky bitch came up on gay ass Buster. She thought that shit was a secret. My hair stylist, Marcus Darlin, knew all of his clients' business. Acting had to be Goldie's passion the way she kept her husband's beard manicured. Her personal life seemed dazzled with materials, but that bitch was boring. Maybe I'd befriend her. Set her ass up. Take her spot. Devereaux knew I should've been Ebony Waterhouse, but she didn't want to hire family.

A couple got up from a table behind me. Maybe that jerk who'd touched my hand had done me the favor of my not having made it to the restroom. I sat on the stool facing the exit, leaned back against the chair, crossed my legs, swung my foot back and forth waiting for Spencer to arrive.

Say what? Straightening my spine, this could be my lucky day. Phoenix and Goldie entered arm in arm, side by side. I captured a few photos with my cell, then watched them. No doubt. They appeared booed up. I couldn't believe I had pictures of Mercedes's husband, Benjamin, cheating and now Phoenix. I could be that bitch to expose these trifling pretenders.

Stirring up shit in both of my sisters' households was not my intent. Okay, yes it was. My life was screwed. Theirs were too. They just didn't know it. I texted a pic of

Phoenix to Mercedes knowing she'd show it to Devereaux. To level the situation, I sent Devereaux a picture that I'd taken of Benjamin out on a date at Houston's restaurant months ago. I might snag my role sooner than I'd expected.

My brother was a twenty-seven-year-old in heat born February 17. I was a year younger than he, July 28, Leo. My vagina was always turnt up. Being with child made me hornier. I could tell the moment I saw Spencer working behind the bar at the Cheesecake Factory on Lenox Road pouring my mother a birthday drink that he had a big dick that I wanted to ride. I didn't care that it was my mother's fiftieth, or that Spencer was interested in her. He was hot for me. I'd admit, I didn't care about a lot of people or things. I was out to get mine all the time.

Didn't believe my mom would go all the way with a man almost half her age when she'd let a sixty-year-old married man move in with her. Guess she caught a break when Fortune suffered a heart attack and died the day after she stepped over the hill. His death was worth celebrating. No one missed his broke ass. Trifling men like dude at the bar should never get laid, but there were always females like my sister Sandara who'd lay with the lames, have their babies, then bitch about what the daddies didn't do for their kids.

Whatever.

At least I can no longer say I didn't know my father. Now that I knew the truth, I didn't give a fuck about his old deadbeat decrepit ass. His tired one foot in the grave, high blood pressure, bent over behind with gout in both feet was calling every day begging to see me. My father was a stranger to me. Having met him hadn't changed that situation.

I smiled. A half smile as my brother entered the bar. Noticed Phoenix and Goldie were seated at a booth up front. Spencer was six feet two. Had them light brown bedroom eyes and full lips. Slim, sexy, 180 with that creamy milk chocolate complexion. I liked his hair trimmed low; preferred those shoulder-length locks he'd recently cut off, though. Told me the energy in his dreads wasn't the same after knowing he'd sexed his sister.

Female heads turned toward him. If they knew he had those indentions in his lower abs that curved toward his inner thighs, a big dick that hooked to his left . . . *Alexis, that's your blood!*

I could've waved at Spencer, but decided

to check my face in my compact mirror while letting the ladies enjoy his view.

I didn't believe in regrets, but that was one good dick I sure 'nuff should've passed on.

Chapter 3
Spencer

Ah, yeah. Inhaling slow and long, the aroma of chicken and waffles greeted me the second I opened the door. I spotted her right away. I swore that woman never took a holiday from ultra sexy.

Vinyl-covered cushioned stools lined the bar. This was my favorite joint. Knew lots of shit like how men approach dudes, hook up, then leave together. What they did wasn't my thing or my business. The food and hospitality kept me coming back.

Wooden high tables on the perimeter. Dining-height seats in the front, private cigar lounge upstairs. My man Tom was mixing. I rubbed my palms together. That was what was up.

Should've known there was something beyond decadent about Alexis the moment she tilted her sweet chocolate indulgent ass in my direction at the Cheesecake Factory. Damn. Sidetrack. Her mama's number-one

44

dessert was our Godiva.

Alexis was that female version of me. Our mannerisms and mental outlook on sex, love, life, and situations made us twins at heart. Wish I would've known she was my sister, man. Yeah, a brotha got dick control issues, but I'd never get it in with family. If we didn't share DNA, my "D" might be in her "A" before sunrise.

Spence, dude. That's kinship, nigga. Squash the thoughts, bruh. My doggie-dog territorial got-to-bone the baddest babes was another reason my boy LB was gonna flip when he found out the whole truth about my sexing Alexis.

I watched her check her hair and makeup; her blemish-free, smooth skin was just like her, flawless. Bronze lipstick covered those full puckers with that dimple in the middle of her bottom lip. Her long jet-black wavy hair flowed to her breasts below where I recalled her areolas were. She stared in the mirror. I smiled, nodded my approval.

A feline stood up from her seat at a booth, diverting my attention. Damn! Shorty was nice. Black lace catsuit. A half-dozen studs lit up her ears. That necklace couldn't be real else she'd have security nearby. Whoever dude was at the table she'd left, nigga was crazy. A woman that fine, I'd have to go in the restroom and watch her piss. Sleep with one eye open to make sure no other man slipped into her dreams. She strolled toward me. I waited for her to get within my three feet of space.

"You real chill," I said, giving her a comp.

"Thanks, handsome." She pivoted, strutted real slow in Alexis's direction. Wait. So she'd only come this way for my reaction? I followed her to get a close-up on that outrageous booty and tight frame. Shorty's hypnotic opened my third eye.

"What's up, Alexis?" she said to my sister, not waiting for or getting a response.

Finding out Alexis and I were siblings made it easy for me to tell my woman — her mother — the truth about checking out of her spot at a wee hour. *My sister needs me.* What was Blake going to say? *At this time of the morning?* Or, *You can't go.*

The latter would've never settled on her taste buds. I'd told Blake the night I'd met her, I was legal. A real man didn't need permission. He gave his woman respect . . . not control. Dude at the bar trailed me up and down with a mean stare. I was already knowing. He'd hit on my sister and she'd checked his hairy nose ass. I returned dude the favor, then stood in front of Alexis wondering how she knew shorty.

"I'm glad you could steal away for a few," she said. "I'll try not to keep you past curfew."

"Whatever, man."

Standing, she parted her arms for a hug. Her Viva La Juicy perfume made being close to her sweeter. "I couldn't sleep. Thanks for meeting me."

"No prob," I said, wrapping my arms around her bare shoulders. I held on a few secs to piss off the dude behind me. Letting go, I hoped Shorty would sweep back by. Stepped back. A lingering view of Alexis's fit, I had to shake my head. For sho I was the envy of every man in this joint, especially fat boy behind me. So was bruh who was seated up front waiting on Shorty.

Giving attention to my sister, I told her, "You look nice."

Softly, she answered, "Thanks," all provocative and shit.

Felt my third eye shut. Good boy, I thought. Shaking my head again, I sat across from Alexis. "Who would've thunketh? You my lil sis." I had to say that ish to keep my dick in alignment. Fam did not fuck fam under any circum— glad I was all cised up.

"Oh, so now I'm lil sis, huh?"

"For the rest of our lives. Yup. But I still can't believe this shit. Then again," I told her, "I can. Our dad is that doggish ho. You ordered yet?"

She shook her head.

"You hungry?" I didn't bother picking up the menu. I never strayed from my true and tried.

She nodded.

My eyes shifted, lingered on Shorty as she swayed that blond hair and those magnificent hips at the same time. She winked at me, then said to my sis, "Keep rising to the top, Lex," and kept it moving.

Had to ask. "Y'all familiar? Classmates? What's the affiliation with Shorty?"

The last time Alexis was this quiet she was in my arms. We were on my balcony chilling, listening to the poolside waterfall. She'd confided in me about not knowing her dad. How bad she wanted to find him. Her mom listing her father as "unknown" on her birth certificate. That was the ultimate illegit. I believed that caused Alexis to hate. Her mom. Our dad. Men. Women. Maybe even herself. I wasn't sure of her internal but on the surface, Alexis was beautiful.

"Cool. I'm hungry too," I said, breaking the silence. "You wanna share the chicken wings?"

Smiling, she said, "You know it, chick."

Mirroring her expression, I said, "That's

48

my lil sis."

Finding out we were related didn't shake me. I was pissed off at my dad, not my sister. Felt natural like when I'd met my ex-girlfriend Charlotte. Talking for hours on the phone. Hanging out for days, never getting tired of being with her. I missed Charlotte's crazy ass.

"Okay, you can chill on that. I'm only a year younger than you, my brother."

True that. She was twenty-six, didn't need me or any other man's protection, but I'd be there for her from now on. This was cool. Letting a female I'd never sex again lean on me made me feel needed. No ulterior. My heart opened. Made space for Alexis. I didn't have to play "d" or keep my guard up. A sister in my life was essential.

Needed my sis to be there for me as well. I'd seen how Alexis got down the day my ex-girl showed up at my spot without an invite. Alexis had done the same cruising to my unit like Charlotte. Alexis's apartment was in the same complex but spaced like East coast, West side. When Charlotte accosted Alexis, then called Blake a bitch, Alexis slapped Charlotte three, maybe fo' times — I'd lost count — straight in the face, then pulled out her forty.

Snagging the waitress, I ordered Alexis

49

her favorite drink, a mai tai. "A dirty martini for me with three olives." Blake had me on that sippy sip drank. "We're sharing the chicken wings, throw in an order of fries, and that slammin' gumbo. Two orders of that." Looking at Alexis, I asked, "You want a vegetable?"

She twisted her upper lip. Cute.

I told the waitress, "That completes."

"Be right back with your drinks," the waitress said, walking away.

"So what's up with you that this couldn't wait for the sun to rise? Trippin' off of the ole man's desperation to get to know us? I refuse. I hope you haven't punked out on our agreement not to see him again."

She shook her head.

"Good. 'Cause I don't give a fuck about that nig. Beatin' on my mom and shit like she was his punching bag. His punk ass damn near killed both of us. Now he wants to let bygones be." I started moving my head side to side. Felt my jaw tightening.

Clenching my teeth, couldn't say my reasons for despising that nigga was more solid than hers. He knew Alexis was his and he still disowned her. Blake told me about the paternity test he took right after my sister was born. Probably didn't want my mom to find out how big of a whore he

50

really was. And what was his bitch ass point of making me do a DNA and Alexis do another one? I did it so Alexis wouldn't have to go it alone. Secretly, I'd prayed mine would've come back negative. That way I would've had no reservations of beating him down one solid for me and my mom.

I felt my throat tightening, eyes started watering. I blinked a few times. Tucked in my lips. Slid my palm over my nose, then rested my chin in the arch of my hand.

Conner Rogers sent my mother to an early grave. Venus Domino got the courage to leave him when I was ten. If my dad hadn't almost killed me, I think my mom would've stayed with him until he killed her. My mother, the love of my life, the only person who has ever loved me unconditionally protected me when I couldn't fight for myself. She left my dad. Became a self-made millionaire, but I supposed the excruciating memories were etched so deeply she couldn't forget that shit. I had no idea she was suffering in silence.

My mom accidentally overdosed on prescription meds. That was the cause of death on the certificate I had. But I knew it was no fucking accident. She was too Einstein to swallow more than the recommended. All I knew was she left me alone. I'd give back the house and apartment building that were paid in full. I would've never collected on the million-dollar insurance policy if she could've gotten out of that coffin and walked with me. I would've left that check at the altar. Never looked back.

Our drinks arrived in time for me to douse my sorrow. I finished mine before I placed the glass back on the table. Alexis sucked, and sucked, until the ice in her glass was higher than the alcohol.

Looking at my sister, Alexis's tears spilled onto her silk dress, one chasing after another. Guess we were both trying to drown the sadness inside of us. Buoyancy was a muthafucka. Some shit you can never forget. I unrolled the black cloth napkin, handed it to her, then I placed the silver fork, spoon, and knife on the table.

"I don't want to come between you and my mom, but I need you more right now and since you're the only brother I have —"

I interrupted. "That we know of."

"You're right. That we know of," she agreed. Polishing off the rest of her drink, she ordered us another round.

"Sis, I don't know how much longer my arrangement with your mother is going to last. I'm thinking about letting her go. Since I found out my sorry ass father is yours, too, I care a lot for your mom, but it feels weird sometimes . . . you know."

"The sex must be good; otherwise, I know you. You would've moved out of my mom's house by now."

Shorty crossed my mind. Sex with her was probably amazing. Could probably spin her small curvaceous ass on my big dick. Pick her up. Flip her upside down. Eat her pussy while she sucked my dick. Shouldn't think about that when I was discussing my cohabitation arrangement.

"We didn't know we were related. Come on now. You can't hold my being with your mom over my head." I added, "I met her first," then gave a half smile.

Her lips curved but didn't part until she told me, "Whateva, chick."

I hadn't quite moved in or out. My unit was still fully decored. But it was more than just sex with Blake. She was attentive, considerate. Every day we didn't eat out she cooked. She checked on me, not up on my whereabouts like Charlotte used to do. Wondered if my ex had slipped to the ole dude she'd spread for while she was mine. Fuck Charlotte.

Sleeping with my sister's mother . . . I'd done a lot of things with and to females. Continuing the relationship felt as though I was betraying Alexis, but there was genuinely nothing wrong with my relay with Blake.

Staring at me, Sis said, "Nah, we just need a break from yonies."

We both had a way with words. Both often had the same closed-lip smile. I used mine to conceal my thoughts. I laughed. Alexis did too.

"Wild child. How long you been straddling the sexes?" I asked.

"For felines, since I was fourteen. Dicks, fifteen and a half."

We equally had a voracious sexual appetite. Were extremely passionate. Freaks by nature. And we'd both mistreated the people who loved us most. I prayed we'd never hurt each other.

"I'll be your best friend, if you'll be mine," I said. Placing my hand on the table, I opened it.

Unexpectedly Alexis started crying. I moved from my side of the table to hers. Sat on the stool beside her, gave Alexis a firm hug. "I got you, Sis." I meant that.

Sniffling, she said, "I sure hope so, Spencer, because I'm three months' pregnant and the baby might be yours."

That shit threw me all the way left, slamming my conscience into a brick wall. I held her closer. Gave what she'd said more thought. Considered the source. My sis was probably lying. Maybe not about expecting a child, but Alexis was capable of trying to ruin my relationship with her mother.

"I'm here for you, Sis. Of course you're not keeping it? Right?"

I prayed she said no. Being a father was not on my short-term goal's list. Being an uncle-daddy was all kind of foul. For real.

"Whichever way, I'd better decide soon. James," Alexis paused. Stared toward the door. I glanced over my shoulder. My jaw went south. Charlotte was more beautiful than I remembered and I thought that shit was impossible.

Her long blond hair was in those dangling curly twists I loved to play with. Inhaling, I recalled the scent of the Angel perfume she lightly stroked in her hair. She wore a sexy classy red romper with a belt sashed about her waist. The receipt for those come-fuck-me red stilettoes had my name on it. I'd bought them.

Worse part . . . Charlotte looked happy with ole dude.

"Sis, don't trip. I got you. But right now, I gotta go check that nig with my ex."

CHAPTER 4
BLAKE

Where was he?

The break of dawn crept through my vertical blinds. Lying on my side in my bed, I held my churning stomach wondering where was Spencer? Was he okay? Had he gotten into an accident? Held up by an Atlanta police officer? Was he caught drinking and driving?

I prayed not.

Georgia troopers didn't hesitate to issue DUI tickets. The average fine was ten grand. I'd bail him out, but if his privileges were revoked . . . I tried convincing myself that he wasn't between my daughter's legs. He wouldn't do that to me again knowing Alexis was his sister.

Click!

"What was that?"

I sat in the middle of my bed. Stretched my ear toward the entrance of my bedroom. The noise came from one level below.

56

Anxiously, I listened, hoping I'd hear a door close. The next minute was filled with silence.

Must've been the wind whisking tree branches. Leaning over the edge of the mattress, I smiled. My baby was in his pen sound asleep.

Fluffing my pillow, I lay back on my side. Curled my knees to my breasts, then pulled the cover up to my neck. I was cold from the inside out.

If he wasn't doing her, what was he doing with her? Didn't trust either of them when they were together. What was so damn important that he got out of our bed for her? Spasms in my abdomen caused me to roll onto my other side. I balled back into a fetal position.

The time those two got together at his place, the sex (they professed they never had) was probably equally amazing as when Spencer had given me my first squirting orgasm during the consummation of our relationship.

"Shit." Their fucking was my fault. Should've put Conner Rogers on her damn birth certificate.

Touching my clit, I hadn't showered him with my fluids since the day I'd suspected they'd done it. The fact that I knew in my gut they'd both lied about their not having sex with each other probably was the reason my body couldn't totally submit to Spencer anymore.

I checked my cell. No missed anything. Placed it on his side of the bed.

That wench looked me in my eyes. My daughter had said, "Mom, nothing happened. He couldn't get an erection." That child could lie standing on one foot in a six-inch heel on a stack of bibles and never wobble or waver.

Spencer had said, "I tried, but I couldn't do it."

I'd love to believe he had no reason to fabricate a story, but I was seasoned enough to know that when a man cared, he lied. It was only when he had no regard for my feelings that he'd blatantly tell me the truth about sexing another woman and didn't give a damn how I felt afterward.

I pressed the button on my cell, glanced down. I checked his Insta, Twitter, and Facebook pages. No posts. None on Alexis's either.

"Liars." They both were. That I was sure of.

The temperature inside of me started rising. I flipped the covers away from my naked body, jumped out of bed. Perspiration oozed from my pores as I raced to the bathroom. I sat on the toilet. Should've brought my phone with me.

The onset of sweat slithering from every pore gave me a reason to focus on something other than my man not being home. Turning on the water, I'd become accustomed to the midnight and early-morning showers. The cool water made me cold again. I'd deal with the flashes. The alternative, taking hormone replacement therapy drugs, wasn't worth the risk of getting cancer. It was easier to get up than to drench and then change my bedding every day.

I straightened the comforter, sat on the bed.

By chance, if any of what they'd said about Spencer not being able to get an erection was remotely true, instinctively his dick had all the sense not to get hard for Alexis. I believed he was flaccid because they were family. Guess I wanted to . . . it was best not knowing. What difference would it make now?

Standing beside my bed, I looked into the pen. My puppy was buried underneath his cashmere blanket. He wiggled his head out, stared at me. "You are so cute, baby." That little fella brought me pure joy. Whenever I saw, held, or walked him, instantly I felt calm.

Checked my phone, no messages. It was 5:29.

Too early to get ready for work, not enough time to rest well, I lay on my back in my bed. Stared at the ceiling. He said Alexis needed to talk. Didn't take four hours for a conversation.

Spencer hadn't texted since he'd left home. Didn't have the decency to answer any of my calls. I knew I shouldn't have told Alexis who her father was. She met her dad one time, three months ago. Then told me she didn't care to see him ever again. The whole search was pointless. I knew that would be the case, yet I still gave in to her. Everything was always about her!

Shouldn't have had my attorney, Kendall Minter, locate Conner Rogers. I was calling Kendall later today advising he cancel the search for Mercedes's, Devereaux's, and Sandara's dads. I knew who their dads were. Just didn't know where they were. My kids were grown. Let them decide if they want to dig up their dads. There were better investments for my resources. Max for starters.

Men. I knew they weren't all dogs, but I knew even the purest of breeds had doggish tendencies.

Flipping my hand to the air, I said, "Thanks to my giving in to *that* little girl's demand, nobody was happy." *Nobody!*

The day Conner came to my house to meet Alexis, I'd gotten all dressed up to show Conner I'd made it without him. I was the branch president of a major financial institution. Owned a mansion in Buckhead free and clear, drove a white Benz or a fire-engine-red Ferrari wherever I wanted. I'd sent each of my girls to college, had a hefty six figures in the bank, and the day Conner stepped his crippled feet into my house, I had a man twenty-three years my junior living under my roof, sexing me real good.

For once in my life, Blake Crystal had it all.

No one was going to cast shade on my sunshine, not even my flesh and blood.

I exhaled. Checked my cell. No missed anything. I knew that. Wasn't as though I'd heard a tune. I scrolled through old text messages from Spencer.

One that stood out read, The one thing I asked you not to tell anyone, you told a complete stranger. The knots in my stomach returned. The pain was more intense.

From that devastating moment, distrust plagued our beautiful relationship. I'd messed things up. That day when I opened my front door, I was shocked Spencer had overheard me tell my girlfriend about his having been molested by his uncle. I'd broken our bond. Since that day, Spencer hadn't kissed, held, or made love to me the same way, but we were still together. Lots of couples trampled through quicksand and survived to celebrate ten, twenty, sometimes fifty years of being with each other. I was just trying to make it to our first anniversary.

Pressing my palms together, I prayed, "Dear God, please give me patience, understanding, and wisdom. I love this man, Jesus."

Soon I'd have to get up. Get dressed. I wasn't ready. Didn't want to be in bed either.

I said aloud, "Give him time, Blake." Rebuilding our trust was hard for me too. I hadn't forgotten about his ex, Charlotte, calling me a bitch.

Being with Spencer made me feel thirty again. Not in a good way. Those were the days when ten pounds would disappear from my hips and thighs with my constantly worrying about my man while eating very little food.

Racing to the bathroom, I leaned over the toilet, then heaved. Nothing came up. Where was Spencer? Who was he really with? Alexis could be home alone.

I was doing it again. Driving myself crazy with the unknown. No matter how many thoughts crossed my mind, I couldn't make him come home.

I stared in the mirror. My irises were red, lips curved down. "Girl, you look old." I splashed cold water on my face.

Was Spencer penetrating some woman? If he was, did she feel the way I'd felt when his dick was inside of me? Was she a better lover? Did she suck his dick better? That wasn't hard to do. I never enjoyed giving oral. Was she younger? Prettier?

Lifting the sides of my cheeks took ten years off. Maybe I should get Botox.

I knew if Spencer entered this bathroom, wrapped his arms around me, told me, "Baby, I love you," his few words could erase hours of my pain. If he was lying, once he'd penetrate me I'd forgive him.

Tomorrow wasn't promised.

Tears mixed with cold water. I kept washing them away.

I dried my hands, got my phone, texted Alexis, You'd better not have told Spencer about my sexing Billy Blackstone after my fiftieth birthday party!

I meant to backspace to delete the message. Instead, I pressed send. My heart raced and I went into a daze. My screen became a blur.

Again, I worried what would become of my unintended confession that was in print. I was the master of confidentiality, in my professional life. All of my girls had been unusually quiet for the past month or so. Something was going on that my girls didn't want me to know.

I texted Alexis again, You're jealous! You thought Spencer was going to leave me after he found out you're his sister. What you're doing is wrong, little girl!

She was so sure my man was going to bail as she'd said. This inviting him out after midnight — siblings or not — that wasn't happening again. She needed to tend to her man and her woman and put the right ring on the proper finger.

I backspaced, deleting the second message. Wished I could erase the entire night. Start over. Spencer wouldn't have gone out.

Alexis was the only one who'd relentlessly questioned me from the day she could speak in complete sentences. She was the one who always challenged me. Now, for the first time since Spencer had moved in with me, he was not in my bed at the break of dawn.

The sun had started rising.

"Hey, you. Good morning," I said softly, talking to my puppy. I scooped him up with both hands.

I went from having the finest man in Atlanta in my bed to stroking a three-month old Yorkshire terrier that Billy gifted me.

King MaxB was adorable.

For my fiftieth birthday, my eldest daughter, Mercedes, threw me the biggest surprise birthday party I'd ever had. All seven of my siblings came. Their kids. Their kids' kids. To top it off she'd managed to find my first love, Billy.

So much had happened since that affair with Billy, if I could call it that. It was three months ago, that night (and the following morning) when we'd had sex, I had no idea he was married. I gave myself to him to get back at Spencer for not being by my side on one of the most important nights of my life. I was never going to turn fifty again.

My cell in one hand, rubbing Max with my other, it was six in the morning. In an hour I'd have to start getting ready for work. Corporate still hadn't given me my well-deserved promotion from the branch level. I wanted out of the daily responsibilities of operating a branch. If I resigned, what would I do? Maybe I should apply for a lateral banking position at a different institution, then work my way up.

"Hm."

I sat on the side of my bed, placed Max in my lap. Gently touching his back, I dialed Spencer's number. My Yorkie rolled over, spread his legs. Kind of how I'd done for Billy that night, but I'd gotten a lot more than a tummy rub. If Alexis showed Spencer my text, I'd never forgive her.

I smiled until I got Spencer's voice mail. Smooth hang-up. I'll see your missed call.

Calmly, I said, "Yeah, Spencer. I've called you every hour since you've left. I deserve a call back." Then thought, *Don't make me pack your stuff.*

The only thing that kept me from making a hasty decision was this precious, delicate, five-pound baby staring up at me. Max licked my hand three times.

Since Spencer worked the evening shift at the Cheesecake Factory bartending, he watched Max during the day. Calling in would give my supervisor a reason not to promote me.

I placed Max on my bed on his tan cashmere blanket. I got dressed with the intent of going to Spencer's apartment. I undressed. Dressed again. Sat at the foot of my bed, looked at Max. He tilted his head sideways. Stared at me.

66

"I know," I said to him as though he could understand.

I changed into a black pencil skirt, red fitted blazer, and red heels. I phoned my youngest. I'd have to take my puppy to work with me and hide him in my office if Sandara didn't answer. Didn't trust leaving him home alone for nine hours. Didn't have a kennel for him. Probably would never get one. This little guy was too cute to cage. Maybe I should enroll Max in doggie daycare.

"Hey, Mom. You okay?"

Her concern was valid. Normally, I wouldn't call this early. "I'm fine. Spencer's not here and —"

"Oh, yeah. That's right."

"That's right what?"

Sandara sighed, "Nothing, Mom. What is it?"

Oh, it was something I'd address later. "Can you watch Max until I get off from work?"

"When did you start working on Saturdays?"

"Can you watch him or not?"

"Well" — she paused, then said — "of course, Mom. Bring him over. I'll be here. Bye." Sandara ended the call.

I dialed Spencer again. The ringing

stopped. I held my breath. Then I heard Alexis? Arguing? I recognized Charlotte's voice, but what the hell? Increasing the volume on my cell, I pressed the mute button and could not believe my ears. All the back-and-forth shouting sounded as though someone was about to get assaulted.

I heard Spencer say, "Alexis, no!" right before the call ended.

I froze. I couldn't inhale. Exhale. Felt like Alexis, Spencer, and that other woman had stabbed me in my head, my heart, and my back at the same time and Sandara had watched me bleed to death.

Going to work was definitely the smartest decision. Getting in my Ferrari, I prayed my emotions did not override my better judgment and I did not go directly to Spencer's place.

Chapter 5
Spencer

Soon as I heard Charlotte popping off, "Bitch, what do you want?" there was no time for a third wipe to make sure I'd cleaned all the shit off of my ass. I raced out of my bathroom naked.

"Damn. Chill, y'all." My flaccid dick flapped side to side. Wasn't like both of them hadn't seen all of me. I looked at my sister, "Alexis, what are you doing here?"

I hadn't posted up at my apartment since I'd moved in with Blake. Didn't take much for Alexis to detect the lust in my eyes when I saw Charlotte at T.I.'s Scales 925. My sis knew me well.

"I couldn't sleep. Was hoping you'd be home and we could finish our conversation." She scanned Charlotte up and down with her eyes. "Should've known this thirsty bitch would be here."

Charlotte fired right back with, "You couldn't sleep 'cause it's your *pussy* that's

69

tired. Literally!"

"Charlotte. Don't go there." I knew my ex hadn't forgotten the last round when my sister straight punched her out. I'd rather ultimate fight Demetrious Johnson than to get caught up in a mix with these two.

Dipping to my bedroom, I put on a pair of sweats, then I heard: "Yeah, that's right. I said it. You a ho and your old, dried-up mama is a geriatric ho!" Charlotte said.

Fuck the shirt. I tossed it to the floor, ran back to the kitchen area where they were.

Alexis handed me my cell. How'd she get my damn phone? It was in my bedroom on my nightstand. *Wow.*

"Back up off me, Charlotte. I'm being polite. I'm not going to ask you twice," Alexis said.

Charlotte boldly moved closer. "Tell that ho—"

"Alexis, no!"

The light on my screen distracted me. I looked at the caller ID. The seconds were ticking. Blake's birthday photo of her dressed in red looking all fabulous was on my shit. I ended the call. "Who in the fuck answered my phone?" This was what I got for leaving my ex unattended to empty my colon?

"Let me go, you crazy bitch!" Charlotte

70

brought this on herself. If you know a feline isn't mentally stable, you gonna provoke her? Really. I was tired of both of their asses. Wish I could walk away from the insanity.

I put my phone in my pocket. "Alexis. Let her go."

Alexis had both fists locked into Charlotte's hair. "Who's the ho now?! I'ma make you my bitch! That's my mother. Apologize."

Charlotte's fingers were clamped onto Alexis's wrists. She struggled to keep Alexis from pulling harder. Charlotte calling Blake out of her name had little to do with what was going down. My sister and my ex got off on firing off on people. Difference was I'd only witnessed Charlotte opening my cabinets, sweeping all my expensive dishes to the floor. One time she clawed my back like she was auditioning for Mufasa on *The Lion King.* Charlotte went off on me 'cause she knew I'd never hit her.

I grabbed Alexis's forearms. "Sis, please let her go. Charlotte, just try to keep still."

Someone had to remain calm. This was the second time these two had an altercation. I felt bad. The first time I didn't know I was related to Alexis. I'd said Sis to let Charlotte know Alexis wasn't my gurl. Bent over facing the floor, I doubted she'd caught

71

that part.

Last night when I approached Charlotte with her dude, I'd told her to be at my house in an hour. I went to Alexis's, reassured her she had my support. This was serious. This kid's DNA could be jacked up if I were the father.

When I got home, Charlotte was waiting at my front door. Honestly, I didn't expect her to show. Fake-ass apartment building's security system. Charlotte had her ways of getting into places, especially into my heart. I'd let her in my spot. We had that wild and crazy breakup, makeup sex. Talked dirty to each other the entire time.

A few hours ago my dick was down Charlotte's throat, in her pussy. Her clit was in my mouth for about sixty minutes straight. Filled up on her secretions. I slid on a condom and went straight in her ass. We did all that. She rode me cowgirl, reverse cowgirl, she backed that ass up on me doggie-style. I spanked her real good. After working up a serious sweat, we'd dozed off. My dick and balls had become her pillow. She liked sleeping down there. Said the scent turned her on.

I went to empty my canal and here I was. This time Alexis should not have come by unannounced. She was styling her usual, but this short halter mini with high heels was fresh. We were all in the kitchen that was right near my opened doorway. I wanted to shut it. Scared as hell to let go of Alexis for two seconds, I prayed no one passed by.

Yes, Alexis was my sister. Yes, she might be pregnant, but we just had a conversation at her apartment — I glanced at the time on my microwave — nearly five hours ago. The reason she was here was obvious.

I shouldn't have told Alexis I was thinking about ending my relay with her mom, but I wasn't doing that for her. Once I got back with Charlotte, I realized I missed her young, gorgeous, wild, and crazy ass. Okay, truthfully. My ego wanted to let dude know Charlotte's pussy was mine always and forever and I could fuck her anytime I wanted.

"You want to go to breakfast, Spencer?" Alexis asked as though she didn't have my gurl's hair on lock.

This time I squeezed Alexis's wrists so hard her fingers uncurled. I backed her up to the open door.

Charlotte motioned for me to close the door in Alexis's face. Alexis rushed in, snatched Charlotte's hair again, dragged my gurl into the hallway. I swear I did not see that one coming.

"Alexis, please. Let her go," I yelled.

Alexis shoved Charlotte's head down. My gurl was bent over, again. Her titties pointed toward the floor. Her asshole was wide open. My dick and nuts were hanging low and swinging fast inside my sweats.

"Bitch, let me go!" Charlotte cried.

Alexis pulled harder. "You gon' stop calling me out of my name."

This time I couldn't blame the madness on Charlotte. Alexis's fists were locked in at Charlotte's scalp this time. She pulled. I tried to restrain her without hurting my ex any further. Thankfully, Alexis didn't have her purse, which would've meant she would've had her gun. This tragedy could've turned homicidal.

The door across the hall opened. I told my neighbor, "Don't call the cops. I got this, man." He nodded, then went back inside.

Staring into Alexis's eyes, I pleaded, "Sis, you can't be fighting carrying a baby," thinking that might convince her to let go of Charlotte's long, beautiful, natural blond hair.

Oh, shit! I prayed Alexis didn't say it was mine. That would give Charlotte fuel to whup both Alexis and my ass.

I didn't want to do this, but my options

were limited. Digging my nails into Alexis's wrists, one finger at a time uncurled. I exhaled. I was relieved until I saw clumps of Charlotte's luxurious hair falling to the floor.

"What the fuck, Sis?!" I felt like shit. This was the second time I hadn't protected Charlotte from Alexis.

I hugged Charlotte, kissed the top of her head. "I'm so sorry, baby."

Charlotte looked up to me, cried on my chest. I held her closer.

Alexis shouted, "You're taking up for that bitch?"

Charlotte stopped sniffling, looked up at me. Her eyes were blood red. Her lids narrowed, lips tightened. She turned to Alexis.

Bam! Bam! Bam!

"Charlotte, no!" She'd popped off three quick punches to Alexis's face like an alter ego of Laila Ali kicked in.

Couldn't say good gurl, Charlotte, but I wanted to. Alexis grabbed her head and stomach, then fell to the floor and started crying. Charlotte backed into my apartment. All I thought about was Alexis and the baby. Thankfully, Charlotte hadn't hit Alexis below the breasts.

"Charlotte, go to my bedroom, baby. Now." She moved from the entrance to the kitchen. Stood there.

I needed to make sure Alexis was okay, but I was not letting her back in.

Alexis moaned really loud, "Our baby."

Why the fuck she do that shit? I went to the kitchen, got my cell, dialed 911. "Oh, shit!"

Charlotte rushed Alexis. I dropped my phone. Charlotte had Alexis by the hair.

"What the fuck is wrong with you? Stop kneeing her in the stomach!" I snatched Charlotte, shoved her into my apartment. "Get your shit and get the fuck out!"

Charlotte stomped to the bedroom, returned dressed. Her purse was on her shoulder. "Bitch, you fucked with the wrong one. Don't turn your back, you nasty bitch. I ain't done."

Angrily, I said, "We are done and yes, you are, Charlotte. You'd better pray she doesn't lose this baby or we're going to have you arrested."

She told me, "Try it." Then she said to Alexis, "And yes, your mama is a ho and you are, too, bitch. I'm not crazy. All that sis bullshit. I know that's your baby, Spencer. Fuck both of y'all."

The sex was phenom, but it'd clouded my judgment with getting back with Charlotte. Had to let her go after this showdown. I watched her walk away for the last time. Any woman who kicked another in the stomach knowing there was a baby inside was certifiably mental. I didn't want Charlotte anywhere near me again.

All I did was shake my head. I'd never hit a woman, but this shit right here made we want to beat Charlotte's ass.

I went inside, got my phone, keys, and wallet, and locked my door. Stuffed everything in my pocket. I placed my arm under my sister's knees, the other behind her back. "Hold on."

"Okay," Alexis said.

When she coughed, a little blood spilled from her mouth. I didn't want to, but I couldn't help but shed a tear.

Charlotte came back toward us.

"If you're coming back for more, Charlotte, you're going to have to —"

Scooping up her hair, she said, "I'm going back to my other dude. Don't you ever contact me again in your life." Then she rolled her eyes at me and left.

Wanted to say, take your ass on, ho! But that would've started another fight. Ole dude could have my sloppy seconds. I was done with her trifling ass.

I carried Alexis to my car. Piedmont Hospital was less than a mile away south on

Peachtree Street. Helping my sister into the emergency room, I reassured her, "You and the baby are going to be okay. I got you."

CHAPTER 6
DEVEREAUX

"Thanks for believing in me."

This was the type of emotional transparency that bonded me to Phoenix early in our relationship four years ago. He was different from most men in Atlanta. I passed on the guys who were chauvinistic. Self-centered. Showed no respect for intelligent women. Openly had more than one woman simply because they could.

Last night my fiancé had picked up our daughter from his mother's house, gone to Publix grocery, come home, and cooked his favorite dinner for the family. The grilled snapper with asparagus was delicious.

This morning he'd prepared a nice brunch with French toast, fresh strawberries, smoked salmon omelets, and blueberry smoothies. Nya and I cleaned the kitchen, then our daughter went upstairs.

"You're the best, babe," I told him, putting the china plates in the cabinet.

His response, while texting on his cell at the same time, "I know you have to write, I'll be in the living room watching television."

Unlike some men, Phoenix respected my insane schedule. If I weren't on set, I was at home penning pages. I went upstairs, worked on my new series, *Notches.* In the mood to share quality time with my fiancé, I shut down my computer.

I peeped in Nya's room. "You okay, princess?"

"I wanna go to T-Cedes."

"Okay, sweetie. But not today. Daddy and I are taking you to the aquarium later," I said. "You need to take a nap."

Shaking her head, Nya said, "Brandy wants to go."

"Nap, Nya. Now."

Closing her door, I texted Mercedes, Leave it to my daughter, Brandy would move in with us. Mercedes's twins, Brandy and Brandon, were almost twice Nya's age. My sister Sandara's sons and daughter were closer to Nya's age, but Mercedes spoiled my daughter so much I wished I were my sister's child.

She texted back, Of course. I'll have her ready. What time?

Wanting to chill with my man for a few

hours, I replied, 4p.

I got a bottle of champagne, added canned sliced peaches to my flute. "Hey, you," I said.

Cozying up to Phoenix, I shared the love seat. The indoor water fountain flowed down the wall of stones behind us. I picked up the sound system remote, turned on smooth jazz, went to the kitchen, snagged a second bottle of bubbly, and then cuddled with my man. Depending on how much we indulged, our taking Nya might turn into Mercedes chaperoning the girls.

I had tons of unfinished business that would have to wait until tomorrow. Once we start filming, I'd barely have time to tend to my own needs.

Picking up my phone, I noticed it was noon. I powered it off. The next eighteen hours were exclusively for Phoenix and Nya.

"Seriously, Dev. Thanks for believing in me."

I told my man, "You don't have to keep saying that."

The first. The second. The third, fourth, even fifth time I'd heard him say that was cool. I'd lost count of how many times my fiancé had credited me since my agreeing to his managing Ebony. Positive reinforcement was what couples were supposed to give each other.

Phoenix had been excited all day. I was, too, since Ebony had gotten her act together. I wasn't surprised she'd given approval to let Phoenix manage her. Secretly, I'd hoped her husband would've objected to having my man oversee Ebony's career.

Truthfully, I wasn't sure how I felt about Phoenix having a valid reason to be on my set on a regular basis. The fact that the director, Trés Vinsaunt, was interested in dating me wasn't my concern. I'd never remotely shown interest in another man since I began dating Phoenix.

Business was always my focus. Being a bitch with my staff and cast when necessary, I did not hesitate. Maybe Trés enjoyed witnessing that dominating part of my personality. Men loved bitches like my sister Alexis. That was why Ebony was perfect for her role. I never wanted her to hold back.

Alexis tried to convince me to give her the part of Ebony Waterhouse. I refused for two reasons. One, she's family, and family felt they were entitled to privileges not given to others. Two, my sister was slick, flip, cute, but she was not a trained actor. The latter could be rectified. I'd told her, my show was scripted like reality. It was not reality.

I sipped my champagne. "This is delicious, babe."

I preferred cabernet. Phoenix liked Mumm's brut.

Phoenix placed his strong hand at the base of my neck. Meeting me halfway, he pulled me closer, kissed my lips. His tongue circled around mine. He suctioned the peach out of my mouth.

"Not nearly as delicious as you," he said, eating my fruit.

Having to check Phoenix in front of my staff or hold my comments until we got home was already concerning me. I didn't want to bring that kind of drama inside our peaceful home. I prayed that things would work out for the best. If it got too hectic, I could politely ask him to leave the studio.

The way he admired me with his deep brown eyes made my heart beat for him. I removed his frameless, rectangular-shaped glasses, placed them on the table behind the sofa. The black skull cap he wore over his shadow low-fade cut gave him that artist appeal. Phoenix never wore T-shirts or jeans. Casual or dressy, he had tons of long and short-sleeved button-ups and slacks in almost every color.

"I do have to thank you, Dev. You're making my dream come true. You just gave me the green light to your hottest rising star.

Ebony is going to make us a lot of money, babe. This is the start of . . ." His eyes grew with excitement. "Um, um, um."

"Um, um, um, what?"

He rubbed his brow, held my hand. "I'm going after all the A-list actors. TV. Film. All that."

"Well, don't pitch for anyone else associated with SSC." I wasn't asking. "Ebony is in your hands. She's going to potentially make *you* a lot of money," I said, not wanting him feeling as though what was mine was his. Plus, whenever a person paid another, the one getting a check seldom made more than the person signing the check.

I did lots of things for Phoenix, but blending assets was not happening until after he signed a prenuptial and said, "I do." For once it would feel good to have my man take me on an all-expense-paid vacation. I'd never complained about his limited resources. I understood how hard it was for him, but four years was long enough. Just because I made more money didn't mean he had to let me pay for all of our pleasure.

I was twenty-eight. He was thirty. He'd better make branding Ebony work well. I was getting weary from carrying him.

He placed his glass beside his eyeglasses.

"But you, babe. I admire you. You're the best mom, fiancée, friend. Not to mention brilliant." Phoenix stood. "You blowin' up, Dev. You the man," he said, bowing toward me three times with his palms faced down.

I hated patronization. I put the capital *T* in our team. We both knew that. I was not looking for accolades. I'd prefer his partnership on every level.

Picking up his drink, he sat and then continued. "You work too hard, baby. It's time for you to take a break and lean on me from now on."

Seriously? I felt my skin crawl with agitation. What exactly did he mean? Two days out from filming the series and I'm supposed to do what? Turn down because he's got this.

He held his glass up high. "Cheers."

Can we wait until the signature on the contract dries and the first payment clears his bank account? False promises, bounced checks. One thing I'd learned was not to prematurely count my money.

"Who's handling your legal contract, babe?" That was where his focus should be.

"I'll figure that out," he said casually.

"I have Goldie's personal information. I can ask Kendall Minter to do the draft. How much are you charging her?"

His brows drew closer together. Lips twisted to the side. "Hmm."

My shoulders and head flopped. "You have no idea how much you're going to charge her?" I asked, suctioning a long, slow intake of my drink.

"I was trying to think of what was fair. Maybe two grand a month."

Champagne almost flew from my mouth into his. I swallowed. "Are you afraid to request what you're worth, babe?"

He hunched his shoulders. "Ten a month? Is that too much? I don't want to scare her off. You're paying her eight hundred thou. Maybe I should tell her I want ten percent of her salary."

Here we go again. Bright ideas. Clueless on the details. Dreams. No plan. You do not request a percentage of a person's revenue if you didn't negotiate a deal for her in advance. I disclosed her pay to him in confidence.

"Don't let her know you're aware of how much she's getting paid. You'll figure out what to request. Start higher than what you expect to get, but don't be outrageous. Let me know if I can be of assistance." I'd decided to stay out of his business unless he came to me.

"After we get back from our outing, babe,

I'm having drinks with the fellas to bring them up to speed on my new company."

Smacking my lips, I sighed. Even with his boys, no celebration was sensible at this point. Phoenix had my support. Ebony was my concern. Regardless of how things progressed, my lips were shut. I was generous with him as my fiancé. He would never survive sitting across from me as an adversary.

Women had a way of changing directions faster than men. Underneath a pretty face, inside a sexy smile, cloaked in an attractive physique, shrewd businesswomen could be cutthroat champions.

My man didn't know the behind-the-scenes gritty details. I'd clawed — wicked witch pointed nails screeching against a chalkboard — to earn a spot for my show. I definitely had a few foes who'd love to see me fail. I didn't play games, but I had fight in me that Phoenix had never seen. Ebony had best not try anything shady. If she did, that was the only way I'd intervene. The one thing Phoenix wasn't doing was working for free.

The longer I gazed at the handsome, vulnerable, somewhat naïve man before me, his innocence filled me with fear and love. Enough of being on this couch. My pussy was tipsy. I wanted to feel him penetrate my body. Give me a head-to-toe orgasm. Hadn't had one in . . . damn. It's been that long? I hated to ask Mercedes to pick up Nya. I'd promised my baby we'd take her to the aquarium. Now I see why it's been so long. I kept putting my pussy's royal treatment on pause. That was my fault.

"You do a lot for me, for us. It's going to work out for you this time," I reassured him. "Don't get ahead of yourself. Your company is going to thrive."

"I sure hope you're right. I'm tired of falling short."

Failure wasn't a bad thing. No successful person I knew had become wealthy without hard knocks.

"I came from nothing, Dev. My own mother didn't want me. She still doesn't need me for anything. I feel like she looks down on me like I'm a disappointment." A tear fell from his left eye first, then his right.

My pussy stopped puckering. I sighed. Resumed drinking. Wish he'd stop playing the victim. Stop believing he had to prove himself worthy of his mother's love. Time would do what I couldn't. Heal his broken heart. I witnessed the reunion between Phoenix and Mrs. Etta Watson-Henry. She was trying to bond with him. Abandoning

Phoenix was never her intention. Etta had explained she wasn't ready to be a mom, so she'd left him with her mother. What was done couldn't be undone.

The positive part he hadn't learned to appreciate was Phoenix had reconnected with his mother. When he told his grandmother we were pregnant and having a girl, his mother contacted him the same day. He wasn't her only child, but he was the eldest and the only one she hadn't parented. At least he knew who she was. I wasn't going to allow myself to join his pity party by my bringing up who my "unknown" father was.

Mrs. Watson-Henry had been a blessing to us, to me. A year ago she started keeping Nya whenever we needed, to give us time together. She'd watch Nya every day if we'd agree. My mom was too busy enjoying her younger man, Spencer, to babysit. To give Nya a balanced schedule and time with her cousins, my sister, Sandara, kept Nya several days a week. Mercedes pitched in too.

My mom's relationship with Spencer was going to end soon. Even if I knew who the father of Alexis's unborn child was, I was not going to be the one to tell my mom that Alexis might be pregnant by Spencer.

I told my man, "You have to let go of the pain and be thankful." I would've worded what I'd said differently if I didn't think he'd get offended. Tiptoeing around his ego was better than ruining a decent moment with him today.

Phoenix could go from hot to cold in seconds. He'd better not act a fool on my set. I had to mute the dialogue in my head in order to enjoy the rest of this day. This opportunity would not repeat for at least eight weeks.

"I love you, babe. You're amazing." I told him the truth.

Sitting our glasses on the table, I planted kisses on his cheeks, then passionately pressed my lips to his. Squeezing his dick, I sucked his tongue.

He leaned back. "I'ma go check on Nya. Hopefully she's asleep." Picking up his cell, he walked away, saying, "You stay right here."

Bam! Bam! Bam!

Phoenix stopped. We stared at each other.

Bam! Bam! Bam! Bam!

He hurried to the front door. I followed him. He reached toward the shelf mounted high upon the wall next to the door, then opened the box. Got the gun, handed me one.

There were no chairs, stools, or benches close enough to the door where Nya might

90

climb. All of our weapons were stored where our child could not reach them. At night we unlocked the drawers on our nightstands where we kept loaded forties. Each morning we secured the lock, then placed the key in the top dresser drawer.

Phoenix peeped through the hole.

I whispered, "Who is it?"

He took my gun, put both back in the box. Opened the door.

Staring at my sister, I asked, "Why are you trying to knock down my front door?"

Mercedes said, "Get your purse. Alexis needs us! We've got to go now!"

CHAPTER 7
PHOENIX

"Call me a bitch!"

It wasn't her first time asking. I rattled my head. Had never said that word to a woman other than her. Never referred to her as such outside of the bedroom. Didn't want to obey her right now. Wanted to do to her what I couldn't do to my fiancée, fuck the shit out of her real good.

Smack! Her palm landed on my jaw. She started choking me. There was no script. She wasn't acting. We were not role-playing. This was how she got down.

"Call me a bitch!" This time she was more demanding.

Unable to breathe, my eyes scrolled so far back if they could do a 360, they would've spun completely around. I wanted to howl at the moon outside her window like I were a wolf in the night surrounded by darkness and that was my only light. This shit was so intense I couldn't yelp like a pup if I wanted. But I loved it!

She pushed me deeper onto the mattress. Releasing her chokehold, she grabbed my dick, stared into my eyes. I gasped for air. This small-framed chick was a mighty strong woman.

"I'm getting ready to suck you dry. This here is my dick. Do you understand me?"

Started to respond. The "I need you" intro to Chris Brown and Tyga's song "Ayo" played on my cell back-to-back-to-back, interrupting the moment. Ebony knew the text tone was my fiancée calling.

"Forget that bitch." Ebony picked up my cell, put it on vibrate, and resumed what she was doing to my dick.

Drove me fucking nuts when she dominated me. Talked dirty to me. She didn't do it all the time, but her timing was always perfect. I didn't want to take the lead on this session.

Watching her stroke my dick with precision, up, down, left, right, round and round she rolled my balls at the base of my shaft. I fought to suppress exploding all over her face when she rubbed my dick between her flat palms fast enough to start a fire.

The combination of her aggressive attitude and her jacking my shit every which way as though she were possessed made me nervous. I had to rescue my man. I cupped my hands over my shaft.

"Slow down, babe."

She snatched my wrists, broke my grip, flung my arms into my chest. "Who the fuck you talkin' to? Did I give you permission to speak? Did I tell you to touch *my* dick? This here is my dick and you gon' stop giving it to your baby mama. You hear me?"

Smack! Her palm stung the hell out of my cheek. All I did was stare at her.

The seductive rasp in her voice could've made me spat seeds semiautomatic-style on those perky nipples. Before I answered, she started sucking the head. I was hypnotized at the sight of my pole sliding in and out of her mouth.

One of her hands was clamped at the base. The other stacked on top. Saliva streamed from her mouth. She hawked, then spat on my shit. Next, all I saw was my swollen mushroom going in and out each time she bobbed. I swore my copperhead felt like it was about to blast off of my chopper. Seeing her work that black magic with her flickering tongue felt as though I were on the verge of a tsunami.

Wedging my erection between her firm breasts, redirecting her eyes only, she stared up at me, twirled her nipples. Spoke in between sucks while sandwiching me tighter between her twins.

"Nigga, you gon' learn to stop fucking her before coming to my house."

I nodded.

"Your dick gon' need crutches when I'm done." Licking her lips, she moaned. "I got some popsicles in the freezer."

Aw, hell yes! The way she chilled her mouth with those strawberry, orange, and grape pops. "Whew!"

"That's right, you sexy muthafucka. Don't make me go downstairs to the refrig. Ain't no telling what I'll surprise you with. Is my dick happy, baby?"

"Fuck yeah." Going to check on Nya was my way of avoiding sexing Dev. Ebony always made holding on to my nut worthwhile. Mercedes rescued me from the excuses floating in my mind at that time. Talking business, playing ignorant, that was my way of taking Dev's libido down a notch or two.

I nodded again. "Chopper is about to bust!"

"Good."

Ebony's twisting was painful and pleasurable. *Yeah! Break my third leg, babe.* My eyes shifted to the left, paused, then focused on her. She dove into my genitals like twelve starving seagulls descending on a single piece of sourdough. This time I couldn't see my dick at all.

I wasn't sure what she'd done next, but the spot my corona hit deep inside of her throat at that very second made me say, "Right there, bitch!" I screamed like a girl. I thrust my hips forward. The roof of her mouth hooked, then snapped the upper side of my head, hooked, then snapped again as though she was trying to flick off the top of a beer bottle. I held the back of her head so she couldn't move.

"Fuck! Bitch! Yes!"

Her jaws suctioned in.

Ebony had made me do lots of things I'd never done like cum from getting head. It felt amazing every time a woman's mouth was down there, but no one had made me bust, not even Dev. The first time it happened with Ebony, I thought it was a fluke. The second time was impressive. But she was consistent. So was Dev. The score had to be something like Ebony 99, Dev 0.

Chilling on the love seat earlier with Dev, I'd already plotted my getaway to Ebony's tonight. I'd never planned on hanging with the fellas. Took Ebony to T.I.'s Scales 925 for a post-midnight date soon as she'd finished memorizing her lines Friday. I saw

Alexis, pretended not to. Hope she hadn't tripped off of my being with Ebony. Didn't really matter since I was Ebony's manager. If Alexis put me on blast, I'd tell Dev I was with the fellas and I ran into Ebony.

When a man cheated on the regular the way I did, countless comeback lines were programmed into my mind to defuse any and all situations.

My day was preplanned. After we took Nya to the aquarium, I was headed here. Not wanting to disappoint Nya, once Dev got swept away by Mercedes, I took my baby girl as promised, then dropped her off at my mom's. Nya was going to my mom's house in the morning. She just got there a little sooner. Told mom we had a family emergency. That wasn't exactly a lie.

Ebony swallowed.

"Yeah! Right there. Suck your dick, bitch. Suck it like it's the last time you gon' taste this muthafucka."

Etta would snatch me up if she heard what I'd just said. We may have an almost decent relationship now, but Etta did not tolerate profanity or disrespect of any kind. If she knew where I spent my weekends, she'd probably stop watching Nya. If she knew what I was doing behind Dev's back, my mother would disassociate with me . . . again.

Ebony glanced up at me, smiled, but never stopped jacking me off.

This was the life! I wasn't different from the average dude. Our dicks wanted more than one pussy. Only the strongest dudes didn't stray. Trust me. It took a large degree of willpower to have sex with one and only one woman throughout an entire relationship. Actually, fucking Ebony on the regular was the only reason I was still with Dev.

I'd never call Ebony the B word outside of the bedroom, but I had to admit, it felt Tarzan pound-on-my-chest good to unleash the beast inside of me. I hated being a fucking gentleman in the bedroom.

I yelled, "Aah-eeh-ah-eeh-aaaaaah! Bitch!" cumming into her mouth.

The expression was intended as a compliment to Ebony for the way she rocked the mic. She didn't let go of my dick. She turnt up.

"Ahhh. Damn." I was spent. I tried to relax. Couldn't. Knew better than to touch my, I meant, her dick.

Two wives would serve me well. I wish I could openly marry them both. Dev wasn't enough in the bedroom, but she'd just made my sexing Ebony on the regular less complicated. I appreciated her for that. I was truly blessed to have a lady and a freak. Starting next week one would be to my right, the other on my left side.

One in front of the camera. One behind. Me sandwiched in the middle.

Ebony stayed ahead of my ass. Always gave me a reason to chase that pussy. Dev relentlessly held on to my rear, making sure I didn't leave her.

I was glad when I'd gotten Dev pregnant. My ace card with her was, with her daddy issues, I knew she'd never want to raise Nya without me. I played that to my advantage. Gave her a ring to make her feel worthy, but I was not close to being ready for marriage. Had to respect Dev telling me not to solicit representation of any more of her folk, but I had an idea that would draw her cast to me. I wasn't as dumb as Dev thought, but it was best to let her believe that she controlled me.

Ebony picked up a bottle off of the headboard, then slowly drizzled orange tequila liqueur along my flaccid dick. Parting her lips, she took a swig, squished, swallowed the alcohol as a chaser to my cum, then placed the bottle back where it was. Her lips lowered toward my crotch.

"No, my babe. Please. I can't take any —"

Her shut-the-fuck-up stare silenced me.

Seems like all Ebony wanted to do was suck every seed out of my sack. Covering my dick with both hands, I had to ask, "Who else you been fucking?"

"If you want some pussy, Phoenix, all you have to do is take it, nigga." She crawled out of bed, put on her robe. "I could ask you the same. Who did you screw last night?"

She had me frowning. "You know my situation," I said, sitting on the edge of the mattress. Had to admit, her getting up was a relief. My chopper was sprawled atop my nuts marinating in sticky liqueur.

"I know my position. I'm your side. You're my main. Remember? It's not the other way," she said, swaying her ass in my face.

"Goldie, look at me," I said, slapping her booty. "I didn't give her your dick last night or before I saw you today."

"Yeah, right," she said. "I don't think it's a good idea for you to manage me. We are with each other and Devereaux is going to find out if you're on set. If she finds out, I'll lose my job. You'll lose me as a client. Neither of us will get paid. We'll be two homeless bitches with one blanket."

We laughed.

What was the worst that could really happen? I'd have to move in here.

"That's exactly why I have to manage you," I insisted. "She'd never suspect us if we're around her all the time."

"Yes, she will. That's exactly why you are not going to brand me. You're fired."

What the fuck did she mean by the tone of her word *brand*? There was no way I was going to let Ebony break it off with me for the career I got her. I felt tension tightening in my neck. I massaged my shoulder, picked up my cell, and took it off of silence as I entered the bathroom.

"I need you . . ." played. Ignoring Dev, I placed my phone on the vanity, stepped under a hot, steaming shower for about fifteen minutes.

When I entered the bedroom, Ebony was fumbling through her drawer. Stuffed something in her pocket.

Placing my cell on the bed, I oiled my body, toweled off, got dressed, told her, "I'm your manager. That's final."

Ebony untied her robe, stood in front of me naked. Those perky nipples made my dick swell a little. Mind was willing, but a low blood flow was all he had. I pulled her to me, started sucking her titty. My man mustered up enough thickness to penetrate. He wanted to feel her insides. I picked her up, carried her to the bed, unfastened my pants, and began fucking Ebony missionary.

My chopper was sore as hell. Should've kept him tucked.

She ripped open my shirt, grabbed the collar, yanked me toward her, then thrust her hips into mine. "Okay, I'll let you manage me under one condition."

It didn't matter what she was about to say. I was shocked that I was on the verge of firing off another nut.

"Anything for you, my babe."

Her pussy spat out my pole. She gripped my shaft, then said real sexy, "Promise me you'll never fall in love with Devereaux."

My chopper went from heaven to hell. Serious nosedive. I never should've confessed to Ebony that I loved but wasn't in love with Dev. That was a real mitch move. Dev was solid, but I couldn't give my heart to a woman who didn't need me for anything except a manny to our kid, and a last name change. Yeah, yeah, yeah, Dev's money was cool and all, but that empathic bullshit she dropped on a regular was emasculating.

"I want to be the only woman you're in love with."

"Cool." If I gave up my emotional and financial security for this girl, would she have my back? Or leave me on the doorstep the way Etta had done?

"And," she added. Ebony held my soft dick head close to her pussy. "I want this," she said, squeezing so hard I yelled, "Damn!" She continued as though I hadn't screamed. "Inside of me every day."

Her pussy felt so amazing I could hit it three, four times in twenty-four hours and never become bored. Fall asleep dick-deep in her hole, but what she'd ask for wasn't possible and she knew it. The only way I could hit this daily . . . I was not doing her on set. Ebony had fucked up my sexual high. I suspected she might be aiming to set me up for failure.

To end this session, I told her, "I'll work it out."

Maybe it was the way Ebony held me in her arms after sex. Or the way she made me feel needed all the time. Her orgasmic gourmet dishes were the best. She could heat up the bedroom, but Ebony had never cooked me a meal.

All the things Ebony did to pleasure me, I wish Dev made time to tend to me this way. I rolled onto my back, still had on my shirt. Ebony slid on top of me. She still had on her robe. We embraced each other. I kissed her. Already in hot water, I'd get up in a few. Ebony's hug was healing.

"I need you . . ." played on my phone.

Stretching my arm, I felt for my cell, read Dev's text, Call me now. The prior six messages read the same.

I flipped Ebony onto her back. "I've got to go, babe."

I took a three-minute shower, put on my pants, grabbed a fresh shirt out of Ebony's closet. I had extra everything here. Clothes, underwear, shoes, ties, deodorant, lotions, body wash, were all at Ebony's house. She'd put me up on buy two of each outfit, leave one at her place. Said women noticed everything and Dev would definitely know if I'd ever come home looking or smelling different.

Stepping into my shoes, Ebony said, "Babe, come here."

"I can't. I gotta go. Come lock the door."

"Just come here for a sec," she insisted.

I stood by the side of the bed.

"Since you're going to manage me, you're going to need this," she said, handing me a key.

"For real?" Aw, shit. The only other woman who had given me complete access to her without my asking was Dev.

Ebony nodded, then rolled over. "Lock the door."

Before I left, I told her, "I love you."
"I love you, too, my babe."

CHAPTER 8
ALEXIS

I wasn't sure if I was about to deliver good or bad news.

There was no way I could please them all. Sympathy, empathy by any means was what I needed. I had to live with my decisions. I was in this conspiracy alone. Me. Myself. And I.

To show up at Spencer's without calling. To pull out Charlotte's hair. To put myself in a position where another woman hated me so much she could've killed me. The time had come to face my demons. Wasn't certain how those closest to me would treat me after they heard what I was about to say.

Charlotte was right. I was a ho. Not the kind she'd thought. I'd never spread my thighs or licked a pussy without a purpose. I was a control whore. Pathological liar. I was mentally, physically, and financially abusive. I was my father's daughter. I was guilty of being those things because of him.

My mother.

God made me special. If no one else would forgive me for my sin, He would.

He was the only one who knew my secret. I was never pregnant.

I'd been upstairs in my loft waiting to confess to everyone who was downstairs. A few more people needed to arrive.

Getting to know my dad for myself was necessary if there was any chance of changing my manipulative behavior. I texted my dad, Come over to my house now. I need you.

He replied right away, What's your address? Three months after having met Conner, I'd never told him where I lived. Didn't want to betray Spencer. Yeah, my brother took me to emergency but before Charlotte kicked me in my stomach, he'd sided with her. It was time for me to confront everyone. A sharp pain jabbed me in the stomach, causing my teeth to clench.

Rolling onto my back, I texted my location to him along with the gate code and where to park. Had only seen him once the day we'd met at my mom's. We'd texted a few times afterward. He might as well come over, too, so I didn't have to give the same speech twice. He hadn't done shit for Spencer or me. Figured he could make it up to his unborn grandchild by financially supporting us. Had to admit. I wanted to change, tell everyone I'd lied. But I wasn't ready for all that, knowing I could benefit royally from letting them believe I was having a baby.

My rent was almost due. Somebody had to pay it. The old, rich men I used to entertain, like Goldie's seventy-something husband, Buster, I refused to backslide to shaky hands.

Recovering in my bed from the maniac's attack, I thumbed through my Instagram. Ebony had gone ham on social media hyping up her photo shoot tomorrow for #sscatl. The beat on her face was brilliant. I snagged her makeup artist IG @alleyezongg. That should be me boasting. No, I claimed it. One day that will be me.

I whispered, "Whatever, bitch." That was meant for Charlotte. I'd better not see her ass anywhere. Spencer had begged me not to press charges. Said I'd be implicating myself.

I heard my brother's heavy footsteps coming up the hardwood stairs to my loft.

"I just let your mom into the garage. She'll be here in a minute," he said, standing beside my bed.

Blake was the only person I didn't want involved. I'd sworn my sisters to secrecy.

The only way my mother knew about my pregnancy was if Spencer told her.

"Why did you invite her when I told you not to?"

"Because she gave birth to you," Mercedes said loud enough for me to hear. "When are you coming down here? We've been waiting on you forever. I'm about to leave, lil girl."

My cell rang. It was our dad. I buzzed Conner in. "Leave," I told her, staring at Spencer. "I didn't want you guys to come over here anyway."

I heard Devereaux say, "She's ungrateful. I could've been with my man."

I'd stayed away from the rail in my loft. They could hear me but hadn't seen me. My arms and legs were unmarked. My face and stomach were a hot mess. I'd covered my facial bruises best I could with foundation.

I swear if I ever saw Charlotte, I was going all in on that chick without notice.

Spencer defended me against Mercedes. "I only wanted Alexis to tell you guys once. She'll be down in a few."

"Tell us what?" my mother asked after letting herself in.

Spencer asked me, "You ready?" He mouthed, "I love you, Sis. Your makeup looks great."

Holding back tears, I eased out of bed. I looked at him, then whispered, "I don't know why they have to know. The fight was no big deal."

"I got you," he said, holding my hand. "Let's go."

I paused between steps. When I turned the corner into my living room, Mercedes, Devereaux, Sandara, my father, and my mother stood holding her new dog on her shoulder like he was a baby. Who I didn't expect to see was James and Chanel.

Narrowing my eyes at Spencer, I shook my head. "You wrong chick."

"You wrong man." He shifted his eyes from me to our father. "You know I hate his ass."

Conner commented, "The feeling is mutual, Spencer."

My mother approached us. Gave Spencer a one-arm hug first, then motioned toward me. I backed away, shook my head.

"Max is cute," I said, then walked passed her. I squeezed in between my allies, Mercedes and Devereaux. Mother sat in a chair.

I was quiet.

Mercedes spoke first. She looked at me, touched my chin, then smeared my foundation. "Well, Mr. Big Stuff. Stop wasting our

110

time, girl. I see somebody finally stood up to you. I know you didn't call us here for that." Sarcastically, she asked, "You and Spencer getting married or what?"

Wow, I was all the way wrong about her being on my side.

My mom stood from her armed chair, held her dog across her forearm, squinted at Spencer. He rattled his head.

"You okay?" Chanel asked me. "What's this about, Alexis? Marriage?"

"Yeah, what? Are you calling off our engagement?" James asked.

Twisting my lips to the left, those two, make that three including Blake, were not supposed to be here. At this very moment I hated Blake more than before. Her inviting James and Chanel was inappropriate. What had Spencer told my mom?

"This is fucked up." I stood, headed toward the stairs. Regardless of what I said, everyone was going to view me as the tramp. Not my mother.

Spencer blocked me. Escorted me back into my living area. "You want me to tell them?"

My eyes scrolled the inside of my lids. Opening them, I stared at my mom, then nodded at him. "Yeah, why don't you do that." That way I wouldn't have to tell another lie.

"Sis," he said, holding my hand. "She's your mom. It's *our* family."

"Get to it, boy!" Mercedes shouted.

Best for me to remain quiet. I was kinda sad that they could tell I'd been in a fight and nobody cared to ask me what happened.

"Spencer," Mercedes boldly stated, "you've got two seconds. If I get up, I'm leaving."

Spencer said, "My sister is twelve weeks' pregnant."

Mercedes said, "That's it. We know that already."

Mom stared at Mercedes. She scanned to Devereaux, who nodded. Finally, Sandara hunched her shoulders, then said, "It's true, Mom."

"He's lying," my mother said. "So who kicked your ass? The woman, or man, that you slept with?"

It was quiet. The eerie kind of silence in a horror movie filled my head as I imagined strangling my mom.

Chanel was the only one crying. She came to me. Opened her arms to embrace me. The only reason I'd let her was in hopes of gaining empathy from the others. I didn't hug her back. I was numb.

Spencer continued. "I had to take Alexis to the emergency room earlier. There was an altercation, as you all can tell." He eyed Conner. "No, I did not put my hands on her. I'm not a woman beater like you."

Conner remained silent.

My mom retorted, "I know who kicked her butt. Charlotte assaulted her. Probably more like Charlotte was defending herself from what I'd overheard on the phone. Whatever, Spencer. Get on with it. I have to take my baby shopping," she said, kissing her dog on the forehead.

James stood, balled his hands into fists. "Tell the truth, Alexis. Did Spencer lay hands on you and you guys are trying to cover it up?"

"No, James. Please, sit down. This is difficult for me."

"For you?" my mother mumbled.

James said, "Alexis, why are we here? Why did your sisters know about the pregnancy and I didn't? Why this gathering of the whole family? Why —"

I shouted, "Shut the fuck up, James!" Lowering my voice, I asked him, "How's your fling thing, Mz. LA doing? Flying her in anytime soon?"

My mom stared at Spencer. "I knew you two lied to me. I didn't want to believe it, but I felt it in my gut."

"Lied about what?" Chanel asked, sitting next to James.

In my perfect world, I could have my guy and my gurl. Since they showed they cared about me, having a baby might be what I really need to work it out with both of them. If James' and my relationship survived this fiasco, I could have his baby.

Spencer said, "It's a girl."

That was another lie I'd concocted. People are more sensitive to mothers carrying a girl. I touched my stomach. The first fake tear fell.

My brother added, "Thanks to you, Dad, yes. Yes, it's feasible that the fetus is mine."

Conner said, "What the hell do I have to do with whom you're fucking?"

"Shut the hell up, old man?!" The veins in the side of Spencer's neck bulged. "If your ass would've done the right thing —"

Shaking his cane, Conner lamented, "Don't raise your voice to me, boy! I'm still your father. This is Blake's fault! Not mine!"

"Don't blame this shit on my woman! What you wanna do? I don't need a reason to whup you up and beat you down like you did my mom. Make a move, old man. I dare you!"

James interrupted, "If Alexis would've

114

done right by me . . . wait a minute. You fucked your brother? That's some sick disgusting make me want to throw up shit."

Conner said, "James, calm down. Spencer is right. It is my fault. They didn't know they were related, but I did."

"No disrespect, Conner, but fuck that. That's the problem. Everybody always comes to Alexis's defense. Who the hell do you fight for?" he asked me. His eyes were filled with tears. His voice lowered. "We've been engaged for two years. I can't do this. Where is my ring? You don't even wear it."

Fuck James. His cheating ass wasn't innocent. I asked him again, "How's LA?"

Calmly, he nodded. "Better, now."

"You guys are engaged?" Chanel asked. "Where's my ring, Alexis?"

Ignoring Chanel, I stared at James. "Ask LA where's the ring you bought her. Don't forget I saw her naked pictures and sex texts in your damn phone! You started this! It doesn't matter where my ring is. It's mine!"

"I'll do that text to LA," James said, tapping on his cell.

My mom stepped to me, raised her hand to slap me. Spencer grabbed her arm. "Blake, don't. This is not completely her fault. Things with us haven't been right since I found out Alexis is my sister, and you and I know this."

"Wait, so you're penetrating the mother and the daughter," James said. "I'm out." He stood at attention like a soldier but didn't take a step.

Wasn't sure who was in shock the most right now. Mercedes gave a slow side to side with her head. "I knew one day your deceptive ways would catch up. But I swear you have nine lives, Alexis. Everyone in here is mentally screwed, except you."

"How can you sit there and say that? Alexis almost lost the baby," Spencer said, protecting me once more from Mercedes. "That's why I wanted you guys to come over. So you'd know she needs us to support her, not to judge or attack her."

"I need to get home to my family. Can we move this forward? What are you going to do, Alexis?" Devereaux questioned.

"Keep it," I said.

"You can't," Mercedes said. "If it's by Spencer, your DNA is too close. The child is going to be deformed."

Sandara spoke for the first time. "You think you're so smart. You don't know that, Mercedes."

"What you don't know, Alexis, is if it's mine?" James asked. "You're the worst. I'm out for real." He made his way to the door, didn't open it.

Spencer said, "Now that everyone knows, everybody can leave."

"So you fucked her last night? Is that why you didn't come home?" my mother asked. "Or did you screw Charlotte. Maybe y'all had a threesome, huh?"

Calmly, Spencer replied, "No, I did not."

"Then where were you?"

It was time for me to return the favor to my brother. "The only reason you're not in my position, Mother, is because your scrambled eggs are fried."

Conner laughed so hard he leaned on his cane. "You got that right."

Spencer stared at me. My mother's brows drew close together. Her eyelids narrowed almost to a close. The dog was cute. Glad she had a living animal occupying one of her hands or I was certain all of her fingers would be wrapped around my neck.

"You're cheating on me?" Spencer asked my mom.

My mom questioned, "How did you get my cheating from what she said?"

Now she was in the spotlight. I told her, "Tell my brother who gave you that dog."

Max growled at me. My mom's lips curved up a little.

Mercedes commented, "Max seems to be

a better judge of character than you, Spencer."

Ignoring her, I continued. "And tell Spencer how you spread for Billy Blackstone on your fiftieth birthday."

Mercedes glanced up at the ceiling. "Lord, Jesus. Forgive that lil girl, for she knows not a thing about respect or discretion. Alexis, I did not confide in you for you to throw this in our mother's face. You have no conscience."

Devereaux hung her shaking head. Sandara looked at the door. My mother stared at me.

I didn't care who stayed or left. "I just decided. I'm having an abortion."

"You can't kill my granddaughter," Conner protested.

Perfect timing. This was my opportunity to win over my father's wallet. "I can't afford to keep her." To add effect, I started crying. "You want to raise her, Daddy? Huh? Just say so and I'll sign the adoption papers today."

"Good decision," my mother said. "Have two abortions. One for Spencer and one for James."

"I can't let you do that knowing it might be mine," James said. "I'll be here for you. I'll call you later," he said, leaving this time.

"You're doing the right thing, Alexis," Mercedes said. "Get rid of it."

"Have the baby, Alexis. I'll help you raise her," Chanel said. "We can have the family I've always wanted."

"I'll support whatever you want, Sis," Devereaux said. "But seriously, I've heard enough. I have to go."

"Me too," Sandara said. Giving me a hug, she left with Devereaux.

"We'll get through this as a family," Conner said. "Text me your bank account information."

My mother howled, "Whoo!"

Conner ignored her howl. "I know you guys hate me. You have every right to. I'll financially support you and my granddaughter. I'm going to contact my attorney soon as I leave here and have him make some changes to my trust. And I'll send him an email. That's the least I can afford to do for you Alexis. Can't take my money to my grave," he said. Then he looked at my mom, "Blake, find someone your own age and leave my son alone."

That was the first thing I'd heard all night that made me laugh.

Conner gave me a hug. When he motioned to embrace Spencer, my brother held up his palms, stepped back. "Fuck you man."

The only person who hadn't expressed his desires, I already knew what his wishes were. Spencer wanted me to have the baby.

Turning away from my mother, I left her with Spencer and her dog, then went upstairs. Those two could let themselves out of my place.

I heard Chanel ask, "Can I come up, Alexis?"

Sex always made me feel better. I needed someone to hold me. I told Chanel, "Yes."

Right now I needed a lover and a friend. Spencer couldn't fuck me. If he stayed, he could watch the girl-on-girl action. Then he could do Chanel and I could watch them.

My night might not end badly after all.

I called out to my brother, "Spencer, we need you."

CHAPTER 9
BLAKE

"You'll never get this dick again."

Boo. Hoo. I picked up my Yorkie.

Spencer's best decision would've been not showing up at my house after watching me walk out of my daughter's apartment yesterday. Last night he wasn't here. This morning he strolled in all casual.

"Really, Spencer? You and your dick could've stayed wherever you were last night. You come at the break of dawn talking mess to me. You can get out of my house." I put Max in his pen, gave him a toy.

Our being in my bedroom was uncomfortable for me. He sat at the foot of my bed. Thoughts of us spooning, his making love to me every night, then again in the morning made me weak. I did not want to start over hoping to find a man to call mine. Yet, there was no way I could move forward with this one.

He sat there wearing loosely fitted sweat-pants, no underwear. The black Nike shirt with "We Run Atlanta" hugged his firm abs. The caramel smooth skin, square chin, full lips, and captivating dreamy eyes I'd fallen in love with had transformed into a complete asshole.

"How dare you have the audacity to tell me what I'll never get knowing you're the one at fault." Staring into his face, I didn't want his beautiful, young, hard dick or him. Spencer was just like all the rest of these men in Atlanta. "You're a male whore."

He sat there speechless. Stared at me. Picked up the remote. Turned on the tele-vision. I snatched the controller, pointed it at his face, then powered off my seventy-inch flat screen.

"That's cool, Blake."

The scream I suppressed was not to scare my puppy. My lids did not blink when I told Spencer, "I hate you. I wish I'd never met you. My life wasn't the best on my fiftieth birthday, but —"

"Or the day after when Fortune gave you two black eyes. He's probably the one bet-ter off being dead. Don't forget who was there for you, Blake. Who never left your side for two solid weeks?"

"I don't owe you a damn thing." I wasn't

indebted to Spencer. Wasn't about to play this immature mind game with his attempt to make me feel guilty.

My lips tightened, then quivered. I fought to hold back tears. No bow or standing ovation from me was in order for his slinging mud in my face. I could strike back. Ask if Alexis strapped on and fucked him in the ass like his uncle.

Men started shit, overlooking that women harbored enough ammunition to ambush them. Softly, to throw him off, I agreed, "You're right. Thanks."

He frowned. "I doubt that Billy fucks you the way I do." He stood, grabbed his dick. "He can have you."

I saw the impression and the left hook of his shaft. Not raising my voice, I told him, "Fucked. Past tense."

Billy Blackstone was my first love. First lover. But he wasn't the man for me. What I hadn't known when I had sex with Billy that night (and the following morning) was he already had a wife. Was there one man in Atlanta not out to fuck and then fuck over a woman?

Fortune was an inconsiderate asshole who made me feel like a meal ticket, not a sexy, hot woman to feast on the way I admit Spencer had done! Fortune's heart attack was the best gift he'd given me.

"I'm glad Fortune is dead. And —" I stopped. Wanted to add, I wish you were dead, too, but that wouldn't have been true.

Spencer relocated to my chaise, reclined, placed his hands behind his head, then stared at me. "Is that your idea of a comp, Fab?"

Comprise? Not hardly. Seriously. After all I'd said. That was his comeback? I was not trying to flatter this man young enough to be my son. I sat diagonally across the room from him in an oversized chair with my legs folded like a chicken wing so he could see underneath my nightgown that I wasn't wearing panties.

"Don't refer to me as Fab, or Fabulous!" I lowered my voice. "My eggs have never been scrambled or fried as my disrespectful daughter, who uses her vagina as a credit card swiping device, claimed in front of my entire family." Then I shouted, "I'm nobody's whore!"

Shit. My Yorkie started barking and clawing at the side of his pen. I rushed and picked him up. Instantly, he calmed me.

Spencer replied, "That's debatable. Listen, Blake. This isn't a pissing match and it's not about my sister, Alexis. You lied to me. Before I gave you the relationship ring that you've stopped wearing, I asked you if any other dick had been inside of your pussy since we met. You looked into these eyes," he said, pointing two fingers at his face. "You and women like you are the reason why I don't trust bitches, especially the old ass ones like you!"

Hairs sprouted on the nape of my neck. I put Max in his pen, sat back in my chair. Rubbing my hands, I blew so hard my jaws puffed. I squeezed the toes on my right foot, exhaled hard. I got up, walked toward Spencer. Stood over him. Looked down at him.

"Call me a bitch again and I'll give you a reason. You. You were the one who lied first. You. Slept with my daughter and she might be pregnant with your child. You. Stayed at her house with Chanel and God only knows what happened last night. And this morning."

"Precisely." He placed his feet on the floor, put his hands on my hips, gently pushed me back. His touch felt good.

"You need to get that out of my face," he said to my pussy. "If you were fertile you might be carrying Billy's, Blackstone is it, baby. You fucked him before I had sex with Alexis."

"That's debatable."

"Cute. Lead. You're too old to follow. I

hadn't planned on doing your daughter. It just happened because you betrayed me first."

I stepped back. "Regardless to whether I'm leading or following, I'm not slow. Okay. I'm supposed to understand because you're a man? Oh, I see. I provoked you. Is that it?"

He nodded. "Yup."

Moving away, I gave him a good six feet to keep from slapping his face. "Get your shit and get out of my house."

Spencer stood. "Fuck you and all this shit. Keep it. Burn it Angela Bassett–style and hold your breath for the next twenty-seven, thirty-seven, forty-seven, fifty plus nigga that'll make you squirt the first time he taps your ass. I'm done with you for good."

Decent point. Took me five decades to experience ejaculation. Damn, why'd he have to go there? I tried to conceal my flashback to the first time we made love. The mind-blowing sex didn't make me feel he was the one. It was how he cared for me after Fortune had beaten me. It was the way Spencer dabbed witch hazel on my bruised eyes, cheeks, and lips several times a day for two weeks. I missed our chilling in my Jacuzzi sharing intimate details about our past.

Spencer Domino could still be my man if my daughter wasn't pregnant. Secretly, I sided with Mercedes. I prayed Alexis got an abortion. The fact that they slept together, I could deal with his unfaithfulness if he could forgive mine.

He'd said he was done with me before and here he was. Here we were.

"You don't mean that," I said. "If you were serious, you would've been gone by now instead of standing here arguing with me."

"Cuddle up with your dog. You two deserve one another."

No he didn't go there. "Good-bye, Spencer. Let yourself out. Go fuck your sister and her girlfriend. Go take care of your unborn daughter, son, niece, nephew. One better. Go get fucked."

On that statement, he headed downstairs to my front door. I hadn't intended on stooping to his level, but I refused to allow him to trash me without scratching his eyes out.

I refused to chase Spencer. Thank God for Max. I put a cute orange Ralph Lauren polo shirt on him; then I changed into a sexy fitted orange crop-sleeved dress with a pair of three-inch heels. I smeared on pussy pink lipstick, released my ponytail. Wasn't trying to look half my age. Opening my jewelry box, I put Spencer's ring in my purse to give myself a reason to show up at his place. I eased into a red thong, oiled my legs, put Max in his RL tote bag, picked up the keys to my red Ferrari, and trotted downstairs.

"I apologize, Fabulous. Forgive me," Spencer said.

He was seated on my leather sofa . . . naked, stroking his big, long, black dick.

I gasped. My breathing became shallow. Max barked at Spencer. I had to laugh.

Opening my purse, I removed my relation-ship ring, flipped it to Spencer as though he could choose heads or tails. He released his dick, caught it midair.

My last words to this young, disrespectful asshole were, "Let yourself out."

CHAPTER 10
DEVEREAUX

By the time I got home at midnight, Phoenix was snoring as though he hauled bricks for a living.

Alexis wasn't the only one dealing with problems. Our mother, Mercedes. Seems like my baby sister Sandara was the only one without all the extra. But her situations with any one of her baby daddies could pop off in a split second.

I'd dozed off around two in the morning once the snoring subsided. Woke up at five forty-five, fifteen minutes before my alarm was schedule to sound. Almost four hours of rest was great for me. Phoenix was still asleep. He remained that way when he didn't have a reason to get up, which was most days when he didn't have to care for Nya, meet a client, or have breakfast with the boyz.

My biggest relief was Phoenix's mom, Mrs. Etta, had volunteered to keep Nya the first half of this week, allowing me to focus on overseeing marketing and promotions. Midweek my baby was going to Sandara's. Dropoffs, pickups, Phoenix was not getting out of doing that regardless of his managing schedule for Ebony.

Careful not to disturb my fiancé, I went into my bathroom, closed the door, washed my face, and brushed my teeth. Removing my bonnet, I combed my hair, snapshot a photo, texted it to Marcus Darlin, with a message: I need an appointment.

When would I find time to let him care for the natural mane on my head?

Marcus Darlin replied, Dang! Dev I almost dropped my flatiron. Let me know when. I'll come to you.

Staring in the mirror, I texted back, Will do.

The wide and pointed nose, not full yet not thin lips made me wonder if my father was white. The thickness of my hair suggested he could be Jewish, African. My face was flat. I smiled. There was no real definition in my cheeks. Glossy brown eyes surrounded by long, dark lashes people paid upward of two hundred dollars for. I fingered my brows.

"You need to eat more," I told myself. Stepping on the scale, 160. "I'm good."

Easy to put on. Hard to take off.

I adjusted the water to warm. The pounding soothed my body as I scrubbed head to toe. Straight strands curled more as I applied shampoo, then thoroughly rinsed what was all mine before turning the faucet to off. Massaging in a leave-in conditioner, I checked the time. My hair would have to air-dry.

This time next Monday I'd be practically residing at the studio and filming at different locations for eight consecutive weeks. Promotional photo shoot starts today with my leading ladies Ebony, Brea, Misty, and Emerald. Their respective men were joining in tomorrow for their pictures. Yesterday at Alexis's was complete mayhem. I had enough jaw-dropping cliffhangers in my head to spin the first episodes of *Sophisticated Side Chicks New York* and *LA.*

What was up with Alexis questioning James about LA? I wasn't going to say Alexis should have an abortion, leave Chanel alone, and marry James. At least he was still ready to commit. Obviously, my sister wasn't. I doubted James would call off their engagement if the kid weren't his. Whatever "it" was that drove men insane, Alexis should share with me.

I selected a comfortable pair of yellow

cotton pants, a shirt, and a pair of tan split-toe sandals with jewels on top. Entering my office, the scripts for each episode were printed and laid out on my working table. I returned to my bedroom.

Watching Phoenix breathe heavily, I couldn't help but wonder where my man was last night? I didn't want him to open his eyes to drama, but I was disturbed. Misery was not going to become my bed companion. Chaos outside of our relationship was trying to creep into my psyche.

Yellow represented the sunshine of my profession. Blue, the way his balls must've felt each time I'd said, not tonight. Blend the two colors . . . the episodes in my mind were not going to be my reality.

What were my mother and my sister thinking screwing the same man? One of them could've said no to Spencer's dick. Should've been Alexis. More material for me.

Phoenix fluttered his lids. His dick didn't pitch the usual morning tent under the sheet.

I sat beside him. "Babe, I was having a family crisis. You were supposed to have Nya at home when I got back. I left shortly after noon. You dropped her off at your mom's at three o'clock. How long did you stay at the aquarium with her? And you didn't respond until my seventh text message asking you to call me. That's not like you. What were you doing?"

His brows damn near touched. He rubbed his eye. Slowly he propped his pillow against the headboard, sat up, leaned back. He didn't look at me when he said, "What difference does it make?"

Reaching for his cell, he asked, "What time is it?"

I grabbed his phone. He took it back.

"Where were you?"

"Man, I was with the fellas."

Politely, I asked him, "Where? The room tone was above your ringtone? Was the strip club jumping at three, four, and five o'clock in the afternoon?"

Gesturing with his hands, he said, "It's not my fault you couldn't go with us. I took Nya to the aquarium by myself."

Seemed more like a drive-through shark tank for my baby. While we were waiting for Alexis to come downstairs, I'd spoken with Nya. She said she saw a shark. A shark. No star or jellyfish. No turtles or penguins. What the hell! I wasn't going to tell him I'd had a conversation with our daughter.

His eyes shifted side to side. "Then I met up with my boyz at the Rose Bar."

Maintaining my composure, I repeated, "The Rose Bar?"

The tension in his voice increased as he said, "Yeah."

"I was at the Rose Bar last night," I lied.

This time he stared at me. He was quiet. Hunched his left shoulder.

"Was the music thumping so loud at six, seven, and eight that you couldn't hear your cell? Where were you, Phoenix? What time did you get home?"

"I left the bar early. What's up with the cross-examination? You getting brand new." He became defensive. "I'm not doing this." His voice started cracking. "You've always been cool with my hanging out. Your family had a crisis when your mom's ex-married man slash boyfriend or whatever you want to call him assaulted her. When I did call you, this time Alexis is possibly pregnant by her brother who is also your mother's boyfriend. Even if I knew you were dealing with all of that, Dev, what could I do to change the situation? Babe, you worry too much. I love you. Don't let your family's drama ruin our good thing." He pressed his lips to mine; then he leaned back onto the pillow.

Typically, I wouldn't drill Phoenix, but I'd had a brief conversation with my sister Mercedes at Alexis's apartment. Mercedes confided that she'd hired a private detective to follow her husband, Benjamin. I knew spying on my fiancé would push him away.

That Alexis, I knew her well, her sending me that photo of Benjamin with another woman. Alexis had an ulterior motive, more than likely to take the focus off of her. The way Conner offered to help Alexis, I was beginning to believe that I should try to find my father.

What if my dad felt like Etta and wanted to be in his granddaughter's life? What if Phoenix and I were related? We didn't remotely resemble each other, but we could be second or third cousins. God, why did my mother have to do this to all of us? What was she thinking?

"What if we're siblings?" I said to switch the subject.

Laughter filled the bedroom. "We're not kin. Trust me. Where are you going with this? Do you want to find your father?"

I wasn't taking our communication where I wanted. Wasn't leading my relationship in the direction my sister wanted either. The fact that Mercedes mentioned last night she had something important to discuss with me tonight, then showed me a picture of Phoenix and Ebony at T.I.'s Scales 925 on

Friday night. That was when my trust wavered. If he had nothing to hide, why hadn't he told me they'd met up?

"Sometimes, I want to find him. My mom is right. I've done well, the rest of us had done good despite not knowing and I . . . I don't know, babe."

"You see what happened with Alexis. If this is what you really want, I'll support you. Do it in two months after the wrap-up on taping our series. I gotta concentrate on building Ebony's brand."

Real seductive, I said, "You know what I want you to focus on, babe?"

Phoenix smiled. "Yeah, I know." He tossed the cover to the floor, lay flat, spread his thighs.

His dick plumped. With each rise, I touched the tip.

Sex wasn't on my mind. I cupped his face. "Let's set a wedding date."

His shaft quickly deflated. The head rested on his balls. Resuming his position against the headboard, he said, "A piece of paper isn't going to change how I feel about you. We've got each other. Getting married can wait."

I was tired of our living arrangement but clearly understood why he wasn't. I wanted my status to become legal. Change Nya's and my last names from Crystal to Watson. Introducing Phoenix as my fiancé at all the prescreening events, I didn't want that. I had the ring on my finger. I deserved the next level of his commitment.

Phoenix lived under my roof because I was determined to make sure my, make that our, little girl never had to wonder what a hug and a kiss from her dad felt like. My, not his, big day was tomorrow.

The odds of meeting a man in Atlanta who wasn't gay, bisexual, or pussy hopping was challenging. My mom never married. I didn't want to be her shadow. The one man who put a relationship ring on her finger was younger than me. Mercedes had a husband. Benjamin was a great guy. Wild as Alexis was, she had a ring from James. James wasn't leaving Alexis even if that baby inside of her wasn't his. Sandara had three kids. No ring.

I'd never have another baby out of wedlock.

A part of me was envious of my sister Alexis. She knew her father. I texted my mom, I want to meet my father.

On my own, I'd found my way to a place where love and trust were sacred. Phoenix made me feel safe. I wasn't going to ruin my engagement. We'd be okay.

My mom texted back, I told Kendall not to do it. If you want to find him, do it without me.

I replied, Since you're pissed with Alexis this is how you treat me. Fine. I'll do it on my own.

I knew my man was right about our feelings for each other, but after four years of wearing this heart-shaped diamond engagement ring, I was ready to put on a beautiful designer gown, ease my way down the aisle one small step at a time, and stand beside the man I wanted to share the rest of my life with. *Who would give me away?*

"Babe, we really need to calendar a date for the wedding," I said.

"Do I love you?" he asked.

"Yes."

"Do you love me?" he asked.

"Yes."

"Do I treat you like a queen?"

Frustrated, this time I hissed, "Yes," wondering what his definition of queen was.

"Do I lick your asshole during sex?"

That made me cringe each time he'd done it. Hearing him say that made me uncomfortable. Assholes weren't sanitary.

I nodded. "But you know how I feel about it."

"I can't help that, Dev. How we gon' set a date and we can't . . . besides, you know my business is about to take off with Ebony. I appreciate your holding me down, but let me be a man and take care of you. Let me make you comfortable in and out of this bedroom."

"Don't change the focus. Marriage is about taking care of one another."

"You know I just took her on as my client," he said proudly. "And —"

"And she works for me. I pay her! So indirectly I pay you. Don't act like you got her the role on your own. What does your taking on my main celebrity have to do with our setting a wedding date? First, it was business was slow. Then, you weren't making enough money to pay for the wedding. Then you needed time to redo the business plan I've never seen so you could get a loan. I told you to talk to my mom. She's the president of a bank that services customers all over the world. But no. You don't want her counting your coins." I wanted to say, what coins? "Being on *my* set twelve plus hours a day, starting today, I'll be busier than you. Now is the time, Phoenix. It's not like I'm asking you to go on vacation. This is our wedding I'm trying to set a damn date for."

After everything I'd said, he countered, "I'm not spending six figures for one day of making other people happy."

"I'm not other people! I'm your fiancée!"

"I just need a few more months. After filming we should be financially prepared to discuss a date. I'm not letting you foot the bill by yourself."

"You said that six —"

"I'm tired of arguing about this shit, Dev!"

"Fine. Fine!" I wanted to give him an ultimatum, but I loved this man and didn't want to lose him.

I felt as though I was starting to become an embarrassment to my colleagues, casts, friends, and family. What was a reasonable amount of time? This ring had been on my finger for three years. The only time I'd taken it off was to shower. The money didn't matter more to me than my man or my status. I'd pay for the entire ceremony if it meant being Mrs. Devereaux Crystal-Watson.

He got out of bed.

"Where are you going?"

"I have an early-morning appointment with Ebony. Have to prep her on the shoot today. Make sure we get all the shots we need for my promoting her. I'll see you on set."

"She's my star. Not yours."

He smirked. "Everything is going to be all

right. The most important thing is, we love each other."

He gave me a real sweet tongue kiss. That would have to do for now. He headed toward the door.

"We'll see you later, babe. I love you."

I thought but didn't say, *I love you too.*

Looking over my shoulder, I watched Phoenix until he entered his bathroom.

I couldn't let his not committing to a date consume me. I had a long day. First the shoot, then a late dinner with Mercedes at Ocean Prime restaurant.

CHAPTER 11
EBONY

#mynewlife #nextchapter #Sophisticated-SideChicksATL #SSCATL #iamebonywaterhouse

Videotaping strawberries, banana, blueberries, protein powder, and unsweetened almond milk blending in my Magic Bullet, I posted it on Instagram, then poured twelve ounces of ice-cold aloe vera gel in a squeeze bottle, added a small tube of Neosporin, and shook it up. Flipping over my Bullet, I unscrewed the top, filled a tall glass, and then carried my breakfast and beauty treatment out back. Inhaling the fresh morning air, I placed both items on a round table, then covered the lawn chair with two beach towels.

I was young, not foolish. After marrying Buster, moving into his house in Conyers, I'd kept my home in Brookhaven. BK was a quiet community adjacent to Buckhead. Houses here were close enough to call the people next door my neighbors. Immediately after closing escrow three years ago, my sponsor had a ten-foot brick wall built to deter anything with two or four legs from crossing onto my property. There was a gun in every room. Never had to, but wouldn't hesitate to use any of them.

A call came in from Buster. I answered, "Morning," with a smile.

"Sounds like you're ready for this day."

"Getting there," I told him.

"I believe in you, Goldie. Your fans are going to love you almost as much as I do. Don't tarnish my last name. Keep all our business personal."

Crossing my fingers, I said, "Promise."

I heard a male in the background ask, "Buster, should I wear the light or dark blue briefs?"

"Sweetheart, I'll call you tonight. Bye."

Placing my cell on the table, I reclined, sipped my smoothie.

Older men weren't rude. They were set in their ways. Thinking about my ex-man, the one before Buster, I'd met him online where all types of people were seeking a plethora of arrangements. Couldn't vouch for other pussies, but my Colombian pussy was more beautiful than the sun rising. Lots of men with money flew me all over the world, bought me expensive jewelry, clothes, cars, in exchange for dates. Some wanted sex; others simply needed me to listen to their problems, or Facetime and talk dirty while they jacked off. What I wanted most was U.S. citizenship and financial security. In that order.

A few times I ventured outside of my sexual comfort zone and masturbated during Skype sessions to get a quick five to ten grand. I wasn't trying to be labeled a porn star. The best part of meeting men on the site was most of them were upfront about what they wanted and what they'd invest to get punany. Occasionally, thousands of dollars still posted to my account. Dining at five-star restaurants in exchange for the pleasure of my company was how I'd first met Buster. No woman should be broke. Coochie coupons were recyclable. If I could only have one, I'd rather sex an old rich man than fuck a young broke dude.

Sunshine beamed on my body. I spread my thighs. It was time to get my money flowing. This was the most important morning of my career thus far. I'd filmed the pilot with Devereaux, but today signified day one of working with her for nine straight weeks. I rubbed the icy aloe and ointment all over my face and naked body to soften and tighten my skin. I sipped my smoothie waiting for the moisture to absorb into my pores.

Buster was a seasoned romantic freak. He loved for us to watch the sun rise and set every chance we had, which wasn't often. My backyard faced north. Looking to my left, orange hues slowly blanketed white scattered clouds. My husband also enjoyed stroking himself while watching a young black man with a big dick and sexy ass fuck me. Phoenix didn't know that I was married to a bisexual seventy-one-year-old man or that I had a home in Conyers. Most women talked too damn much. There was a lot men never revealed. Where they lived. Whom they lived with. If they had a woman, wife. Hell, I'd been the side believing I was the main.

Juggling men at an early age taught me that no man needed to know everything about me, not even my husband. Starring in a role on #SSCATL was #mylife.

I covered my hair with a large pink plastic cap, turned on the outdoor shower, rinsed with warm water. Lathering an exfoliate cloth, I scrubbed all over. I squeezed jojoba oil into my palms, massaged my body, changed the water to cold, then shut it off.

I heard Phoenix call out, "My babe, where are you?"

"I'm out here, my babe."

Joining me on the patio, he said, "Damn, you look hot."

"I am. Go take off your shit. Come get this sweet pussy."

Phoenix went inside. Two minutes later he came out undressed. I restarted the water, braced my palms against the wall, and spread my legs. Soon as he put the head in I started cuming. Our chemistry was incredible. The deeper he penetrated me, a small orgasm led to a bigger one. By the time he was all the way in, not caring who heard, I screamed with pleasure.

He pumped faster until he announced, long and loud, "I'm cuming!"

Looking over my shoulder, I told him, "Cum for me, daddy."

Phoenix pulled out. "Damn, she really was hot, wet, and ready for me."

There was no time to bask in the moment. Turning off the water, I said, "We have to get to set. We shouldn't show up at the same time. I have to get hair and makeup done, then wardrobe, so you arrive about thirty minutes after I get there. I'll text you."

"Let me taste you," he said. Sticking out his tongue, he knelt before me.

His mouth on my clit made me wet. I wanted to have another orgasm, but I was not going to be late behind letting a man who thought I was going to pay him to lick my pussy make me climax. Again.

"That's enough for now. Meet me back here after we're done. I wanna ride my dick tonight." Galloping, I touched his chopper.

Instantly, he got hard. "Why you teasing him like this?"

There was no time for that conversation. "Don't stand over me on set. Don't give me direction. That's the photographer's job. Did you remember to bring your iPad?"

"Yes, it's in the car," he said. "We need to discuss compensation. I was thinking ten grand a month plus ten percent of what I get you in endorsements and sponsorships."

Ten what? Phoenix was straight tripping if he thought he was going to get monetarily compensated. Every check would be payable to Goldie Jackson, and his return was open access to my home and my good pussy.

That five thousand I'd gotten from my husband to give to Phoenix to find me a gig had finally paid off. Damn, it took him three years. Phoenix couldn't rep me. Outside of Devereaux he did not have any viable contacts.

The day we met, he approached me all professional talking about how he could make me famous. His pitch was strong. Two months after we'd met I let him hit this 'cause I could tell from his mannerisms he had serious bedroom skills. He wouldn't have gotten paid if we'd had sex first.

I didn't want him managing me. That was his idea. He could quit right now. Nothing in my life would change, unless he became vindictive. Confessed our affair to Devereaux to get me fired. I might have to rethink my plan.

"Have your lawyer send me the contract, babe."

"So you agree to what I'm asking for?" he asked, all surprised.

"I've got to get ready. Let's discuss this later."

I knew if he were the big star he'd expect me to respect his obligation. Hated when men were inconsiderate. "Don't break with me. Break with Devereaux or stay to yourself."

"Dang, what's up with the long list?" Phoenix said. Following me upstairs to my bathroom, he stood in the doorway.

Walking past him, I turned on the shower. "You can't give her a reason to suspect us. This is day one of nine straight weeks for me."

"But I told Dev I was meeting with you this morning. Won't it look odd if we show up separate?"

"Stop! Telling her every damn thing. She doesn't need to know every time we meet. Oh, I need you to figure out how to get away for the weekend. And do not tell her you're going to be with me. We're taking a mini vacation."

"How am I supposed to do —"

"We leave Saturday, be back Sunday. It's a surprise. You always lie about being with the boys, one more lie isn't going to matter."

"Yeah, but not overnight. She does come home."

"Figure it out," I told him, stepping into the shower.

Recalling the changes to the script for the first episode, my pussy was on fire. My scene with West-Léon was what made me wet now. West-Léon was getting a cool four hundred grand. Not bad. He was so fine I prayed I did not have an orgasm while filming.

I was glad Phoenix was gone when I walked into my bedroom.

#bossbitch #photoshoot #today #SSCATL #iamebonywaterhouse

CHAPTER 12
ALEXIS

"You want to go to Stone Mountain with me?" Spencer asked.

"Chick, this time of the morning?" I said. I knew the attraction park opened at ten thirty during the summer, but man. I checked my phone, then told him, "It's nine o'clock."

"Your mom is tripping. Worse than kicking a bruh out, she left my naked ass stroking my shit on her couch, told me to let myself out," he said.

Cracking up! I almost fell on the floor.

My mom was like most females. Considering ending the best relationship she'd probably had in years over her dude cheating. I knew her. Although Spencer left my place an hour after she had last night, Blake was wondering if Spencer had dipped his dick inside of Chanel. Wouldn't be surprised if she believed he'd fucked me too. When would she learn, chicks couldn't police good dick.

"Wait, don't laugh. That's not all. She told me to go fuck my sister *and* Chanel."

I sat up in my bed. Smirked. Nodded. A burst of laughter escaped, causing me to hold my stomach.

He paused, I guessed waiting for me to stop hollering. It was cool that he could share details with me of his personal situation with my mom. Blake had no concept of how people my age got down. Sex wasn't sacred. Cuming was recreational. We did not have sexual hang-ups. That was for people her age.

Spencer's firm tone was filled with annoyance when he asked, "You done?"

Smothering my last few chuckles, I told him, "I know you put the D in her real deep when you got home. You did go straight home right? Or did you detour to Charlotte's?" I cracked up.

Silence came before, "I went to Blake's, man, but all that backlash kept my shit flaccid. What you gon' do besides ridicule?"

"Hold on. You woke me up with this hilarious stand-up. What did you expect?"

"Then I probably shouldn't tell you Max stared me down like he was the man and my black ass had better not be home when he got back."

That was it. I let loose and couldn't reel in for damn near a whole minute. "Yeah, you need to release some tension. Come get me in an hour. I might not get on the rides, though. Gotta take it easy after those blows to my stomach from your gurl."

"Chill," he said, ending the call as though he hadn't heard my last comment.

I needed to get out of bed anyway. Ordinarily I'd hit the gym and get down with Kanye's workout plan station on Pandora. I amped up "Do Ya," a single by DaBoy-Dame. He was my generation's P. Diddy and Jay Z doing collabs with artists we loved like Ty Dolla $ign. I showered to the beat. Washed every nook and cranny. Layered sunblock all over my hourglass figure.

Everybody needed something or someone to love. Billy Blackstone had no idea how much joy he'd brought my mom by giving her King MaxB. Blake had a fit anytime anyone called her pedigree a dog. Sandara's kids adored Max. He had that laid-back attitude I'd want my pet to have. Maybe I should get tropical fish.

Scanning my halter minidresses, my selection was more about what color I was feeling. Purple stood out. Money green four-inch stilets. Any heel shorter was for the conservatives. Not certain of what part of the three thousand plus acres park we were going to stomp on, I put a pair of mint leather flat sandals in my purse.

The only breathing animal I needed to love me was me. Wasn't sure I did the best job of taking care of my emotions, but for sure I had no problem keeping myself first. Unlike a lot of these females in Atlanta trying to keep GPS on their dude, I'd never chase pussy or dick.

My cell rang. Hopefully, that was Spencer calling to say he was on his way. I didn't mind people waiting on me, but I hated being the one sitting around.

I looked at the caller ID. It was my sperm donor. Hopefully he was calling to make good on his offer to financially support me. Knowing there was no baby in my belly, I'd take every penny he offered and call it restitution.

Still couldn't call him dad, I answered, "Hey, Conner."

"Alexis, this is not Conner," she said.

Well, that was obvious. "How can I help you?"

"This is the nurse at Grady. Your father told us that you're the only living relative he wants to see. He's in ICU. He may not have much time. You need to come to the hospital right away."

My heart thumped in my chest. "What happened? I just saw him yesterday. He was fine."

"Honey, he was shot several times early this morning. You need to hurry," she said.

Shot? Frowning, I became speechless. I'd only known Conner a few months. Didn't care much for or about him. But his offer to help me yesterday had softened my exterior.

Only living relative he wants to see?

"Are you there?" she asked. "I have to go. Hurry. Please."

"Yes, I'm on my way."

Before Spencer knocked, I opened my door to gasp fresh air.

"You look nice, as always. You ready?" Spencer asked, then paused. "Oh, no. What's wrong?"

Covering my mouth, with wide eyes I stared at him. There were no tears to shed for Conner. Didn't know him that well. Wasn't going to visit him without Spencer.

"Let me get my purse." I removed my gun. Placed my forty on the kitchen counter.

"Now I know something is wrong. Sis," he said, holding my biceps. "Tell me."

Afraid he'd bail on me if I told him the truth, I said, "It's a beautiful morning. I don't want to ruin it." Then insisted, "I'll drive."

The stop we had to make, I knew Spencer wouldn't agree to if he were behind the wheel. I headed south on Interstate 75. We didn't have far to go to get to the hospital.

"James really bought you this ride?" he asked, reclining his seat.

I was glad he'd asked something that eased my concerns about our father. In a few minutes, Spencer was going to be pissed. I replied, "I earned this bitch."

"Cash? Is that how he paid?"

I went from being alone in my bed, cool with hanging out with my brother, to traveling into the unknown. My immediate future was scary. I didn't want Conner to die.

"Did he pay cash?"

"Oh, I guess. All I made sure of was that my name was the only one on the title."

"So why you cheating on the dude?"

"The question is why not? You guys do it all the time. James has a white girlfriend in Los Angeles. What you call that?"

Spencer sucked his teeth. "Females always suspect, but y'all constantly suspecting. And you know she's white and she's his woman . . . because?"

"Saw the texts on his cell. I said that yesterday. I wasn't being nosy. We were in his car, I picked up his phone, and there was her naked pussy spread across his screen. She said she missed him already."

"You shouldn't have done that."

"You shouldn't have had sex with my mother, then me, then left the restaurant Saturday morning and fucked Charlotte." Recalling the throwdown with Charlotte, I started getting mad all over again.

"Well, she's history. Your mom is too."

Men, I swear I hated their double-standard bullshit rationalizations. I drove into the entrance at Grady.

Spencer stared at me, then sat up. "Why are we here? You have an appointment?"

I got out the car; Spencer trailed me. His question about an appointment gave me the perfect idea. The only way to get out of being pregnant without confessing my lie was to fake a miscarriage. I could do that later.

Standing at the information desk, I said, "We're here to see Conner Rogers."

Spencer stepped back. He became quiet. His eyes shifted left, then back to me. "For real. This is how you gon' do this shit?" he asked. "Why you spring this fucking trickery on me? This is the second time you've broken our agreement without telling me." He yelled, "We are not supposed to deal with his ass!"

I chose not to say a word hoping he'd calm down.

The receptionist gave us directions to the intensive care unit. I led the way. Spencer walked beside me. He muttered, "I hope that muthafucka die."

"Don't say that, Spencer. Conner was shot early this morning."

Crime in Atlanta had increased rapidly. Robbers were invading people's homes while they were at home, then beating, sometimes killing them. Purse snatching in daylight was happening. Carjacking had taken a more organized approach with thieves stealing keys from valet attendants. Anything could've happened to my, I meant our dad.

Spencer nodded, became quiet, slowed his pace. Standing in the hallway, my brother held my hand. We stopped. He faced me. "How do you know he was shot?"

"After I spoke with you, a nurse called and told me."

"Why would she call you?"

No need to lie. Wasn't sure how my brother was going to feel. "She told me Conner said I was his only surviving relative."

Letting go of my hand, he became quiet again.

I gripped his hand. "Go in with me. Please. I need you."

"You're his favored. I'm sure he doesn't want to see me. I'm chill. Don't tell him I'm here. I'll be over there when you come out," he said, going toward the seating area.

Maybe if my brother hadn't cursed out Conner yesterday, things would be different. Taking a deep breath, I approached the nurses' station. "I'm Alexis Crystal here to see Conner Rogers."

"Certainly. Right this way."

I followed her to a door. I peeped into the window. If Conner hadn't offered to help me and my make-believe unborn, I wasn't sure I'd be here.

The nurse opened the door. "Go on in," she said, entering behind me. She checked his monitor, looked at me. Her eyes shifted to Conner, then back to me. She nodded.

A breathing cup covered his nose and mouth. He looked at me through eyes that were halfway opened. I shouldn't have but had to ask the nurse, "Can you tell my brother I need him? His name is Spencer Domino. He's in the waiting area."

Conner's eyes shifted left to right, then back.

The nurse nodded once, then left.

Removing the cup, Conner said, "Thank you for coming, Alexis." His voice was low, weak. "I'd hoped to get to know you better." He took a long, slow, deep breath inside the cup. "I want you to take good care of my granddaughter."

No need to confess now, I said, "I will." Sitting beside his bed, I held his hand. My throat began to swell. I swallowed. Asked him, "Why did you deny me? Why didn't you at least let me know that you knew I was yours?"

"Please don't cry," he said, watching my eyes fill with tears. "I can't change what I've done. I was hard because I thought that was what made me a man."

Since my brother wasn't here in the room yet, I asked, "Did you know your brother was molesting my brother?" I was entitled to an answer. If this man knew and did nothing, I was walking out and never going to see him again.

Saying nothing was worse. I pulled away my hand. Stood. "So I'm your only living relative? Is that what you told these people?"

He sucked more oxygen. "Alexis, wait. That's not exactly what I told them. Please don't leave. I asked you to come for a reason."

"And I asked you a question about my brother. I'm listening," I said with one hand on the door.

"I've changed my will. I'm leaving everything to you and my granddaughter."

I let go of the door. "You did what?" He mentioned last night that he'd email his attorney but that was fast.

"I don't want my only grandchild to want for anything. Please, come here."

I moved closer. This time I held the cup over his face. Waited until he'd inhaled several times.

"Open that bottom drawer. Take my keys. They're to my house and the car I was driving when I got shot. If I don't make it out of here, everything is yours," he said as though he knew he wouldn't. "A copy of my revised trust is in my mailbox. Upstairs in my office, inside the top drawer of my desk you'll find the keyless remotes to all my vehicles. My lawyer can help you work out the details."

The only attorney I trusted was mine. I was going to contact Kendall. He was the one who'd located Conner.

Conner took a deep breath. "All I ask is that you do one thing for me."

Better not be something crazy. "What's that?"

"I want you to name my granddaughter Venus Domino Blake Crystal and call her Domino."

I was in shock. Wondered what else he'd

left. Why didn't he say he'd left something for Spencer? My brother was abused and abandoned.

Spencer pushed open the door, entered the room, stood over Conner, then asked, "Did you know, old man?"

Conner took a deep breath. "Son, I forgive —"

This time Spencer's voice was deeper. "You don't deserve to call me your son. I need to know before you check out of here, old man. Did you know?"

Conner's chest heaved as he nodded his head.

Spencer yelled, "You bastard!"

Faintly, Conner responded, "No, son. Hear me out."

"No, nigga. Fuck you!"

A nurse rushed into the room. "Is everything okay?"

I hugged my brother. Spencer cried on my shoulder. Snot rolled down my arm. I didn't care. I lied to the nurse, "Yes, he's okay. Just a little upset."

Relieved she came in when she had, there was no telling what Spencer would've done. The nurse looked at our dad.

Conner's eyes slowly closed. I held my breath until he opened them, then said, "We're good."

Soon as the door closed, Spencer stared down at Conner. "I swear if you weren't in this hospital, I'd kill you." Grinding his teeth, my brother asked, "Tell me why?"

"Conner, please. Tell my brother the truth," I pleaded.

He took a deep breath. Blew it out of his mouth. "Until you took the DNA test, son, I honestly thought your mother had cheated on me. I thought you were his son, not mine."

"So you'd stand by and let him screw his own son. Man, that's bullshit and you know it." Spencer left the room.

I started crying.

Dropping Conner's keys in my purse, I told my dad, "I have to go."

He opened his mouth. Gasp after gasp no words came out. I stood there waiting, hoping, praying he'd die for knowing and not stopping the molestation.

"Did you leave anything to Spencer?"

Shaking his head, he dragged air into his throat.

"You hate my brother. Why?" I stood there not caring if he were short of breath. If he'd take his last, I wouldn't call for the nurse.

Gasping, he said, "Spencer."

"Spencer, what?" I asked.

"Hates me."

Shaking my head, I hated him too. If I didn't have access to his possessions, I'd curse him out. "You can't blame my brother for how he feels. You created that situation."

"True. But he didn't have to shoot me," Conner said. Alarms on his monitor started beeping. Nurses ran in. I walked out.

My tears were for my brother. Not for Conner Rogers's lying ass. I needed to drown my sorrow with a mai tai. Knew Spencer would agree.

I texted my manager friend at Suite Food Lounge, You at work.

William Alfred William hit me back, You know it beautiful.

Set me up man in a corner booth. Coming through in 10 to 20.

Al, that was what everyone called him, texted back, For sho.

Make that an hour and forty-five. I knew Conner wasn't dead yet, but I wanted to see his house, car, trust, and whatever else he claimed he'd left me and his granddaughter.

Chapter 13
Spencer

"This is so sweet, man." The smile on my sister's face was so wide I saw her pink upper and lower gums plus damn near all thirty-two.

"So Conner punk ass just breaking you off? He ain't leaving me shit?"

Sis glanced at me. Focused back on the two-lane road. "I got you," she said, using my line.

"What exactly did he tell you?" Knowing Alexis she could be lying. Or inheriting a lot of debt. Conner didn't own shit when he was with my mom. He never remarried. His ass was probably undercover like his brother.

Alexis turned off of West Paces Ferry Road Northwest into a stretched driveway and cruised about a hundred feet. Conner's spot was three stories. I noticed she didn't need Siri to assist with directions.

"He said you shot him."

That shit silenced me.

"I know you didn't do it. But if you did, don't tell me. Even if you had, I'd understand. I can't be a hypocrite if Conner doesn't make it. The way I see it, he owes me."

Owed her? I nodded.

Dude parked her convertible in front the double-door entrance. The plush green lawn was manicured to perfection. An eight-foot concrete wall painted black and white lined the perimeter along the sidewalk.

"Not bad for a deadbeat," I casually said. If I were driving my SUV, she'd have to make this pit by herself. I trailed ten steps behind her as she opened the mailbox, pulled out a large yellow envelope, then she unlocked the front door.

Standing inside, burgundy, black, and chestnut leathers covered the antique sofa, bench, and two high-backed chairs. Large framed paintings of Tuskegee airmen, Dr. King, Malcolm X, Colin Powell was on one side of President Obama's photo. Al Sharpton, Jesse Jackson, a few black men I didn't recognize hung to the right. The first floor had an art gallery vibe.

Had to admit, I liked the layout. If I didn't hate dude, we might have had some intellectually stimulating convo. Scrap that sentiment. I did what had to be.

"He lived here by himself?" Sounded more like a statement than a question. I was still tripping that he'd confessed he knew what happened to me and Sis was acting as though that part of the convo never happened.

I'd never lean on her shoulder for support again. Didn't need her to have my back either. Why the fuck would I waste my time putting six bullets in Conner's ass?

Watching Sis, women were the greatest pretenders. Relay was sacred until you pissed them off. Then all a man's business became a public announcement. Thought about Blake for a sec.

I told Alexis, "Let's go to his office, get what you came for so we can bounce."

"Can you believe he said this will be all mine?" Alexis's face glowed. She was probably already redecorating in her mind. Deciding where she'd put the nursery. Damn, I was going to be an uncle. Hopefully not a daddy-uncle. If the kid was mine, this joint would be partially mine too. Kind of.

Turning on the lights in each room we walked into, we finally located the office on the third-floor corner facing the driveway. All of his blinds were closed. Now that I thought about it, no windows, curtains, or blinds were pulled up or back.

Sis headed straight for the desk, a heavy-weight mahogany piece. Before putting down the yellow sealed envelope, she waved it in my face.

She sang, "Here it is," with that wide smile.

Across the front read, *"Living Trust."* When did he have time to do this shit?

"You think he's lying? It might be fake," she said, carefully prying the edge.

I was next to her. "Why should I care? Check it out. It's all in your hands. Literally."

She slid out the first page. "Well, Alexis Crystal is right here," she said. Flashing the page in front of me, she pointed at her name, then put the paper back in with the rest.

Something wasn't adding up. "Don't you think it's strange he arranged this last night and someone shot his ass this morning? It's like he knew there was a hit out on him, so he put your name on everything; then when he found out about your being pregnant, he wanted to make sure his granddaughter was broken off." Mad as hell my name wasn't there, too, I was rambling.

"It's not strange. He may have added my

name three months ago right after we'd met."

"And not mine?" I pressed my lips together. Stared down at Alexis. "The only way for you to have known before today was you lied to me. You've been communicating with him. We agreed to ostracize not fraternize. Your ass couldn't be trusted to do that solid for me?"

She hunched her shoulders. I gave her a few nods.

"All we did was text," she said as though that was better. Then she removed a metal box from the bottom drawer. "What do you think is inside?"

My opinion wasn't needed. I remained quiet, turned around. Scanned the books on his shelf. Lots of the same sexuality and psychology titles I had on mine were on his. Out of consideration, he could've willed me something. What the fuck I ever did to him he deserved.

"Spencer, look." Alexis held four remote keys in hand. Porsche. BMW. Ferrari. Bentley. Then she held up a rack of C-notes. "How much do you think this is?"

Being no stranger to stacks, I told her, "Looks like ten grand."

"No way." She started counting. "You're right." Alexis put the money along with the car keys in her purse.

A call came in for Alexis while she was stuffing the envelope inside her purse. She stared at me. "Let's go."

I was so ready I led the way to the stairs.

"Hello," she paused. "Yes, this is Alexis Crystal, the daughter of Conner Rogers."

All of a sudden she was Ms. Professional? *Whatever.*

There was another break in her conversation; then she said, "Okay," and repeated, "Okay. I'll have to call you back with the particulars."

We stood in the living room. The expression on her face wasn't one of a grieving child and sure as hell didn't match the contrived sadness in her voice. "Thank you so much. Yes, I'll get that information to you soon. Good-bye."

She grimaced a little, ended the call, then shared the news with me. "Well, now I know what the cash is for. He's gone to glory and I have to make his arrangements."

"No, you have gone to glory. I reassure you he's in hell. And I don't give a fuck what he's left or who he willed it to. My mom gave me everything I needed and more than I ever wanted. I'm glad he's dead."

"Stop saying that. You don't mean it,"

Alexis told me.

"I have zero regrets."

The only reason she cared was her purse just got real heavy. That spill was to appease herself. Bet if Conner hadn't left her a dime, she'd side with me. Still be pushing up on her rent money.

Now the only person alive who I hated was my uncle. Wish his ass was dead, too. If what Conner had said had any truth, that meant he thought my mother was a whore. The only place I knew where to find Bishop was at Blake's church behind the pulpit. "Whosoever shot Conner, I hoped they never find 'em."

"You still want to grab that drink?" she asked. "You need one chick."

I could've bailed Alexis out of her financials. But how much was enough for a woman who didn't value money or people. Hope she didn't spend all her riches in one year. You haven't lived until you know who or what you were willing to kill for and die for. She should thank me.

Answering her question, I said, "Sure. Why not?"

"Forget Suite. Bones? Lunch is on me," she said, patting her purse. "It's Devereaux's and Mercedes's favorite spot."

A text came in from my manager, Derrick, at Cheesecake. Can you come in at 6:00?

Hit him back with a quick, definitely. Needed a distraction, but I was taking Sis up on her offer to pay. Even for lunch, two entrées plus four cocktails couldn't close out a tab for less than a hundred fifty, tip excluded.

My sister valet parked her Lexus. The restaurant wasn't crowded. We grabbed a couple of stools at the end of the bar. Immediately I scanned the menu on their iPad.

"Why would he leave anything to a kid that's not born?" she asked, tossing the yellow envelope in front of me. "He'd planned this before the fam came to my place."

"That would've only been valid if you told him you were pregnant with a girl before he showed up at your spot. Maybe he didn't want you to abort his grandchild. Who knows? Who gives a fuck?!"

"You mad at me?" she asked, pointing at what she wanted to eat.

"Nah, not at you, Sis."

She offered. "You want to open the envelope?"

"It's already open." I ordered, "Martini with three. Scratch that. Two mai tais, a jumbo lump crabmeat cocktail for me and . . ."

171

Alexis added, "The lobster bisque as my main."

I continued. "I'll have a Caesar salad and the bone-in twenty-ounce rib eye medium." After the bartender walked away, I had to say, "So you don't care how you come up? You know this shit ain't adding up."

"Don't judge me, Spencer. This ten K in my purse can pay my rent for four months."

"Do it. Ain't nobody gonna be front row at his funeral but you. Cremate his ass."

"I can't do that," Alexis said, removing the stack of papers. Her eyes scanned side to side. She flipped page after page. Her eyes grew large. She stared at me. "Oh, my, God."

"Save it," I insisted.

I was glad the drinks arrived. Gulped mine. "Damn!" Good. Strong. Just what I needed.

"Listen to this," she said, then read, " 'I leave to my unborn granddaughter my entire estate.' "

I laughed. "What happened to you? Even dead he still full of shit, man."

"No, wait. It says, 'my unborn child will receive 2.5 million at the age of thirty.' "

Now I was holding my stomach, bent over, belting the way she sounded when I told her about Max. I wanted to beg Sis to stop reading, but I had to hear the rest.

"If anything should happen to my unborn grandchild, Spencer Domino and Alexis Crystal shall inherit the estate and divide it equally."

Snap. My laughter became silence for a moment. Nah, I was no damn hypocrite. "You can have it, Sis. I don't want or need his money."

"Are you crazy?"

"My mom left me straight. I got a mil cash, a house, and an apartment building free and clear. Seriously, you come up on it."

Her eyes shifted toward me. "And you're renting? Right?"

"Don't have shit to prove to you, dude." Money she hadn't got was changing her already.

She kept reading. "Wait, it says in the event there is no pregnancy, one hundred percent of the estate goes to . . . his brother?"

"Aw, hell no. Let me see that." She'd read it right. "Fuck that. He's not getting a dime. If I could prove he violated me, I'd send his ass to jail."

Teardrops clung to her eyelids. Sadly, she told me, "I have something I need to tell you. But you have to promise me that you won't tell anyone, especially my mom."

Holding her hand, I told her, "I promise."

"The day we went to the hospital."

"Okay," I said, waiting.

"After Charlotte kicked me in my stomach and I coughed up blood." Alexis held her stomach. Sis started crying.

I bit my bottom lip real hard. Shut up. *Let her tell you what it is.* I closed my eyes. Opened them real slow.

"Spencer, I didn't want to tell you. I lost the baby."

Damn. That shit fucked me up.

CHAPTER 14
BLAKE

Spencer's picture was replaced with a photo of Max as my screensaver.

Placing my cell on the vanity, I checked myself in the restroom mirror. The green blazer, matching skirt with my closed-toe black and cream three-inch pumps I'd worn to work was cute. Days of walking in five- and six-inch heels were long gone. My hair was smoothed back into a bun style that Alexis wouldn't dare wear even in her sleep. I removed, then reapplied my chocolate matte lipstick glad I'd made it through the day.

Bypassed Brandon, he was at his desk, on the phone. I'd say bye to him later. Unlocking the door to my office, I sat at my desk, then called Sandara.

She answered, "Mama, you don't have to keep calling me. Max is fine. Ty thinks he's hers. She's taken over feeding him and cleaning his bottom with baby wipes after he craps."

Max was doing well with his pad training. I'd placed his toy, extra everything — treats, food, pads, change of clothes, bowl, wipes, and water in his RL designer tote. Caring for him was like raising a toddler. Smiling as I scanned through his photo album on my phone, this fella had saved me. If I didn't have Max, I probably would've had sex with Spencer yesterday. God knew it was hard walking out on an erection when I knew how good his dick felt inside of me.

Exhaling, I replied, "That's good. I'll have to put Ty on payroll."

Ty was my four-year-old granddaughter and Sandara's middle child. Her brother Tyson was five. Tyrell was the youngest, three. He was probably jealous of Ty attending to Max since she was always fussing over wiping his face, brushing his teeth, and dressing him.

"Mama, you sound sad."

"I'm fine, honey. A hectic day at the bank, that's all." That was partially true.

I prayed I was closer to getting a corporate promotion. I'd find out next week whether or not I'd get passed over again. My salary was great. There wasn't anything I didn't know about my job. I needed to challenge myself, learn a new position.

Wish I had a man to share my money and success with. Thought that person was Spencer. Make that, a good man. I have to start being more specific when I ask God for a companion.

"Mama, you should really let us have Max. Now that you and Spencer aren't together, can I wear your relationship ring?"

It was refreshing to hear myself laugh aloud for the first time today. Sandara was serious. I wasn't offended. "Girl, don't even think about it." That went for my dog and the diamond on my right ring finger. "I'll see you at six. Sharp."

My relay, as he'd called it, with Spencer was over. Didn't mean I shouldn't enjoy his gift. It was mine to keep.

"Mama, let Max stay the night. We all know Alexis is going to be Alexis. Men like Spencer never change. Take it from me. Call your best friend Echo. Go to happy hour. Have some fun."

Fun. Wow. The last time I felt desirable was my birthday. Being with Spencer was the wildest sex I'd had in over a decade, make that two decades. I had to give going out tonight consideration.

"I'll let you know. Bye, baby."

"Mama, wait."

The excitement in my baby girl's words

made me perk up. "What is it?"

"I have a go see."

Now that was great news. I didn't care where. I just wanted my child to get off of welfare, support herself and my grandbabies. "Where? When?"

How was Sandara offering to adopt my baby and she was going to need preschool for her own. I'd better enroll Max in day care.

"I don't want to jinx it, but if I get hired, I'll be traveling."

I frowned. "Traveling where?"

She screamed, "Internationally! Can you believe it?"

"No, I mean, yes. But, baby, you barely go outside of East Point. Just tell me what agency it is, Sandara, so I can have my lawyer check them out. You know human trafficking is real big in Atlanta. You can get lured in, taken overseas, and we'll never see you again."

Suddenly her being on government assistance didn't seem bad. She was safe and her kids were healthy and happy.

"Bye, Mama. I love you. Serious about the ring."

I realized that when she'd asked for it. "Love you, too, baby."

Soon as I stood, my cell rang. I didn't

want to talk to him. Pressed ignore. It rang again. Sandara must've talked him up. I sat down, accepted the call.

"Spencer, what is it?"

"I called to let you know Conner is dead."

And? So? What was I supposed say. I was done having sympathy for men who didn't deserve it. That included Spencer. The tone in his voice was absent of any signs that he was grieving. My bet, it gave Spencer a reason to call me without his saying "I need to talk."

"Does Alexis know?"

"I called to apologize to you, Blake."

His truth came out sooner than I'd expected. Save it. "Does Alexis know Conner is dead?"

"Yeah, she knows. She's here with me. We went to the hospital to visit him earlier."

Give me a break. Nothing positive happened when those two were together. He could stay every night with Alexis and Chanel. I didn't care anymore. That wasn't exactly true, but if I were going to get over Spencer, I could not accept his apology.

"Good." I ended the call not caring about Conner's cause of death. He was a deadbeat the entire time I've known him. Having had sex with Conner Rogers wasn't worth it. Even the child I birthed with his DNA was constant trouble.

My cell rang again. This time it was my daughter.

I answered, "I know. I know that you know that I know. And I don't care about Conner. He —"

"Mama, please," she said. "Stop it."

"Stop what?! What do you want from me, lil girl?"

"We called to apologize, Mama."

"For what! Having sex with each other after I started dating Spencer? You're both grown. Lying about having had sex? I don't care, Alexis. I'm over it. Manipulating the people who love you? You got it from your father. Go bury him. Oh, wait. Is that it? The two of you need money from me to bury him. I wouldn't give you a discount coupon for embalming Conner Rogers if I had one. I hope he burns in hell!"

Alexis started crying. Couldn't recall the last time I'd heard that. Maybe I was too hard, but I was tired of being the considerate one.

"Mama, we're sorry."

"Apologies accepted." I ended the call.

"Knock. Knock."

Before I said, "Come in," my VP, Brandon, opened the door. I was heated, heaving, and started having a hot flash.

"Honey, it's four thirty, the bank is officially closed, and thank God everyone except you, me, and security are gone. I heard you shouting from my office. Get your purse. Let's go. I'm driving."

I was an emotional mess. I did not object.

The drive to the Lobster Bar at Chops in Buckhead was short. We valet parked, went inside to the host stand.

"Reservation for Brandon Cutter."

The host said, "Yes, sir. Are you expecting one more?"

Brandon answered, "Maybe."

The host seated us right away. I sat on the booth side. The host pulled out a chair across the table from me for Brandon.

Exhaling, I placed my purse next to me, then relaxed my shoulders. "Who's coming?"

"Me, tonight, if he's lucky." A smirk spread across his face.

I figured no one was joining us. "I have to keep that reservation for three strategy in mind."

"Works to get a bigger table every time. Besides, I never know whom I'm going to run into," he said.

The well-groomed young waiter placed two flutes on the table and then opened a bottle of champagne. I blew Brandon a kiss.

"Honey, we are going to celebrate your being fifty all over again. You are going to forget about Spencer, and I'm going to help you find some new dick today. Cheers, bitch," he said, holding up his glass.

"I don't know, Brandon. Dick is not the answer."

Covering his mouth, he gasped. "Bitch, you'd better take that back. Dick is always the answer as long as you always wrap it up and never question where it's been, honey. Trust me on this one. If dicks could talk." Brandon perched, then licked his lips.

He tipped his flute to mine.

"Honey, that twenty-something made you squirt. You should never be mad at him."

Glancing at the people seated near us, they looked embarrassed. I was not. I knew who'd invited me out. I had to laugh. Protesting was not going to calm Brandon down.

"So what, he turned out to be Alexis's brother. Who cares if they hooked up? They're not in their forties. That's what twenty-somethings do. Make mistakes. Yes, repeatedly sometimes. My best advice is always assume that your guy is attracted to someone else, but never accuse your man of cheating. A lie hurts more Blake when you decide to tell the truth. The real problem is you women don't know how to take shit to your grave. I —"

I had to interrupt or Brandon would never inhale. "I just need to process all of this." Since there were no kids close to us, I stopped worrying about who overheard what.

"Process what, honey? What you need to do is move forward with your life. Oh, snap," Brandon said, popping his fingers twice. "Am I good or what. Look who just walked in the room? Boom!"

The man who had tried to take me out for years was near the host stand, dressed in a tapered cerulean suit. His six-foot-eight-inch frame commanded attention. The forty-year-old millionaire Bing Sterling was scanning the room as though he was here looking for his date.

"Let me snag him for a sec," Brandon said.

Reaching across the table, I tried to grab his arm. "Brandon, don't. He's looking for someone?"

"And what if he's not."

When Bing saw Brandon, he smiled and headed in our direction.

CHAPTER 15
PHOENIX

Ebony's wardrobe changes were my private show. Wished I could join her in the dressing room, recline in a chair, and just watch her put on and take off outfit after outfit.

Emptying my bladder, texting, eating, all that had to wait. I only took a break when she did. I hadn't missed a single shot of her entire shoot.

Ebony texted me photos of her in lingerie. Red lace, black see-through mesh, thongs, teddies, and a few pussy pics registered while she was out of my sight changing. I watched her spread for the photographer, like she'd done for me this morning. Classy. Sophisticated. I could taste her pussy juices in my mouth.

I licked my lips. In consideration of my fiancée, I should've rinsed and brushed after going down on Ebony. Lucky Dev couldn't detect Ebony's sweet vanilla flavor.

"Phoenix . . . Phoenix!"

Oh, damn. I was so engrossed, didn't see Dev staring in my face. Immediately, I pressed the side button on my phone. I prayed she hadn't seen my screen before it faded to black.

"Hey, Dev. We got this. I approve of your photographer. We're moving on up, babe."

She rolled her eyes, told me, "You're drooling," then walked away. No matter how many steps she took, Dev wasn't going anywhere. I did a few things behind her back, but I never gave her a reason to distrust me.

Wow! Ebony, Brea, Misty, and Emerald strutted out in expensive bras and panties. The kind Ebony wore exclusively for me. I felt like I was seated front row to a Victoria's Secret runway. Shifting my eyes to Dev, she was deep in conversation with the show's director, Trés. That was good.

He wasn't slick. A guy knew when another man was making a move on his girl. Best characteristic about my Dev, she was faithful. Both of my women were.

I rubbed the back of my hand across my lips. Kept admiring the cast. More like lusting, daydreaming about having an eight-hand massage. Ebony was the only one who I'd let touch my dick. She knew exactly how to jack me off. I had to be the luckiest dude in the ATL right now.

Not sure how long I'd be able to reframe from getting a full erection, I exhaled when I heard the photographer say, "That's a wrap."

I had a few ideas of doing a separate set of pics with Ebony. A lot more risqué. A few nude for my personal collection.

The only part of the day I hated was my imagining my gurl sandwiched between West-Léon and Travis tomorrow. My frame was tight. But those guys' pics on social media, shit! They were Trai Byers ripped, from their legs to their neck. Pumping iron, running three miles a day, core training, all that was officially back on my daily schedule.

I'd done as Ebony had asked. Stayed my distance. Did the same with Dev most of the day. Didn't want her to see my dick growing and shrinking, especially when Ebony posed by herself. I was impressed seeing Dev in action. My fiancée was definitely a boss.

"Hey, babe," I said to Dev. "This was an amazing first day. I'm proud of you. I have a few suggestions."

"Later, Phoenix. I have to go over details with AJ Alexander for tomorrow's shoot. We can talk at home."

I thought I recognized AJ's face, but his body was about a hundred pounds lighter. He was that dude who discovered Usher.

"You don't have a minute to hear what —"

"Hey, Dev! Great job. You're a natural at this," the director said, sounding as though he were speaking through his nose. "You have a sec, beautiful? I want to run several suggestions by you for tomorrow's shoot."

Dev? Trés called my fiancée Dev? I was supposed to be the only one with those privileges. She obviously liked it, him, and his proper English accent.

"Of course, Trés. Let me speak with AJ; then I'm all yours," she said, sounding like a high school virgin with a mad crush on this guy.

Soon as Dev walked away, I extended my hand to Trés. "I'm *Devereaux's* fiancé and Ebony's manager. And —"

Trés said, "Yes, Devereaux Crystal. Phoenix Watson is it?"

Obviously, he'd heard about me. Dev should've stuck with the guy who'd directed the pilot. I had to compose myself for Dev. Didn't want to give our company a bad rep.

Knowing exactly who he was, I asked, "And you are?"

"You'll see my name in the credits, ole chap."

Chap? That was fucking rude. I wanted to bust dude one quick time in his mouth.

"Hey, Trés," Dev said, grinning ear to ear. "I have an hour before meeting my sister. You want to grab a drink?"

"You're amazing, darling. I'd love to," he said.

I noticed she didn't say where. That was cool. I had plans. He escorted Dev off set. Neither of them looked at me.

I called out, "Bye, babe!"

She continued talking, to him. Kept walking. I knew she heard me.

Ebony texted me: Something came up. Don't come by tonight.

Yeah, I bet. Dev, AJ, Trés probably put something in my Ebony's head. I could see Trés plotting to get me out of the picture completely. I wasn't blind or stupid. He was making a move on my woman.

Setting a date for my wedding was happening this weekend.

I got in my car and went to Ebony's with the intent to find out exactly what came up.

CHAPTER 16
SPENCER

"My old man wasn't shit to me. Now he's six feet under."

LB stood behind the bar beside me. Hunched his left shoulder. "But for real. You didn't give a fuck about him, Spence?"

I proceeded to shake up a margarita. Salted the rim. Kept quiet. I filled the glass, placed the drink in front the customer.

"My condolences, bruh," LB said, shaking his head.

I told him, "It's all good."

Conner was gone. Alexis didn't care that I was an afterthought. The only way I'd inherit his money was if something happened to my sister's baby . . . aw man.

My brain flooded with what-ifs. Sis probably never was pregnant. If she were and she'd already lost the kid, based on the trust, the money was already ours. Knowing her, Conner never said I'd shot him. He didn't see me. I was at Blake's. Alexis was handling everything as she should.

I had a plan of my own.

How was I going to break down the particulars to my boy LB about Alexis without raising his temp from 98.6 to 102? Betrayal was not my intent. Shit couldn't be undone. Slamming him with the unexpected was unavoidable. But I needed him back in the game, for Alexis's sake, not mine.

Putting on blinders in the ATL couldn't keep a man from being unfaithful, baby! I rubbed my palms together. Men living here had too . . . many choices. Go with the flow of females or catch a one-way flight out of Hartsfield and never come back. Even on a layover a bruh could get laid in one of those private restrooms marked "Family." LB knew we were the masters of "fuck 'em where you find 'em, leave 'em where you fuck 'em."

What we called the "hell well" was the side of the bar where we stacked cocktails for table waiters to pick up. I added two more mojitos to that side of the counter, checked the computer for new drink orders.

You a beast for this, Spence.

Looking beyond the shelves lined with liquor bottles for the bar — through the clear window — I saw cars bumper-to-bumper turning off of Peachtree Street into the mall's entrance for the parking lot. Prime Steak and Seafood restaurant one level up had a better view for customers, not the bartenders. Their prices were higher, food wasn't as good. Our weekday $5.50 an item happy hour bar menu made us the most pop.

Typical hot summer sunset had drop-top throwback classics, Bentleys, Porsche, Benz, Lexus, Tesla, Maserati, Ferrari, cruising up to valet. Breasts half covered, ass cheeks almost out was the norm. Felines made hunting on a Friday night easier than uncorking a bottle. That's why when my manager, Derrick, asked me to close tonight, I was on top of it.

"Are you dining with us?" I asked, keeping my peripheral on those pronounced nipples.

"As a matter of fact, I am," she said with a sultry tone. Reminded me of Sade's song, "The Sweetest Taboo." I'd love to bless her with my skills. Make her hum on my mic.

LB did a James Brown slide, stopped beside me, flapped open a white cloth napkin, plopped it in front of ole taboo gurl. Set up a small plate and wrapped silverware for her, then tapped the bar twice.

Times like this LB was more cute than good looking. One inch under six feet. Slim

180. Had a decent swole on his biceps. Clean, cut and shaved. We were both on the slender side. I was, of course, better looking and three inches taller. A few inches made a huge difference.

Turing my back to the customer, I whispered to my boy, "I'm done grinding Cheesecake chicks. Taboo is all yours. I'm breaking from all babes for a while. Focusing on me."

"Good luck, bruh. I support you, but I know you. You created our 'f 'em' mantra. Putting your pussy grinder on the shelf, that won't last long. Too many kitties in the litter to choose from. Hundred bucks you'll take a number before the end of our shift."

I nodded upward. "Bet." He could line 'em up and lick them all. I was enjoying the view, but I wasn't penetrating for a while.

We had that Morse code for women. One tap. We wanted in on her. Sometimes we'd go for a threesome if she were game. Two taps meant we wanted an exclusive. Too many hot chicks in the ATL to trip off of one the way I'd done with Charlotte.

Blake didn't give me that heart-wrenching, can't breathe, don't wanna be without you feeling. Wasn't sure why I couldn't leave her alone, though. Ego. Maybe. It was easy to let all my shit rest at her place. Gave me a legit to go back whenever I wanted. Charlotte was special. Missed her crazy ass for real. Once I got myself on track we could have a heart-to-heart. We might still have a chance to make our relay solid or at least be friends.

My not keeping it one hundred had hurt Blake, Alexis, and Charlotte. I'd be twenty-eight soon. Getting too old to keep doing the fool. Maybe I wasn't ready to settle with any female. Should stop forcing it.

I poured a glass of chardonnay, mixed a JW Lemonade, Italian margarita, then prepared three cosmopolitans. Placed them on the "heaven well" counter. Those were orders from waiters placed by customers in the bar area but not seated at the bar. Less hectic. We all preferred heaven.

LB serviced new visitors seated at the opposite end from me, took his two taps taboo gurl her white sangria, then stood beside me. "Shutting down the D. This ain't like you, Spence. Keep it one hundred. Charlotte's back? You retraced your steps to Blake? Details, dude," LB said.

Setting up a few more customers, I shook a shaker real hard, hoping the clashing sound of ice would slow the bomb drop, when I lied to my boy, "Alexis is pregnant."

Family first. Had to help Sis find a sperm

donor quick. If she was plotting not to break me off, I was going to do my best to give LB a chance to cash in on Alexis's game.

He faced the window. Stared into the parking lot. He didn't blink. Reminded me of how Max would turn his back to Blake and I whenever we'd kiss. I missed that Yorkie. He was a cool dude.

LB held the wineglass in his hand, bottle of pinot noir in the other. Soon as I'd divulged, I realized I hadn't fessed that I'd been with Alexis too. He'd had her first, though. Begged me not to dig in.

Money. Family. A fresh start would be good for Sis; then she'd know who the father was for sure.

Fuck! Getting deeper into the madness of deception when all I wanted was out was necessary right now. There was no telling what other traps were in Conner's trust. In case it was true, that there was a possibility that my uncle could get the two mil, I'd shoot him first. Just the way I . . . I took the bottle, poured the drink, placed it on the "hell well" counter, circled back to LB.

His expression was the same. "How many months is she?"

"You hit it raw, dude?" I prayed he hadn't. I'd gone down on Alexis. Even in a ménage I had limitations with my boy. No touching one another. No penetration without a helmet. No oral on the chick, but she could slob both of us. Some felines just loved sucking dick.

"Nah, but that was my girl. It could be mine, man. Stranger shit has happened."

"Didn't she clip you for a cool grand?"

"I'm over that. She needed it for her rent. Can't have my girl homeless. It's only money."

What? Not the dude who believes in going Dutch on every date. Alexis had LB in the same position she had James. Fetal with her hand on the balls.

"She's twelve weeks." That would be true if she hadn't miscarried. Laughing to myself, I'd have to take blame for that. Charlotte did what most women would to protect themselves. I couldn't be pissed about that.

LB pulled out his cell. I covered it.

"Nah, man. Don't call my sister."

His head snapped in my direction. "Come again. Your what?"

"Just found out her father is mine too. We got a lot to converse about, man. I'll down you on the particulars right after we clock out." Revealing that truth should make him assume I never grinded with Alexis.

LB shook his head. This might work to my advantage to get those two in bed again.

Alexis would do it for the money. LB for love. He became silent. Busied himself with pouring drinks.

Best not to communicate with LB tonight. After my shift I'd dip. Hit up my sis. She might want to go it with James. That way she could keep all the money and take his too. My boy LB was stable enough and all, but James was definitely the better stock market choice.

I worked the opposite end of the bar.

Heard a voice say, "Haven't I seen you somewhere, handsome?"

Turned around. I froze like my boy LB was a few minutes ago.

She extended her hand and just like that, my dick was out of retirement! He could've greeted her palm the second she'd said, "Ebony Waterhouse." I was ready to let him loose.

I gave her a half smile. No need to tap the bar. I was going to tap that ass. Hopefully, tonight. Holding her hand, I told her, "Congrats on your new show. I'll definitely be watching."

"You'd better," she said with a wicked grin.

A tall white dude with thin, dark wavy hair dressed in a tailored blue suit sat beside her. I let go of her hand. Hadn't seen him in here before. "Bartender, a bottle of your best champagne for me and my lovely wife."

My dick shriveled up. I needed to stick with my original script and chill on chicks.

He said to her, "Sweetheart, I have to take this call. I'll be right back."

Didn't know she was married. I was no suit and tie kind of guy. In about ten years, I might up my casual attire game to OG's elevation. He'd done me a solid by claiming Ebony.

I had enough problems.

"Excuse me, bartender," Ebony said.

"Yes, ma'am," I answered in a formal tone.

"Your name is?" Her grin grew a little larger then vanished.

I shook my head. This babe could be bad and good trouble. "Spencer Domino."

She slid me a card. "Nice package," she said, eyeing my dick. "Call me tonight if you can deliver. My husband likes to watch."

CHAPTER 17
DEVEREAUX

I love my man with all my heart.

Love had nothing to do with what happened today. The fact that I care about his fragile ego was the only reason I hadn't kicked him out of the building.

Phoenix's hanging out on set all day made me want to pull his and my hair out!

A thousand ants crawling on my skin might have annoyed me less than my fiancé answering calls with, "Yeah, man. Let me hit you back. I'm on set."

At one point I thought I was going to go off on him in front of everyone. Yelling at folks on my payroll was my prerogative, but I did it in a professional capacity, when necessary. Shoving Phoenix's phone up his butt, then calling and leaving him a message to get out could've gotten us on Funk Dat on Majic 107.5. Didn't want to give him any further justification to brag.

Traffic on Peachtree Street heading south

was bumper-to-bumper. I exhaled, "Thank you, Lord," reassuring myself that tomorrow would not be a repeat.

Ebony had done a fantastic job. She showed out for the camera. My entire cast did amazing. The women were gorgeous. They had great chemistry. Hair and makeup was flawless. Wardrobe — high-fashion lingerie with real diamonds, sapphires, and rubies the way I wanted — were loaned to me. Everyone added value, except Phoenix. Regardless of what he was doing while constantly checking his cell, his presence was a major distraction.

Constantly trying to ignore him was a chore. He'd have to find another way to service his client. When he wasn't on his phone or standing on the sideline watching Ebony, Phoenix conversed with my staff as they were completing tasks. Even I didn't do that.

If I heard him say "Devereaux's fiancé" one more time, I'd scream. For real.

Trés could tell I was disturbed. I was glad he'd rescued me from Phoenix. My fiancé was so self-absorbed he was oblivious to how disgusted I was, and that pissed me off more. Acting as though he was scared to miss a click of the camera, he barely took a leak. He was better off staying at home with

Nya or being out with his boys. If marriage meant I was going to experience more of what he'd done today, I was starting not to care as much about setting a wedding date.

"Thank you," I said to the valet, took my ticket, then went inside. Trés waved. I headed toward the bar with open arms, then collapsed into his.

The soft tunes resonating from the baby grand soaked into my soul.

Whispering in my ear, "What an incredible mind you have," Trés hugged me tight. He had a masculine embrace that made me feel safe.

I wasn't a crier, but I felt like shedding tears. I resisted. The weight on my shoulders subsided. "Thanks, Trés. You're amazing." I meant that.

Ocean Prime was convenient for us to meet up as Mercedes was due to arrive for dinner in a half hour. I texted her, I'm here. At the bar with Trés. Mercedes and Alexis were the only two family members who had met Trés while we filmed the pilot.

He pulled out the barstool next to him, handed me a glass of wine. "It's not your favorite cab. I order a bottle of Italian so you can" — he paused, then said — "try something new, Dev. You deserve better."

I read the label, "Angelo Gaja, Barbaresco. Okay."

He couldn't have ordered my favorite Gravelly Meadows that cost $850 a bottle at Bones because it wasn't on the list here. Smiling, I sipped, appreciative of his thoughtfulness. "Impressive, man."

Trés let out a little laugh. Held my hand. I pulled away. Didn't want to be rude. Didn't want him to think I was interested. Yes, I was annoyed with Phoenix, but I was still an engaged woman.

This time Trés rubbed my shoulder. My body relaxed with his touch. Gave me the idea to have a massage therapist on set next week.

"Don't thank me, Dev. I pay attention to what you like," he said.

"Mercedes is meeting me here for dinner. You're welcome to join us."

"Is Alexis coming? She's entertaining. If she had acting skills, I'd say give her a part. Maybe we can write her in as a special guest."

"No, I'm not working with family," I insisted. "But I will admit that her personal life is worth writing about. I'll fill you in later."

Trés touched my thigh. "Give me a chance, Dev. We'd make a great team.

Perfect Bollywood power couple."

Trés's wife of twenty-two years passed a year ago from cervical cancer. They married when they were both twenty. He'd shared with me his affairs. Said sometimes a man just wants the feel of new pussy. He swore his wife was the only woman he'd trusted with his heart.

I smiled. Bet he didn't think the same way about a woman riding fresh dick. I indulged in the robust taste of my wine. The subtle spicy kick on the tail made me moan. "Um, um, um."

"I love you, Dev."

I wasn't responding to that. I'd dated enough men to know that was how they baited women and once we were hooked, they suffered from amnesia. Instead, I said, "I can't take another day of Phoenix being on set."

"I concur. Let me be the bad guy. You be yourself. One of these days you're going to let me show you how a real man loves his woman. I have an award-winning track record."

"Let's save that for the Emmys. Emotional infidelity is the worst. You know how I feel about exclusivity. I only give myself to the man I'm with."

"That's precisely why I want you. I'll wait."

I heard myself saying, "Am I supposed to cosign for infidelity? No! I will not give you the opportunity to bait me in, lick another woman's clit, then come home and stick your tongue in my mouth!"

"Hey, Sis," Mercedes said, giving me a hug from behind. "Hi, Trés."

Trés looked over my shoulder. "Hello, Mercedes. You look stunning. Bartender, a glass of wine for this beautiful lady. Please sit," he said offering my sister his stool. Trés finished his red wine. "Mercedes, when you see your sister's premier, you are going to love this woman almost as much as I do. I've got to get going. Dev, don't interfere. I'll see you in the morning." He kissed my cheek, then left.

"I know you're not having an affair with Trés Vinsaunt," Mercedes said, moving her stool closer to mine.

"I have never cheated on Phoenix and I never will."

Mercedes sipped her wine. "Um. This selection is brilliant."

"How're the twins?" I asked.

"Getting more intellectual as usual. Enrolled them for a youth engineering program for the summer."

"And Benjamin?"

"I'm going to get straight to why I wanted to meet with you. I hired a private detective to inform me of the truth about my husband. If I find out Benjamin is having an affair, I'm filing for divorce."

"Are you sure this is what you want to do? Have someone spy on your husband. Raise your children without their father. Most men do not have a clean track record, but Benjamin is good to you and the kids."

"I'm sure Alexis texted you too." Picking up her phone, Mercedes showed me a photo. "So, you know Phoenix is cheating on you with your star actress?"

No, she hadn't. Staring in disbelief, I was not making any assumptions. "It's a picture, Mercedes. That's not proof. And even if I were to confront Phoenix, I'd never do it based on anything from Alexis. I love my sister, but that girl has drama to the tenth power in her life. I don't want chaos in my home."

Knots doubled, tripled, quadrupled in my stomach. There had to be a better way to resolve her situation without my involvement. It was almost as though she hadn't heard what I'd said. My sister had her agenda and I was on it.

"The detective's name is Dakota Justice.

Here's her card. You have too much to risk if you marry a loser, Devereaux. Phoenix is beneath you. Don't marry him. I gave Dakota your number as well because I know you won't contact her."

"Mercedes, this doesn't feel right."

"What won't feel right, for you and Nya, is divorce. If he checks out clean, you'll feel better." Sarcastically, she added, "When's your wedding date?"

I picked up the card. Put it in my purse. She knew we hadn't set one.

Chapter 18
Alexis

I'd let myself into the garage, parked my car, then entered his home.

"If you weren't pregnant, you wouldn't be here," James said, greeting me at the door.

"You invited me over." Brushing by him, I asked, "You want your keys back?" before dropping them into my purse.

His smile brought back memories of when we used to chill on the sofa with his head on my lap. That six-nine man, wrapped in delicious chocolate-cinnamon skin, was the best male catch I'd made. But I wasn't here for companionship.

I'd come to have his sperm deposited directly from his nuts into my vagina. Untying my halter, I let my dress fall to the floor. Kept on my red thong and stilettoes. Posed for him to see my sweet dark ass.

"Since I'm already pregnant and I haven't had sex since I was with you, you mind taking the edge off of your pussy? I'm about to explode."

There were times when telling a lie was better. Men weren't well versed when it came to women. I hated lying to my brother about the miscarriage and perpetuating false motherhood, but to keep the whole 2.5 million I'd have James's baby.

He was moving too slow. I unfastened his belt, yanked his pants to his knees. One leg at a time, he stepped out. I leaned over the back of his couch, spread my ass cheeks.

James rubbed his swollen head from my clit to my vagina, then back again. The next time he approached my opening, I thrust my hips toward his pelvis.

"Slow down, sweetheart. I'ma give you the dick," he said.

Teasing a few more times, inch by inch he fed me what I'd come for. I moaned, "Go deeper, baby. I want to feel all of you."

My donor started grinding with a real nice flow. I squeezed his shaft with my muscles. Held on.

"I want you to cum deep inside of me."

James leaned his chest against my back, held me close, thrust himself far as his head could go, then paused. "I'm cuming, sweetheart."

"Me too." I came when he let me know. Wasn't going to miss out on my orgasm. I wondered if he called LA sweetheart too. Didn't matter. His body shivered. He held me tight until he was done.

"I don't know what I'm going to do if it's not mine," he said, pulling out.

My seeds were spilling down my thigh. I slid over the back of the sofa, left my legs up in the air.

James left, returned with a hot towel, wiped my pussy real slow. "Let me taste her."

I couldn't move. It was too soon. "I'm slightly nauseated. Give me a moment."

He sat on the sofa beside me, massaged my breast. "If the baby isn't mine, sweetheart, I'm moving on."

The reason I was here, at his house, with my legs up in the air. I'd gotten what I'd come for. I had to be nice. Wasn't sure if one of these soldiers would swim the distance.

"I never meant to hurt you."

"You were that messed up that you had sex with your brother? First I had to deal with Chanel. Now this. Really?"

Typical man. He hadn't passed on fucking me. Now he wanted to talk. "I really think this situation with not knowing my father messed me up mentally. Glad I met him before he died." The only reason I bothered telling James was to get us off the topic of my having fucked Spencer.

James held my hand. "For real? Sweetheart, no. You can't be serious. He was just at your house. What happened?"

"Somebody shot him. I can't pretend I'm grieving. I didn't know the man."

"He was still your dad, but I understand. Let the police do their job and find the gunman."

I told him about Spencer and I visiting the hospital. Didn't mention the trust, what I might inherit, or that Conner claimed Spencer shot him. That was nonsense. Spencer was at my mom's. The keys to all of Conner's cars were at my apartment with the ten grand in cash. I'd use the money to make Conner's funeral arrangements.

"You're so beautiful. I hate that your mom did that to you, sweetheart. Now that you're with child, are you going to finish school?"

"I'm going to try. I made it through my first trimester without morning sickness."

"So you're not nauseated?"

Looking at him, quickly I said, "I am. I meant not a serious case of morning sickness. But . . ."

He stared at me.

"What is it, Alexis? Tell the truth."

Doubting I knew how to be honest with

anyone, I kept quiet.

"I'm not going anywhere," James said, stroking my cheek. "Be honest with me. How many men have you had sex with without using protection since we've been together?"

Wish that were an easy question to answer. There was the obvious, Spencer. Then LB, but we used condoms. I'd circled back to a few carryovers during the two years I'd been involved with James. With the exception of Spencer, I always practiced safe sex. The only reason I hadn't with him was we were both in heat.

James picked up his cell, handed it to me. "Read this."

Atlanta ranked No. 1 city for new HIV/ AIDS cases. The article detailed how Grady Hospital, since 2013, had a program to routinely test emergency room patients. In my opinion, that was a good thing. Wow, the fact that from the beginning of the program two to three of the patients tested *every single day* were HIV positive.

Damn! Then there was that Jason Young dude who intentionally infected women. I understood James's concern.

"When was the last time you were tested?" he asked, staring into my eyes. He continued. "Don't lie to me, Alexis."

"You questioning me. What about you? You tell me how many women you've slayed without wrapping it up and I'll let you know."

We stared at each other as he said, "Three months after we started dating there was one."

"One what?" I questioned. "Male? Female? What about LA?" Men were horrible liars.

"Okay. Two. Females," he said with a straight face.

"And, your HIV results were?"

"Alexis, this is serious, sweetheart. So serious that I'm going to schedule us to get tested today."

"Today?" I wasn't prepared for that. Should've told him I had all my blood work done when I found out I was pregnant. I knew him, though. He'd ask to see the results.

"Get tested with me." He got his cell. Began tapping on the screen.

This would be a first. I did need to know my status but . . . Hadn't given it much thought. Spencer had to be cool. I hoped. My mom too. I prayed. Wondered if girls could transmit HIV to girls during sex. Chanel and I shared dongs.

I started sweating but refused to sit up

and spill my seeds.

James was a good man. He was no saint. His dick had taken a plunge in —

He interrupted my mental monologue. "No matter what the results are, I will always love you, Alexis. Get dressed. Let's go. I'm not asking."

"This time of the evening?" It was almost seven o'clock.

"I texted my frat brother who's also my doctor. The lab closes at eight. Long as we get to his office by seven thirty we're good."

So he'd planned this all along. I should decline. A flash shower and thirty minutes later we were at James's doctor's office. It was cold. I was quiet.

"Glad you were able to make it, James. And you are?" he said, extending his hand to me.

Quietly, I replied, "Alexis Crystal." Why'd I let James talk me into this?

"It's a pleasure to meet you, Alexis. I'm Dr. Wallace. I can tell you're nervous. Trust me, you're doing the right thing. I just need both of you to sign your lab consent form. I commend you guys for coming in as a couple."

"Thanks for fitting us in," James said.

"No worries. The lab is down the hall on your left. I'll call you, James, when your results are in. You'll need to come in with James for your results, Alexis. Congrats, you guys."

There was nothing to celebrate. Oh, unless James had told him about our baby.

En route to the laboratory, I asked James, "Congrats for what? Why did he say that?"

"He's proud of you, us, for coming in together. That's all."

I could tell he was lying. Just wasn't sure about what.

CHAPTER 19
PHOENIX

Straight to voice mail for the tenth damn time!

She had to come home at some point. What the fuck she give me a key for? To sit around and wait on her? This time I left the message, "Ebony, where are you? It's ten o'clock. I've been at your place since the set ended. You have to go to work tomorrow. Call me back. It's important." How was I supposed to manage her when I couldn't keep track of where she was?

I hadn't heard from Dev. That was unusual. Texted her, You out with Mercedes or Trés? Didn't want to lie about where I was. Hope she didn't ask. She might be with my girl.

Opening Ebony's kitchen cabinet, there was a box of microwave plain popcorn. No salt. No butter. I put that back. Checked the refrigerator. Fresh-cut pineapples, red grapes, raspberries, blueberries, pomegranate juice, and water. Ice cream, popsicles, and ice in the freezer.

Waiting on Ebony to get home, I'd sat at the dining table, scrolled through her social media pages while eating a bowl of fruit. Drank most of her juice. Sat on her couch, turned on the television, flipped through channels. Got bored. Should go home. Wasn't ready to.

Went into Ebony's downstairs guest bedroom. She'd changed the scheme. Lots of pink, white, and purple. Same colors as Nya's room. It was too late to tell my baby girl good night. Surely didn't want to speak with my mother.

Started going through the closet to see if anything looked different. Nope. Trotted upstairs, took another shower to pass time. Was hoping to do this with Ebony, not by myself. Got dressed, went downstairs, sat on the sofa, and called my boy Marvin.

"Hey, man. Where you at? Home?" he said, then laughed.

"That shit ain't funny, man. I'm at Goldie's."

"Nigga, that's your home away from home. You got access now."

Putting the television on mute, I frowned, started flipping channels. "Why the fuck she gave me a key and she ain't here?"

"Give it back, man. You're going to get your feelings hurt."

"Just say it, man." All this delay of whatever he knew, I had to hear.

"I just left the Cheesecake Factory. Goldie was sitting at the bar tossing back a few with some suave old ass white dude."

"Say what?"

"My bad. He was probably a fan or some shit. They might still be there. Hey, man, I gotta get up early for work. I'ma hit you up tomorrow."

Well, I wasn't a fan. I was her man. I'd bragged about being on set but I hadn't told Marvin or the fellas I was managing Ebony. Hadn't seen my boys going on two weeks. Who was she with? Some old muthafucka? I got in my car, drove to Lenox Square, turned off my car. I sat for a moment. What was I doing? I was not chasing her.

If I'ma deal with this bullshit, I might as well head home to Dev.

CHAPTER 20
EBONY

#lovethesemoments #smartside #morethan-sex #iamebonywaterhouse

Scented musk, sandalwood, and cinnamon candles burned in each corner of the bedroom of our home in Conyers. Fresh zebra-striped satin sheets neatly covered the king-size mattress. Long gold silk scarves hung from the bedposts to the floor. A plush white square rug was sprawled on top of the carpet.

Buster's crystal whisky bottle and four snifters were set up on the coffee table across the room. That was the area where he liked to sit, watch me and a guy have sex, while smoking his Cuban cigar.

He turned on his favorite. Classical music consumed the house throughout. Frédéric Chopin was Buster's favorite pianist.

"Come sit with me for a moment," he said.

I eyed the toys Buster selected; they were arranged on a leather chest within reach from the bed. A few vibrating cock rings, dildos, blindfolds, flavored and heating massage oils. Recalling the imprint in my boy toy's pants, I knew I wasn't going to need that dildo.

I enjoyed getting all dolled up for these sexcapades. Loosely tying my red halter bra, I stepped into a red thong, then wrapped my body with a white silk robe that barely covered my ass. Sitting next to my husband, I put on my six-inch, candy-striped, knee-high boots with the white platform and red heel.

The most expensive bra and panty set my husband had bought me cost twenty thousand dollars. Hadn't worn it since our honeymoon in Bora Bora.

"You look beautiful. I don't want you hot and bothered on that set, so if this bartender rocks your world, we'll put him on payroll, but he can only service you with my permission."

I'd been doing my own thing since before we married. Had to let Buster believe he was in charge of more than paying all my bills and buying me expensive gifts. But #igotthis.

My husband gave me everything I wanted, except great penetration. That was understandable from a seventy-one-year-old.

Good dick with no money would never be mine.

At twenty-six, I needed to be fucked in every hole. Phoenix provided that for me. What I wanted in my relationship with Phoenix wasn't love. It was all about power. Danger. Being risqué. Dominating. Being dominated. The thought of Devereaux finding out about us was exciting, but that was not something I ever wanted to happen.

I massaged my husband's flaccid dick. "You've never mentioned hiring a regular. Are we okay?" The lingering stare made me a little uncomfortable.

"I am, honey," he said. A smile gradually grew. "I can't wait to see this guy's dick. I bet it's big and beautiful."

That made both of us. I was excited to experience Spencer.

Buster cleared his throat. "I'm up in New York more than before. I don't believe you're happy with my being away all the time. If you are, this will be his last time."

There was something my husband wasn't saying that bothered me. Phoenix crossed my mind. I had no intentions on standing him up. Buster surprised me when he told me to meet him at the Cheesecake Factory. There was no way I could tell my husband no.

219

Buster's cell buzzed. We saw Spencer in a black Range Rover at our entry gate. He keyed in the code I'd given him. Buster pressed a button on his phone; the second gate opened. I liked the double security of entering the code and giving access. My home in Brookhaven didn't have either.

"I couldn't be happier," I told Buster.

Buster and I didn't say "I love you" the way I'd ended each conversation with Phoenix. I knew my side was going to be upset when I'd see him on set tomorrow. Every dick had a pecking order. My priority was seated next to me.

I kissed my husband, then stood. "I'll go let Spencer in, honey. You stay comfortable."

"Goldie, make sure I have a good view of Spencer."

"Okay," I said, strutting away.

Opening the front door, Spencer was hot in his crimson button-down shirt and black slacks. I sure hoped he had on sexy underwear. That turned me on. If he didn't, we had options for him to choose from.

"Hi, come in, handsome."

"Wow, you're gorgeous," he said, checking out my twin rack. Scanning my home, he told me, "This is real boss."

Buster didn't like to waste time with small talk. We all knew our intentions. I led Spencer to the bedroom. When he saw Buster lounging in a smoking jacket, ascot, and designer pajama pants, he gave a slow nod.

Buster told Spencer, "Please. Have a drink while you're taking your shower. We'll be right here waiting for you."

"Long as you don't touch me, we cool," Spencer said.

"Oh, no," Buster said. "You guys do all the touching. I'm here to watch my wife."

CHAPTER 21
BLAKE

"I'm glad you accepted my offer to come over, Blake," Bing said. "You look amazing."

Here I was again with a handsome man. The scent of his cologne greeted me first. He had on a white pullover collared shirt with khaki knee-length shorts that were neatly creased and brown leather sandals.

The fact that Bing was ten years younger, and he'd pursued me, made me smile. Better start giving myself more credit for being desirable. "Thanks for inviting me."

I'd worn blue fitted jeans, a crop sleeved pink tapered top, and three-inch open-toed shoes. My hair was flat-ironed with a part down the center. Sandara advised me the combo would take a solid decade off of my fifty.

"I'll give you the tour later," he said. "Follow me."

We shared a lounge chair on his deck. I

could hear myself breathing. Crickets chirped in the distance. In front of the tall trees Bing had told me there was a lake. It was so dark in the distance that I couldn't see water, but the stars shined like diamonds in the sky.

He handed me a glass of red wine. "A toast to the most beautiful woman and the luckiest man in the world."

"Cheers," was all I said, praying there would be many more toasts to come.

We sat, enjoyed wine. I should have more moments like this. Having been with Spencer and now Bing, I realized I preferred a younger, attractive businessman. The mixologist running the bar was not for me. Yet, Spencer was the perfect transition man that helped me get over my ex, Fortune.

Bing interrupted our silence. "I have a confession," he said, refilling my glass first, then his.

"Only if it's good news."

"Okay, then I'll come back to the confession. Blake" — Bing paused, held my hand, then continued — "from what you told me over dinner the other day, I want to let you know, I don't need anything financial from you. I —"

Seriously? I was his banker. I might not be aware of all of his accounts or his liabilities, but the resources at our institution were a comfortable seven figures. My money was no comparison.

"I know that, Bing." This was a man who probably had Swiss bank accounts, stocks, bonds, treasury bills, and more.

"I'm not putting you down. You're a beautiful and intelligent woman. Seems to me you keep choosing to be with men who for whatever reason are, one, not on your level, and two, they don't want you. They simply want to use you."

Appreciate would've been a better word choice. But okay, the fact that he started with, I'm not putting you down, meant to me that he was. I was no charity case. Had to blame myself for sharing too much too soon. That was a fault of mine.

I held the wineglass to my lips, took a long, slow sip, then swallowed. "Sorry if I gave you that impression. That wasn't my intention."

"Think about it for a moment," he told me; then he became quiet.

The more I reflected, I had to admit to myself, he was right. Four daughters, no husband, no fathers listed on my children's birth certificates. Fifty. Single. Lived with Fortune for years while he was still legally married. Didn't want to think about why I fell in love with Spencer. Maybe my not wanting to confront my insecurities was the reason I'd dated down.

"Blake, a real man that you are dating would never consider, let alone have, sex with your daughter. And if you were happy when your ex died, you said you didn't want him because he didn't care for you. No woman hates a man that truly loves her."

I told him all that? Damn. I talked too much. Wasn't going to let Bing make me the solo focus. "You're a great catch. Why are you single?"

"Busy all the time. Travel a lot for business. Don't date desperate women. I do the chasing. I was attracted to you because you partially know my financial status." He laughed, then continued. "And you actually turned me down a few times."

Had my own money. Prayed to keep it that way. If things with Bing and I didn't work out, he could cause me to lose my job. "What were your longest, best, and last relationships like?" I asked.

"Best. College. Three years, seven months, two weeks, and one day. I wasn't ready for marriage. She was. She broke up with me. Met another guy. They're still husband and wife. I missed the mark," he said, nodding. "Should've put a ring on it. Haven't met anyone like her since. You don't have to worry. I'm over finding her twin. I'm in search of my own happiness. Tired of going to bed alone. Don't believe in random sex."

Okay. I was done exploring that part of his past. "What's the confession?"

"Oh, yeah." He laughed. "I knew you were never going to accept my invitation to dinner and I understand why, so I had Brandon set us up."

Smiling, I sat up straight. "Well, that little sneak. I'm going to get him."

"And, I'm going to thank him," Bing said, leaning in for a kiss.

The second our lips touched, I prayed this one would be the one. He was right. I'd never had a man whom I didn't take care of. I was always offering money, cash, keys to my home, or my car to a man. Spencer hadn't asked for those things, yet I'd still done it. My ex Fortune, before he died, had gotten comfortable not only with asking but expecting me to provide for him. I had to accept responsibility for my part as an enabler.

Bing's tongue danced with mine. Liquor and saliva blended as he placed his hand at the nape of my neck. Bing Sterling kissed me harder than any man had. Or maybe it just seemed like it.

"You're amazing, Blake."

"Speaking of amazing," I told him, "it looks like I'm going to get promoted to corporate."

"Perfect timing. You won't have a reason not to go out with me when I get back from Paris."

He was leaving me? For how long? I said, "I've always wanted to go there."

"Consider it done. I'm not taking no for an answer. Call my assistant first thing in the morning. She has my schedule. Give her your details and we'll continue this date in the city of love."

Should I be flattered or annoyed that he didn't consider my profession? Relaxing my back against his chest, I decided to enjoy the moment.

Gazing up at the stars, being in Bing's arms let me know that true love for me was still a possibility.

Chapter 22
Devereaux

"Make love to me, Dev."

Anything he'd ask, I'd do . . . anything. For him. After what happened today, I had to downgrade Phoenix to an almost anything.

I replied, "Not tonight. I have to get up early."

"I do too. Now that we're both on set, we're going to have to find time for making love during the week, not only on Sundays. Nya's not home. We can do it anywhere we want in the house."

I'd taken the private investigator's information from Mercedes for two reasons. One, to help find my father. The other, I looked at Phoenix. He was a man. Yes, he was capable of cheating. After all I'd done for him, I didn't want to believe he'd have an affair with any woman, especially Ebony, but Mercedes might be right. At least I'd know. Being wedded to a liar. I couldn't do

228

that. I closed my eyes. All I wanted was peace and sleep.

He placed his hand between my thighs. Penetrated me with his finger. "I won't take long, babe."

Never opening my eyes, I moved his hand, turned my back to him. My work. My child. My man. That was what made me happy on the inside. I didn't love him any less, but I'd be lying to myself if I'd act as though that picture Mercedes showed me at the bar didn't bother me. I hugged my pillow, buried the side of my face into the plush down feathers.

"Are you seeing Trés?" Phoenix said in my ear.

My entire body cringed. Softly, I answered, "I suggest you don't go there."

"What's that supposed to mean? Why you turn your back on me when I told you I want you to make love to me?"

"Because I'm tired. And I, unlike you, seriously have to work. If I weren't tired, I'd make love to you."

After four years of dating this man, his flesh next to my naked body made me hotter than the day he penetrated me for the first time. Rolling over, I'd changed my mind. What if Mercedes was wrong? I held his face in my palms, then softly kissed his lips.

I was his backbone. I was his ride or die. The protector of his heart. Keeper of his secrets. Comforter of his fears. Fulfiller of his deepest desires. All those things were my responsibility to keep my man from having a reason to sex another woman.

Mercedes's voice echoed in my ear. *What is he to you?*

She wasn't the only one who had questioned why I stayed with Phoenix. My other two sisters thought I was his fool. I might be foolish in their opinion, but I believed in loyalty, monogamy, and true love. I wanted to hold on to those values, yet the truth, I couldn't deny. Deep within my soul I loved this man so much I was terrified of losing him.

I'd changed my mind again. I stopped kissing him. Stared into his eyes. Lovingly told him, "Good night."

Phoenix flapped the cover and comforter off of his body, started stroking his dick.

The things you fear the most shall come upon you.

Nana used to tell me that before she passed. It was my grandmother's way of helping me overcome my challenges by encouraging me to become fearless. Nana was the reason I poured all my passion into the people and things that were important to me. My time was limited. My passion was not.

"Oh shit," Phoenix said.

I felt the motion of his movement. His rhythm got faster, and faster. Hopefully he'd cum soon so both of us could get some rest. I was not giving in to him.

From my hardest days at Clark Atlanta to the toughest days running my business, Nana's advice worked for everything, except my relationship. I was always afraid of losing my man.

Starting right now I was going to try to stop worrying whether or not Phoenix had ever been with another woman since we'd started dating. There was no proof. My man wasn't all I wanted him to be, but he was everything I needed, and Mercedes was not going to pull me into her fire.

His rhythm slowed. My heartbeat thumped in my throat. I could stop being stubborn and give in. Lend him a hand or spread my thighs.

Earlier tonight Mercedes had said, "You can do better." I hated when people told me that as if upgrading men was simple as clicking a button. Get rid of my man and become a single mom? At least I had Etta to watch Nya. That was priceless.

Mercedes's husband, Benjamin, was a great father. He gave her whatever she wanted. I didn't want to find out if dating the director of my television series would make me happier. For now, I'd continue to do more than my fair share if that meant keeping my family happy and together.

"Make love to me, Dev. Please," he begged this time.

The only man I'd ever totally submitted to summoned me to do what I'd do without him ever having to ask. I couldn't deny that I was turned on now. We were naked in our bed, home alone.

I faced him. He eased on top of me.

The beat of our hearts thumped at the same time. Soul-to-soul, his muscular smooth flesh layered atop my body. He stared at me. I closed, then opened my eyes to the most beautiful black man, the color of sweet licorice. The waves of the abs he sweated to maintain, the ones he'd told me were for my enjoyment, I wondered if I had an exclusive.

You're my world, babe. I felt he could read my thoughts.

The energy emerging in my breasts intensified as my breaths quickened. My breathing became shallow. Quietly I heaved, pressing my hard nipples against his chest. My lips parted. Closing my eyes, I exhaled.

He inhaled.

He exhaled.

I inhaled sharp as though taking a whiff of a freshly baked cinnamon apple pie. I loved this man so much. Looking at him, I moaned, "Mmmm." Pressing my lips to his ear in the moment, I confessed, "I don't know what I'd do without you."

Blowing his warm breath into my mouth, he reassured me, "You'll never have to find out."

His nice white teeth illuminated his onyx lips that moved toward mine. I met him more than halfway. Kissed him ever so passionately.

"Make —"

"Shh." I placed my finger on his lips, then whispered, "I got you, babe."

His loving, caring, considerate ways attracted me to him. Our sex had grown more meaningful over the years.

Easing his head inside of me, my walls pulsated. I felt his shaft penetrate me. I wrapped my legs around his firm ass. The fire, the energy, the connection I experienced each time we made love missionary style, it was my favorite position.

I'd never tire of this feeling. Never.

Chapter 23
Spencer

Ebony's bathroom was the size of a studio apartment.

All white marble, tiled walls, all gold fixtures. Jacuzzi roomy enough for six to easily chill. Walk-in shower that could accommodate four people. I bet some real illish sex scenes went down here. My imagination was wild right now, boy.

"Make yourself comfortable in there, Spencer. Use whatever you'd like," Buster said.

Old dude seemed all right. "Cool," I answered.

I closed the double sliding doors. Shit was laid. White plush robe on a warmer. Cherry wooden hangers inside the open closet. Removing my clothes, I hung everything up, including my drawers. Counted a half-dozen smoking jackets. No pajama bottoms. Boxes of new underwear were neatly arranged on a shelf. Briefs, boxer briefs, silk boxers. Gold and white. Black and red. Green. Purple. Orange.

Toiletries, cologne, toothpaste, four kinds, mouthwash, three types, were on a silver tray on the long countertop. This was some beyond the spa shit with face, hand, and bath towels rolled into tubes.

Stepping into the shower, what the hell? There were no knobs to turn, only buttons to push. I set the temperature to seventy-seven, pressure to high. There were no showerheads, but there was a button for it. What the heck, I selected all, then pressed start.

"Mr. Spencer, your shower will start in . . ." An automated system counted down from five. Tiles slid sideways, waters sprayed from above down on the top of my head. Aiming at my hips, my dick and the crack of my ass got sprayed at the same time.

Soon as I thought, *Where's the soap?* Liquid suds squirted from tiny holes in the wall. This was beyond the Matrix experience for my ass.

I started rubbing my body all over. Three minutes later, the automated woman announced, "Rinsing off." Two minutes later, I heard her say, "Blow-drying you." When I was dry, I thought she was going to skeet me with massage oil.

"Thank you, Mr. Spencer. It's been my pleasure pampering you."

Damn! "No, thank you," I said.

"You don't have to thank me."

Okay, I was not getting into a convo with her. I'd save that for Siri on my cell. I stepped into the white and gold boxer briefs, downed the whisky, rinsed my mouth, brushed my teeth and my hair, then eased on the white robe. The heat absorbed into my shoulders. I left the belt untied.

"Aw, man. This joint is paradise."

I decided to try the Tom Ford Noir. Liked it enough to buy it the next time I was at a department store. Slicked jojoba oil on my chest. Had to pick up some of these sexy ass unders too. Tying the belt, I took a deep breath, exhaled, then opened the double doors.

Ebony was lying across the bed dressed in her boots, thong, and bra. She'd taken off her robe, put on a blindfold.

"I like Chopin," I said. "Nice selection."

"Don't look at me." Buster puffed on his cigar. "And don't leave my gorgeous wife waiting. Do whatever she requests," he said, blowing smoke rings.

Cool. The feeling was mutual. Didn't want his old behind looking at me either.

Screwing a man's wife in front of him was

a brand-new, yet exciting experience. I'd heard about it. Long as he kept his ass on the couch and didn't ask me to lick her boots, we'd be all right. I approached the bed, crawled on top of Ebony, interlocked my fingers with hers, stretched her arms above her head.

She was striking. Her titties were north. Couldn't wait to unleash that bra and squeeze them titties to find out if her breasts were natural. I trailed kisses down her arm. Licked her armpits. She moaned, "Spank my ass with your dick."

I felt her hand slide into my briefs. My dick was rock solid. I spoke with authority. "Turn over."

"Call me a bitch," she said.

Ebony was speaking my language. Like a drill sergeant, I commanded, "Bitch, turn your ass over. Now."

Her buttery, slippery butt was in the air. I bit the strap on her thong, pulled her undies to her thighs with my teeth.

"Put it in my ass," she said.

Damn, already?

I didn't have to reach far for a condom. I removed a packet from the headboard, ripped it open. Picked up the lube, squeezed a few drops inside the condom before rolling it onto my dick. Put a drop on the outside of her rectum.

I teased the opening of her ass with my head. I could tell from the size of her asshole this wasn't her first time doing anal. I took my time because that was my warm-up style. Penetrating her felt crazy good. Maybe it was the visual of how sexy she looked, how she smelled sweet enough to eat, or the fact that I didn't want anyone to wake me if I were dreaming.

"Your dick feels so good, Spencer." She called my name in a slick, sexy way. Then she said, "Thank you for fucking me in the ass, daddy."

Didn't matter if she meant that daddy part for her husband. All that shit made my dick harder. Had to apply pressure to the base of my shaft to keep from cuming too soon.

"Go deeper. You have no idea how bad of a girl I've been. Fuck this pretty ass. You like it, don't cha? Is it tight enough for you? If not, I can . . ." She squeezed my man real tight.

I bit my bottom lip. On purpose. To dickstract myself. Picking up the pace, I was about to bust. I paused. She backed her hairless pussy up on my balls, slamming then bouncing her ass into my pelvis. She thrust hard, made her cheeks clap, then paused. Ebony had them stripper moves like

Chanel. I hadn't fucked Chanel, but I'd seen her dance a time or two.

Ebony whispered, "Don't move. Daddy likes it when I cum. You feel my juices on your big cock?"

Speechless. Wanted to say something. Couldn't. Not if I was maintaining control. I waited for her to finish climaxing. Her using the word *cock* helped me out. Hadn't heard a sistah use that word in a minute.

"Put on a fresh condom and come get this pussy. Call me a bitch," she said.

Pulling out, I told Ebony, "Bitch, you're about to get the best dick you've ever had." I put my used rubber in a small empty box, used a wipe to cleanse my hands, reached for a fresh condom.

A swing lowered from the canopy. Dude must've had a remote 'cause she didn't touch a damn thing. She climbed into it, sat up, spread her legs. Her pussy was right in front of my dick.

"Don't move," she said. Aligning herself, she bared down on my dick.

Sliding her hands up, the straps she held on to were bungee cords. "Hold my hips," she commanded.

Ebony interlocked her ankles at the base of my spine, rocked back and forth. Shit was incredible. I was fucked up. When was I going to have this experience again? Surprised dudes weren't lined up outside her gate for this opp. Watching her on television was going to straight up be masturbation night for me.

She glanced in the direction of her husband, then back at me. She whispered, "He's asleep. Take off the condom. I want to feel your dick. But don't cum inside me, okay?"

Wow. I nodded. He said do whatever she'd ask. I took off the condom, dropped it in the box with the other one. Entering her felt like my dick was surrounded by hot, creamy, liquid silk lubrication. I liked heating up my lube before jacking off.

She swung back and forth. I wasn't sure how much longer I could hold out. Wanted both sets of her lips in my mouth.

"I'm about to cum," I said. "What you want me to do?"

"Not yet. Give me a moment," she said, biting me real hard on my chest. Instead of letting go, her teeth sunk deeper. When she let go, I wanted to holler. That shit felt orgasmic in a weird ass way but it took my mind off of busting a nut.

Ebony resumed rocking, rotating, bouncing, and grinding. "Hold my hips. Go deeper," she whispered as though she were cheating on her husband.

That was not the right move. If I looked at ole dude, my shit was going to go south. The second I went all in on Ebony, I screamed like a bitch.

I felt my cum shoot inside her pussy again and again. My dick throbbed. Her pussy pulsated. Her G-spot had to be on full. There was one way to tell. I had to pull out and get out of the way. I put two fingers inside her, slid her G-spot toward me, then pushed hard right above her pubic bone.

She screamed, "Oh, shit!"

Ebony's juices squirted across the room on her husband's dick. Nigga was so quiet I thought he was asleep. When I looked to see how far her juices sprayed, ole dude was wide awake jacking himself off. He busted a nut in the middle of her streaming.

Hope she wouldn't trip off of my ejaculating inside of her, but I couldn't pull out. I just couldn't.

CHAPTER 24
ALEXIS

"Strap on for me. Dominate me."

James was so fuckable when he asked for it. "Go pick out the one you want me to use," I told him, knowing he was not getting what he wanted. These intimate sessions were all about Alexis Crystal cashing in on my inheritance.

He held up a four-inch, then a five-inch. Looked back and forth. Chose the shorter one and my black harness.

Eager, he asked, "You want me to put it on for you?"

"No, I'll do it. Give me a moment."

He sat on the side of the bed. "I don't know why I'm so crazy about you."

Well, there were two reasons in his hands. I scrolled through my Facebook account. Sandara had posted pictures of Ty with Max as though that were their dog. Guess it was hard to give up something that brought you a lot of joy. Ending my relationship with

James wasn't going to be emotionally easy.

It was the control that fueled my feelings. The time was eight in the morning. I locked my phone, put it on the nightstand.

I was going to miss his place. This king-size bed with high posts. The Egyptian thousand thread count sheets. His flat screen on the wall where we watched our porn videos. These two-hundred-dollar pillows that were firm and soft.

"Babe, why do you love me?"

"Come on, Alexis, quit stalling," he said.

He was right. I was taking my time to get him out of the mood.

We'd get our test results later today. Two years of raw, passionate, and unorthodox sex, it would be senseless for us to use protection now. Why did I let him convince me to take that damn HIV test? What was his purpose?

"Okay, baby, but I'm so hot for you. Do me first," I told him.

"We did it your way twice yesterday. It's my turn, sweetheart. Don't be selfish," he said.

"Be honest. You want me to do you for the same reason I want you to sex me. You think this is our last rendezvous until this baby is born. You know you can't ask LA for anal. She'll think you're gay."

243

Adding base to his voice, he protested, "You know I'm all man. If I were gay, you wouldn't be carrying my baby."

"Oh, so now you're one hundred?" I asked just to piss him off.

Lots of women couldn't do what I had no problem doing. Their prudish ways were rooted in someone else's beliefs of how they should live their life. Seeds were planted in the heads of too many people by bishops, pastors, priests, and parents who sinned, too. Some of those standing behind the pulpit were the worst. Like my brother's uncle. I agreed with Spencer. The man would never get a dime of my father's money. Spencer wouldn't either because he didn't want any of it. Was I wrong for hating my bishop for molesting my brother? If God could forgive him, He would definitely do the same for me for using James.

"If you don't want to do me, just say so."

"Give me a minute. I'ma take care of you," I lied.

Spencer was not gay. James was not gay. Doing my fiancé, ex-man, whatever our status was, now was not the time to bring up LA. I was putting him off, didn't want to piss him off too much. Needed him to make another deposit of sperm into my vagina.

Stimulating James in the rear gave him explosive orgasms he couldn't get any other way. I hoped his cuming inside of me one more time would impregnate us. I had to have a baby, not him. Once I inherited my millions, I was letting Chanel go too.

"If the baby is mine, I still want to marry you. I don't want my child growing up without me. She will know that I love her and I love you, Alexis."

She? Damn, I almost forgot I told everybody it was a girl.

Lying on my back, I opened my legs. "Prove it."

Hopefully not for the last time, his lips touched mine. The full experience was what I craved. Oral sex from Chanel was better. James had amazing skills too.

"Take your time," I whispered.

He peeled my labia apart, softly suctioned my clit ever so gently. A cool waterfall oozed from my clitoris. If I didn't have an ulterior motive, he could stay down there, put his finger inside me and make me squirt. Gushing in his bed would soak the sheets and require us to relocate to a different room to continue our session. Wasn't taking a chance on ruining the mood.

"Let me feel your dick inside of me, baby," I said, scooting toward the headboard.

James kneeled, slid my body to his. He teased me with the head before putting it in. "Sex with you is like a fine wine," he said, giving me slow, deep strokes until he came.

He gave me what I wanted. I had to renege on my promise to do him. Fucking him would make me spill all of his seeds. Why did Conner have to put that baby clause in his trust?

"You ready to do me?" he asked, handing me the harness.

I held my stomach. "I don't feel so well. Give me a moment."

"You want me to get you something?"

"No, I'll be okay in a few. Oh, can you hand me my cell."

My phone was on the nightstand. I could've gotten it. Asking James made him feel helpful.

"Here you are, sweetheart. You wanna talk about the situation with your brother?"

I sighed. Not this again. "No, I'm not." What difference would that make? James knew I didn't know at the time that we were related. "Please don't ask me again." Whatever answer James was looking for he'd already concluded in his mind.

"I just need to lay here for a moment. What time do we have to leave for the doctor's office?"

"In an hour. I'm going to make a BLT sandwich. You want one, sweetheart?"

Touching my stomach, I smiled at him. "We'd love one. Thanks."

I didn't pray often but, Lawd, please let me be pregnant with this man's baby.

CHAPTER 25
PHOENIX

Making love to Dev last night felt fantastic!

Still couldn't fall asleep afterward. She got up at sunrise, showered, dressed, left me with a quick good-bye. That was cool. I was out the door right behind Dev. I couldn't wait to see Ebony's ass on set. She had some explaining to do as to why she was at the Cheesecake while I was waiting on her at her place. What time did she get home?

I drove straight to her house, parked in her driveway, used my key to get in.

Stomping up the stairs to her bedroom, I hoped she heard me coming. I called out, "Ebony!"

There was no answer. The noise I heard was from my heavy breathing as I took my last step up and entered her room.

This time I lowered my voice. "Ebony, my babe. Where are you?" It was too early for her to be gone. I texted her, where you at?

The bed wasn't messed up the way I'd left it. Red and gold pillows all different shapes and sizes were arranged to perfection. That meant her ass had been here. Her neat freak behind did this shit every time after we were done fucking. Better not find out she had some other dude in here.

I sent her another text, If you don't want me to make a scene on set you'd best hit me back. Now.

Ebony had me heated! I mean real hot. I should leave her damn key on the kitchen counter.

My stomach growled. I already knew she ain't have shit downstairs in her refrigerator except some damn berries and juice. I checked her walk-in closet. All my shit was how I'd last seen it. Strolled into the bathroom. Shower, tub, sink. All that shit was dry.

"Oh, I see. Your ass was at some other nigga's house all night last night. Came through for a change of clothes, straightened up, then rolled out." Yeah, she must've washed my pussy at his place.

This television show was acting. She'd better not start thinking she's her character. I got her this job. I could get her ass fired too.

Getting in my car, I punched my steering

wheel. I couldn't have my main and my side be more successful than me.

Taking a deep breath, I had to calm down. Couldn't show up at the studio with an attitude. I went through the drive-through at Starbucks. Ordered a white chocolate mocha with extra whip and a breakfast sandwich. Parked in the lot, turned off my engine. Sipping on that sweet ass shit reminded me of how Ebony's pussy tasted.

I had to talk to someone other than myself. I called my boy Marvin.

He answered, "Hey, Phoenix, kinda early for you, bruh. What's up?"

"Haaaa!" I exhaled, releasing my frustration.

"Damn, man. Not in my ear with that. Dev okay? Nya all right?"

The person he should've asked about was me. "Yeah, man. You know my situation with Ebony. It's taking a nosedive since I've been managing her."

"You. Managing, Ebony? Come on, dude," Marvin said, laughing.

He wouldn't know anything about handling anybody's career since he was on the federal government's payroll. "What so funny?"

"What you mean is since I last spoke to you on Friday, y'all ain't together no mo'?"

He laughed again.

Hearing him say it like that lightened my attitude. I had to laugh too. It hadn't been a week yet. "That's why I called you. You put shit in perspective quick. I'ma finish my breakfast, then head to the set."

"I know you been fucking Ebony for way too long, man, but Dev is the priority. Now that they're in the same space, what you need to do is keep your black ass focused and stay off that damn set."

"Gotcha. I'm out."

He ended the call. I listened to V-103 while eating. I heard this chick tell Wanda, "A woman should not have sex before marriage."

"In what country? She sure as hell couldn't be American talking that bullshit. She's probably fucked Tom, Dick, and Harry and neither one of them bruhs put a ring on it, now she's bitter. Bitch get out of here with all that." I changed to 104.

Driving to the studio, I parked next to Dev's white BMW, called my mom.

She answered, "Hey, Phoenix, hold on. Nya, your dad is on the phone."

Damn, she could've said good morning, son. Or, I'm proud of you, son. Oh, yeah. That's right. She didn't know about my new role.

"Hey, Daddy, when you gone come get me?"

"Daddy has a new job. I have to work, but I'll pick you up soon okay?"

"Okay," she said, sounding sad.

Trying to cheer up my baby girl, I told her, "You going to Sandara's house today."

She whined, "I want to play with Brandy."

Nya was smart for her age. Auntie Mercedes gave her whatever she wanted. Sandara was on a real fixed income.

"Next time, princess. This time you get to play with Ty, Tyrell, and Tyson."

"And Max," she said, sounding happy.

"And Max," I repeated. "Daddy loves you. Be good for Grandma."

"Love you. Bye, Daddy."

Before I ended the call, I heard my mom. "Phoenix?"

"Yeah, I'm still here."

"I'm taking a month-long vacation starting this evening. Going on a cruise with my friends. You need to pick Nya up from Sandara's house."

Where was the ship sailing? Around the world? "Cool. No problem," I said, ending the call.

I didn't need this right now. My mom probably wasn't going anywhere. That was her way of forcing me to spend time with

Nya. Oh, wait a minute. Dev might've arranged this.

Getting out of my car, I entered the studio. The photographers were setting up. Checked my cell. No text from Ebony. I texted her, I'm here. Where you at?

Dev was sitting where she was yesterday. I watched her tap away on her laptop.

Walking up to her, I said, "Good morning babe."

Without looking up she replied, "Phoenix, please don't call me babe. When we're here, it's Devereaux."

Playfully, I poked her in the side. She swatted my hand away. "I'm concentrating on something important."

"Lighten up, Dev, it's not that serious."

A person from behind questioned, "Is everything okay, Dev?"

She nodded.

I recognized his voice. I turned to see the director dude. "Oh, so he can call you Dev, but I can't."

"You have a moment." He paused, then continued. "Phoenix, right?"

"Man, you know you know my name. Quit trying to impress my fiancée."

"This is not the place," Trés said. "Dev is extremely busy. Let's take this outside."

Sounded more like a demand than a request.

I looked at Dev. She stared at me, then said, "Oh, Ebony. Come here for a minute."

My head snapped in the opposite direction. Ebony wasn't there. Dev stared at her laptop, started typing.

"You ready?" Trés asked.

"I don't have to answer to you, man." Who did this dude think he was?

"Okay, then answer me," Dev said. "Do you have a copy of your signed contract with Ebony?"

She was still looking at the computer. Typing.

"She's been working. I'ma get it from her by Friday," I explained.

"Then, we'll see you Friday," Trés said.

"Dev, look at me." I repeated, "Dev. Look. At. Me."

"You're so disrespectful. I can call security if you want me to, Dev," Trés said.

"Give him five minutes," Dev replied, staring at her cell phone. "No, make it three."

CHAPTER 26
DEVEREAUX

Watching how Trés handled Phoenix made me uncomfortable. I was relieved and feeling guilty at the same time. I knew what I had to do.

"Tiera, let everyone know we're starting thirty minutes late."

She nodded. "Certainly. Anything else?"

"That'll be all." I picked up my cell, walked outside. Phoenix was in the parking lot shouting at Trés. I got in my car, locked the door, and made the call.

Soon as she identified herself, I said, "Hi, Dakota. It's Devereaux Crystal."

"Good morning, Ms. Crystal. Mercedes told me she gave you my number. Glad you called. What have you decided?"

What all had my sister shared with the detective? I noticed Phoenix jabbing his finger toward Trés's face. Trés told me to stay out of it and I was.

I answered, "I'd like to move forward with

the investigation."

"Great! What's your e-mail address?"

I sat in my car giving her the requested information. A police car drove onto the lot.

"I'll e-mail you a questionnaire and a contract within the hour. Soon as I get everything back, I'm on it," she said. Then she asked, "You still there?"

"Huh? Oh, yeah." I had heard her, but it took a minute for what she'd said to register. "Thanks, bye."

Phoenix got in his car, then sped off. I expected my cell to ring. It didn't.

Having my fiancé spied on was one of the most difficult decisions I'd made. When I'd awakened this morning, I wasn't sure about hiring Dakota. When Phoenix showed up here, I still wasn't convinced. The way his head snapped when I called Ebony's name, that was my deciding factor.

I dialed my mother. Hadn't spoken with her in a few days.

"Everything okay," she asked without saying hello.

"Yeah, Mom. Are you available for dinner tonight?"

She hesitated.

I told her, "It's okay if you don't have time. I understand you're always too busy."

"No, I want to. It's just that I have a date. Can we do eight?"

"Yes, eight is good. I'll text you the restaurant."

"Okay, I'll see you then," she said, ending the call.

I invited Mercedes, Alexis, and Sandara via text message. Not sure what would come out of the investigation, my entire family had to be on my team. I was not too proud to ask for emotional support. Prayed my relationship with Ms. Etta wouldn't change if I had to break up with Phoenix. Nya loved her grandma.

Told myself, "Dev, stay positive." It was hard now that I'd seen the excitement in my man's eyes for another woman.

Entering the studio, Trés said, "What I told the police in front of Phoenix should take care of your fiancé not being around for the rest of the season. Hope you don't mind, I had a chat with Ebony. Told her her having a manager was a good idea, but hiring Christal Jordan, the owner of Enchanted PR is best because Christal is the best. Ebony needs a corporation and a team, not an individual. No disrespect to Phoenix, but what contacts does he have in this industry? Don't let him tag on to your success. Make him build his own."

I was kind of numb right now. My heart didn't feel love or hate. Trés was right about Phoenix making his own way. It was time.

"Tiera, let everyone know I'm ready to start the shoot."

She scurried toward the dressing rooms.

I told my friend, "I've hired a private investigator to find out what Phoenix is doing."

Trés nodded. "Not a bad decision. When *Sophisticated Side Chicks ATL* start trending on the regular, all of our personal lives are going to be all over Dish Nation and TMZ. Best to know what you're dealing with than to have your life become a spinoff of your own show."

"Our show," I said, giving Trés a tighter than usual hug.

Ebony, West-Léon, and Travis came out at the same time. My jaw dropped at how beautiful they looked together.

The black suit West-Léon wore was fitted. I loved the way his blazer hung open to expose his bare chest that had the right amount of shine. Travis's white slacks were tailored to his athletic physique. His shirt was unbuttoned with one side slightly tucked in his pants.

Ebony was that boss bitch standing in gold seven-inch heels. Not many women could walk in those shoes. I might make that height Ebony's signature. Her simple white dress had a plunging neckline that exposed her navel. The edges accenting her cleavage were trimmed in black leather. Her lips were the sexiest blazing shade of red.

Trés and I watched AJ Alexander and his team direct West-Léon and Travis to stand on opposites sides of Ebony. She crossed her arms, placed one foot slightly in front of the other.

Looking at Ebony, I could see how any man would be attracted to her. I was no lesbian but watching her was making me hot.

Chapter 27
Blake

In the words of my youngest daughter, the best way to get over one dick was to ride another.

Sex with Bing hadn't happened . . . yet. I had to face my truth. Believing the next man would help me forget about the last guy, that was the reason I'd given birth to four children by four different men. That didn't make me a whore at the age of twenty-two, twenty-three, twenty-four, or twenty-five. I just desperately wanted a man to love me. Thought each time if I had his baby, he'd stay. Ended up in a cold delivery room in Charlotte, North Carolina, with my sisters — Ruby, Carol, Teresa, and Kim — by my side as I pushed each of my girls out.

Clearly, I was not living by the bible, just waiting for a man to deliver me from what he probably couldn't deliver himself from and that was sin. I struggled, went to college, graduated, got a good-paying job, and offered all my children the opportunity to earn their degree. I didn't need Bing, or my children, or my ex to remind me of my mistakes. I wanted to be praised for the countless things I'd done right.

If I was going to hell for fornication, I'd see a lot of the people who judged me going up in flames too. Changing my ways had to be my decision. I wanted to be in a relationship with a loving, caring, supportive man. Maybe Bing was that guy. Perhaps not. They all started out like Spencer. The ending each time was just the same script with a different twist.

Brandon stuck his head into my office, then said, "The call you've been expecting from corporate is on line one. Can I sit in?"

"Sure. Have a seat," I told him. "Close the door."

One day Brandon might be in my position seeking advancement outside of the banking center. His attire was sharp as usual. Lime green shirt, navy pants and shoes.

Placing the call on speaker, I answered, "Blake Crystal, here."

"Hi, Blake," she said. "This is Wendy in human resources."

Didn't want to delay what she had to say with pleasantries. I waited for her to offer me the position. If I weren't getting the job, I would've gotten a letter in the mail.

"I have great news," she said.

Brandon crossed his legs and fingers. My heart raced with excitement. "I'm listening."

Brandon motioned as though he were clapping. He stood, twerked, sat down. I smiled, shook my head, concealed my laughter.

"I'm calling to offer you the Compliance Operations Manager position. Before you respond, I have to let you know a few important factors."

I should've known there was a caveat. "I'm listening."

"It's based in Charlotte. You'll be provided with corporate housing for up to sixty days. And you'll need to start Monday."

"This upcoming Monday as in" — I looked at the calendar on my desk — "five days from now."

"Yes, I can give you until the morning to decide."

Brandon mouthed, "Accept! Accept!"

I grew up in Charlotte. Had family there. But I'd never lived away from my children and was just getting to know Bing. Who'd watch Max while I went to work? Maybe I should talk with my girls and Bing first.

Wendy asked, "Hello, Blake. Are you still there?"

I answered, "Yes."

"Is that a yes, you're still there or yes, you'll accept?"

I could always come back to Atlanta. It might be another five years or never for this opportunity to repeat.

"Yes, Wendy. I accept."

CHAPTER 28
BLAKE

Two dozen long-stemmed roses — one red, one white — were delivered to my office.

The vase was eighteen inches tall. Baby's breath and lush green accents were nicely arranged. In the moment, my heart was filled with love knowing that someone thought of me today in a good way.

Smiling, I placed my nostrils over the blooming bud, closed my eyes, and inhaled. I paused, admiring the flowers. These were the most beautiful that anyone had sent me. More gorgeous than the ones my staff gave me for my fiftieth. My birthday roses were lovely. Wishing I'd dried them out and kept them, I removed a red and white rose from the bouquet, hung them upside down. I put them back realizing a few days wouldn't be enough for them to dehydrate. Once they fully blossomed, I'd peel away a few petals for a keepsake.

Brandon entered my office. "Bitch, who

beat me to it? Somebody loves your ass. Who're they from? Let me guess. Mr. Sterling," he said, reaching for the card still attached to the bouquet.

Beating him to it, I said, "Bing would be my guess, but no one knows about my promotion." I paused. Eyed Brandon. "Did you call him?"

Bing had class. Breaking the news about my relocation in less than a week, I hope I didn't disappoint him.

Reading the card, *"To the best mom ever. Love, Alexis,"* I was truly shocked.

"Say what?" Brandon's question was rhetorical.

My eyes started tearing. "Give me a moment, Brandon. I need to call my daughter."

"Of course you do," he said, closing the door behind him.

Sitting at my desk, I broke down crying. Maybe being pregnant made her think about the things she'd have to face once her daughter was born. I never wanted to be a single mom. It was so hard for me. And although my baby girl was a hot mess at times, she was still my hot mess.

The long days starting at four in the morning coordinating diaper bags, bottles, and clothes, for each of them. As they got older, dropping them off at different schools, going to work, picking them up only to drop them off again so I could go sit in class to earn a degree. Maybe in addition to not having a father, my girls didn't have their mother either.

But I made up for it by providing them with a great education, cars, and other material things. It was either/or. I couldn't sit at home and provide a better start at life for them than what I had.

Alexis didn't answer. I left her a message. "Baby, you have no idea how much the flowers you sent have brightened my day. This is so thoughtful. I love you."

I should've reached out to my child and extended my sincere condolences for Conner's passing. It wasn't too late. Spencer, I'd leave that alone. On second thought, perhaps he was really trying to find a mother's love in me.

"Can I come back in?" Brandon asked, tapping on my door.

"Yes." I told him, "I'm leaving my flowers here. I need to see this bouquet the rest of the week."

"If they come up missing, don't blame me. If they double up, blame that on me," he said.

I hugged Brandon. "I love you. I'll see you in the morning."

266

"Aw, hell no. You're withholding information. You're seeing Bing again, aren't you?"

I nodded and smiled.

"You can thank me at the wedding. Go get your man, bitch, before I take him from you."

A quick stop in the restroom, I brushed my teeth, refreshed my lipstick. Fluffed, then fingered my jet-black shoulder-length hair.

Driving to Bing's home, in anticipation of an intimate moment with him, I wished I had time for a shower and change of clothes. Dinner with Devereaux later meant Bing and I couldn't go far. At least I was prepared for a passionate kiss. I parked in his driveway beside his white Bentley. The top was down. His leather interior was the same colors as our Falcons, red and black.

The front door opened. "Come on in," he said. "Hope you're hungry."

For him. Yes. I sashayed up six steps. "Haven't eaten since breakfast."

Seven tall white candles were centered on a long dining table that seated two. There was so much room that he could add twelve more chairs. He lit each wick.

"Have a seat. Let's get you fed; then I'll give you the grand tour of my humble abode."

"You're so sweet. I appreciate you." I meant that.

Instrumental music filled the space around us. He placed a small plate with gold trim in front of me. Our first course was three plain red grapes.

"To cleanse the palate," he said. "Plus, Americans think more is better. For me, I prefer less of everything, except money."

The second course was a simple mixed green salad with fresh raspberries.

"The salad is to jump-start the digestive system properly. Another thing people do improperly is drink a lot of water before or during a meal. But if you get thirsty, let me know."

I smiled, trying not to laugh. I was thirsty all right. "Mmm, this is tasty. What's the dressing?"

"If I tell you, I'll have to marry you," he said, then smiled. "It's my grandmother's secret recipe."

There was no perfect time to share the news or the fact that I had to leave early to meet Devereaux. Hope she wasn't setting me up for disappointment. I should think positive. Maybe she had a surprise for me too.

"What's on your mind?" Bing asked, picking up my empty plate.

His question reminded me of how Spencer would say, "The world can wait. In this moment, I need you here with me."

"We'll talk about it later."

"You talk. I'll listen. Timing is everything. I still have to serve you the next course."

Bing returned with a plastic bib, tied it behind my neck. Then he carried in the biggest lobster I'd ever seen in my life!

I laughed. "That looks delicious."

"If you had to choose me or the lobster?" he said with a smile.

"Hmm. Let's see. The lobster is already cracked. Looks and smells delicious." I looked into his dreamy eyes. His question was an easy one to answer. "Definitely you."

"I'd choose me, too, but wait until you taste it. You might dump me. Hope you don't mind sharing."

Peeling away the shell, he dipped a piece of the tail in drawn butter, then fed me. This was a first. I sucked and chewed like it was my last meal. Tempted to devour the whole tail, I drowned his portion in butter.

"Open wide."

He suctioned the tip, nibbled. I shivered. He smiled. By the time we were done, only shells remained on the platter. He removed my bib. Brought me a hot white towel.

"The lemon juice in the towel will take

away the slipperiness."

"Do you always do this?" Soon as I'd asked, I wished I hadn't. "Don't answer that."

"I wasn't going to. Come with me," he said, extending his hand. "After the tour, dessert out on the deck."

No man has ever treated me like a queen. Bing had me wondering if it were too late to change my mind about relocating.

"I have something I want to share with you," I said, standing midway on his wide staircase.

I could see the view through his ceiling-to-floor windows; beyond the pool there was the huge lake that I couldn't see the first time. The tall trees were lined on the opposite side of the body of shimmering water.

"What is it?"

Standing one step higher, I told him, "I got a promotion today."

He frowned. "Congratulations, right? You don't seem excited."

"I am. It's just that it's in Charlotte."

"Charlotte. Not China. That's a drive away," he said with a smile. "And less than an hour flight on my private jet."

Private what? My brows stretched toward my forehead. "Friday is my last day in the office. I start my new position Monday. I just found all this out today."

"Come with me," he said, leading me downstairs. "We can do the tour another day. Dessert and champagne are in order. Blake, I waited years for the opportunity to date you, a few miles is not going to divide us."

Bing held me in his arms. He smelled and felt incredible. I leaned on his strong shoulder praying nothing or no one would come between me and my man.

CHAPTER 29
EBONY

Leaving the set, I got in my Benz and called Phoenix.

"Hey," was all he said.

"What happened earlier? Why did you leave this morning?"

He had reason to be uptight with me about last night, but not today. Like dudes, even when I messed up, I learned to let it go. Either Phoenix wanted to grind with me or not. His call.

"Until we have a signed contract, I'm not permitted to be at the studio. So you ready to execute so your man can be gainfully employed, so to speak?"

The PR referral by Trés made sense. I'd already arranged a meeting with Christal Jordan. I'd seen her on a BET reality show with other publicists. Having her take me on as a client would make me feel more comfortable than doing business with my lover.

"Daddy, I'm hungry," the voice of a little girl announced in the background.

What? "You have Nya with you?"

"Yeah, how convenient. I get kicked out of the studio at the same time that my mother is going out of town on a month-long cruise. Sandara claimed she had something to do this evening. Dev has been texting, but she won't call me. The moment I agreed to be your manager, all —"

"Agreed?"

"I got enough shit to deal with right now, Goldie. I don't need this bullshit from you too," he said.

My getting an attitude with him would've been easy. I had the upper hand. "I'll order us something to eat. Y'all can meet me at my house."

"You sure you're going to be there tonight?" he retorted.

"Damn, thanks for reminding me. What was I thinking? You're the one that's engaged. I'm the one with good pussy and tons of options. Don't come by."

"Goldie, don't say that. I apologize. I —"

"Dadeee," Nya cried.

He need not get our roles twisted. I was the damn star. He was back to being the manny. "You don't have to explain. Don't take Nya upstairs to my bedroom. Y'all can watch television in the living room until I get home. I'll see you guys in about an hour."

"Cool. We can go over the details for our contract when you get home, my babe. I'll have my lawyer get it to yours first thing in the morning, that way I can hand it to Trés. If his ass talk down to your man again, it's on."

Phoenix's problems were not going to become mine. I ended the call without saying "bye" or "I love you, my babe."

CHAPTER 30
ALEXIS

Nervous as hell, I was silent in transit to Emory for our HIV test results.

Why did I agree to this again? James was quiet too. He was probably pissed off about my not doing him. I prayed I was pregnant with his baby. Then I wouldn't have to worry about who the father was. There was no way I was going to do to my child what my mom had done to all of us. My kid would have a daddy even if I had to bribe a man.

I'd better read our dad's trust again. It was a bit confusing. Make sure I didn't miss any buzz words that may keep me from collecting the 2.5 mil.

I texted Spencer, Have you ever had an HIV test?

"You know you owe me," James said, sounding bitter.

Looking out the window, I didn't respond. Just wanted to hear what the doctor had to say and take it from there. He parked. If my news were devastating, no one would know from my slamming body that I was potentially sexually lethal. The thought fucked me up. With so many newly reported cases, what were my odds?

I had on my baby-blue halter minidress, purple thong, and matching stilettoes. Rocked my lavender Dior bag and Cynthia Bailey sunglasses. Swaying my hair behind my back, I strutted into the entrance with James loosely holding my arm.

The receptionist said, "You guys can go in. Dr. Wallace is expecting you."

The doctor greeted us. "Welcome back, James. Alexis, how are you?"

I wasn't down for delaying knowing my stats. "Don't mean to be rude. I'd rather not small talk. I'd like to hear my results."

James waited until I sat in a chair. He sat beside me. Held my hand.

"I have good and bad news," he said. Not asking which one we wanted first he said, "Both tests are non-reactive. Neither of you has HIV. That's the good."

That was all I signed up for, so the bad news must've been for James. "You want me to step out?" I asked him.

"Nah, you need to hear this."

My mind wandered. Did he have prostate

cancer? Some other illness? The doctor did say it was bad news.

"James, Alexis."

"What you calling my name for?" I questioned the doctor, then sat on the edge of my seat.

"Just a minute," Dr. Wallace said.

"No, you wait a minute," I told him. Then I asked, "James, is there something you want to tell me?"

"Alexis, calm down. Let Dr. Wallace do his job, then we can talk over dinner."

James was too damn calm for me. He knew something I didn't. I stared at the doctor. "Well, out with whatever it is, man."

"I hate to inform you but —"

I stood, "Out with it, man! Damn!"

Dr. Wallace said, "You guys are not pregnant. Sorry, James."

I slapped James's face real hard. He held his jaw. "That's fucked up! You had him do a pregnancy test? That's the real reason why you brought me here!" I stared at the doctor. "Are the results for the HIV test real or was that just some bullshit trick to get me here. I should sue your ass for malpractice."

A text registered on my cell from Spencer, You all right?

I replied, You don't wanna know. I'll hit you back later.

"Thanks, Doctor. Alexis, let's go. We can discuss this outside."

I cursed his ass all the way to the muthafucking car! If it weren't too damn hot I would've stood at the bus stop, went to Conner's house, and drove off in the Ferrari.

Starting the engine, he said, "I apologize. I should've told you, but I had to know for myself. I know you. You play everybody for a fool, sweetheart. Now that we both know the truth, no hard feelings. You go your way. I'm done with you."

"No, bitch! I'm done with your trifling ass! I'm glad I had a miscarriage." All I could do now was pray I was really pregnant so I wouldn't have to have sex with a stranger in order to collect my inheritance.

Spencer texted me, Alexis PLEASE tell me you don't have HIV.

I hit him back, This here shit is all your fault! Fucking around with Charlotte and shit!

Soon as I hit send, I laughed. I was so caught up in my lies that I believed I really lost a baby I never had. Oh well, let him sweat it out. I'd call Spencer after I left James's and give my brother the rundown on my test results.

CHAPTER 31
DEVEREAUX

Executed contract and a check for five grand were in my purse. I valet parked at Brio on Peachtree Street. Entering the restaurant, Mercedes was seated at the bar with two glasses of Rosa. She knew to deviate from my normal cabernet to this delicious red sangria I ordered every time we came here.

"You're early," I said, giving her a hug.

"When you're early, you're on time. When you're on time, you're late. You can't walk through the door and start at the same time, but I was hoping you'd arrive ahead of the rest. We need to talk. I changed our seating from the main dining area to the private room."

That was my take-charge don't-need-anybody's-permission sister. Mercedes approached the hostess. "We're taking our cocktails to our table. Don't bring anyone to the room until they're all here. Got that?"

"Of course, Mrs. Mercedes. Right this way."

"And bring the cabernet, chardonnay, champagne, and appetizers I ordered soon as everyone is seated."

So she did order a cabernet. Depending on how my family meet-up went, I might need a bottle for myself.

"Yes, Mrs. Mercedes."

I was immediately relieved. Going from Phoenix being kicked out by Trés and the police to his constantly calling me, I didn't want to coordinate the details for my get-together.

"Thanks for handling everything." Not that I needed to say that, but I was appreciative of my sister lending a hand.

"Not trying to take over your meeting, but I'm paying my nanny by the hour to sit with the twins. I do not have all night to wait for everyone to decide what they wanted to eat and drink."

I whispered in her ear, "Since when did you stop using your last name?"

Mercedes spoke loud. "Since I told Benjamin last night we're getting a divorce."

I waited until the hostess left our area. "Is it that serious? I mean, you had to have just found out for sure that he was doing something." I couldn't even say the word *cheat-*

ing to her. "Don't you want to try to work it out for your kids?"

Please give me inspiration here, Sis, I thought, praying she wouldn't let her marriage end without a fight.

"It's not when I found out. It's what Dakota gave me. I can't make my husband love me if he's in love with another woman. Look at this," she said, clicking play on a video.

The first was Benjamin dining with the woman in the photo Alexis had texted. They left the restaurant, drove up to a modest townhouse development.

"They're going to her house where I assume his ass is right now," Mercedes said, stopping the video. "I put him out. If he were so innocent, why the hell didn't he put up a fight? Huh?"

I embraced my sister. She gave me a brief hug, then pushed me away.

Concerned about my sister and her kids, I asked, "What did he say when you showed him this?"

"Nothing. No explanation. He just packed a bag, told me he'd pick up the kids this weekend, then he walked out."

Whoa. I knew the expression on my face was a blank stare. Mercedes started crying. I gave her another hug. I was the eldest, but she was always the strongest of us all. The one who held it all together. The proudest when she'd dragged out the words, *My husband.*

"If he thinks he's taking our kids to her house, that's not happening," she said.

Wow. I was in shock. If there ever were one, Benjamin always seemed like the perfect husband. "Do you know how long they've been dating?"

My sister stopped crying, removed a tissue from her purse, dried her face. "What difference does it make? My marriage is over. And I'm going to make him pay emotionally, financially, and physically. What did I do to him to deserve this?"

Our mom entered the room with Dakota, Sandara, and Alexis.

"Great, everyone is here," I said, standing, attempting to draw their attention toward me. Giving everyone a hug, I sat at the head of the table, then asked Dakota, "Please, sit next to me."

My mom and Alexis held on to each other. I overheard Mom say to Alexis, "Thanks again for the roses. They're beautiful and so are you." What roses? That was unusual.

Mercedes was to my right. Mom sat next to her. Dakota sat next to me. Alexis sat next to her. Sandara sat beside Alexis. The food and drinks arrived. The waitress filled everyone's goblet with their wine selection.

Regaining her composure, Mercedes ordered the waitress, "Hold off on opening the champagne. Do not come back in. I'll advise you when we're ready."

I admired Mercedes. She'd started her business Crystal Clear Consulting when she graduated from college with a marketing degree.

"What's this occasion for, Devereaux?" our mom asked. "I thought I was having dinner with just you?"

I told her, "Mom, I need for you to support me on this. I didn't want anyone to find out about what I'm doing from another source, so I invited you all here to get the details at the same time."

My mother responded, "I'm listening." She folded her arms as though she'd rather be someplace else.

Dakota chimed in, "If you don't mind, Devereaux, I'll take it from here."

Sipping my sangria, I nodded. "Please do."

"Devereaux has hired me to do an investigation on Phoenix Watson."

Alexis said, "That's what's up."

Mom looked at my private detective. "And you are?" Then she faced Alexis, who was seated directly across the table. "And why is this a good thing?"

Alexis sighed. Her mouth twisted before she said, "Because —"

Trying not to let attitudes escalate to an argument, I interjected, "Mom —"

Dakota interrupted me, "If you don't mind, Devereaux, I'll continue."

I nodded.

"As you should know, the growing buzz for *Sophisticated Side Chicks ATL* has gone viral. Previews of the pilot and photos from the shoot yesterday and today are trending, and taping of the first episode starts Monday. Every week Devereaux is going to become increasingly popular. She is doing the smartest thing any successful woman can do and that's hire a private investigator like myself to check out her fiancé's background and whereabouts." She looked at Mother. "To answer your question, my name is Dakota Justice."

Mom said, "Hmm."

Dakota continued. "Everyone has something they're not proud of. That's understandable."

God knew that was the truth for my family, including me. My disgrace was having a baby out of wedlock. I vowed not to be like Mother. We were different, but Mercedes was the only one who'd married. Although she had problems, it was with her husband, not her fiancé.

"What I'm searching for is anything that would damage Devereaux's reputation or show cause why Devereaux should not marry Phoenix Watson. I'll report my findings immediately. What you do with the evidence I present is up to you, Devereaux."

I glanced at Mercedes, then at my mom and other sisters. "Does anyone have any questions for Dakota?"

"May I have your card?" my mom asked.

We all looked at her.

"Of course." Dakota handed my mom, Alexis, and Sandara a card.

"Mercedes, don't you want one too?" my mom asked.

Mercedes answered, "I'm good. Thanks."

"Well, if no one has any questions," my mom said, "this is a good time to let you girls know I got a promotion to corporate."

"Mom, that's wonderful!" Mercedes gave our mother a long hug.

We all congratulated her. I was proud of our mom. Now that I thought about it, our mother never gave up on anything or anyone of us.

"I want to thank you, Mother, for being the best mom you knew how," I said. "I know I don't always express my gratitude, but I love you, Mom."

I wasn't the best at telling people how I felt. I was learning that good intentions alone weren't always enough. People outside of Phoenix and Nya needed to hear my appreciation.

Tears glazed my mother's eyes. "You don't know how much your words mean."

"You are the best mom," Sandara said. "Because you made it with four of us, I'm working on doing better for my three kids. I got a modeling contract and I'm going back to college."

Mother smiled. "So that's the secret you didn't want to tell me about?"

Softly, Sandara answered, "Yes."

"Well, this is the most awesome news of the day," Mom said.

Alexis hugged Sandara. "I knew you could do it, Sis. If you need me to babysit, I'm here for you. But don't put too much on your schedule at once. College is demanding."

"How are you doing with the pregnancy?" Sandara asked Alexis. "If you need any advice about kids, I've got lots of it."

Tears streamed down our mom's face. Mercedes dapped a napkin on Mom's cheeks, then told Alexis, "Don't call her. Ask me."

Alexis said, "I have a confession."

"Here we go," Mercedes said.

Dakota chimed in. "Let her finish. This is all good healing and cleansing."

"James had me take an HIV test along with him."

Our mother's eyes grew wider than everyone else's.

Mercedes gasped, "Child, you'd better not be."

Alexis rolled her eyes at Mercedes, then vehemently replied, "I'm not. You might want to check your own status."

I hadn't noticed our mother was holding her breath until she exhaled. "Then what's the confession, Alexis?"

"He snuck in a pregnancy test and found out that I'm not pregnant, so we ended it. I was pregnant, but I miscarried at the hospital after Charlotte kicked me in my stomach. It was probably best because honestly I didn't know who the father was."

"So you lost the child before the family gathering at your house and you lied to all of us. You're worse than a man," Mercedes said.

Dakota shook her head at Mercedes. "Don't make Alexis shut down just when she's opening up."

Mercedes said, "She needs to shut it

down. Meaning that vagina of hers."

"I second that," our mother added.

"Whatever. This is my body. I convinced Spencer not to tell anyone and he agreed. You guys know Conner is dead. I hope you come to the service to support me. What I haven't told any of you is, he left me his house and four expensive luxury cars."

When Alexis told us where the house was and what kind of cars she now owned, I could've fallen out of my chair. She added, "And he left me two and a half million dollars. Soon as I get a lawyer to confirm everything, I'll be the richest one in our family."

"What the hell!" Our mom shouted, "That's my back child support!" Mom started laughing. "Call Kendall. Have him verify everything. Knowing Conner, it's more like two dollars and fifty cents."

Alexis opened her purse. Rolled four luxury car keys on the white tablecloth like they were dice. "I inherited these, too, Mother. A broke man cannot afford this collection. Boop!"

Sandara snatched the key to the Porsche. "Mine!"

We were all shocked when Alexis said, "Keep it. If the trust is legit, I'll give you the car. But all of the inheritance isn't even mine unless I'm pregnant, Mother."

"But you're not," Sandara cried. "We could've been ballin'."

"But the good news is James and I tried again and I am pregnant now."

"What in the world. Girl, what drugs are you on?" Mercedes said.

"After the HIV test, I spent the weekend with James. We got down the entire weekend. I took a home test and it's positive. I'm having his baby."

Mother asked, "Chile, one of these days. Does James know?"

Alexis shook her head. "And I'd like to keep it that way, Mother."

"Chile, now I'm glad I'm moving to Charlotte this weekend," our mother said. "I need a break from the madness. My new job is based there."

"That's wonderful! Everything is simply peachy!" Mercedes stood, downed the rest of her wine. "I'm going to request that bottle of champagne. I need another drink. And all this testosterone right here!" Mercedes twirled her finger in everyone's direction. "Devereaux, you can create a new television show. Call it *Crystal Balls!*"

CHAPTER 32
PHOENIX

Dev and I were going to be together forever.

All couples had rough patches that tested the strength of their relationship. For men, we dealt with stress by ejaculating. Like my man Marvin Gaye song, *Sexual Healing*, penetration always helped relieved my frustrations. Since I wasn't getting it at home, at least I had a steady side and didn't have randoms in a rotation.

"Daddy, where's Mommy?" Nya asked.

That was a good question. Nya and I had made it to Ebony's. We were on the couch. Strands of hair had separated from the pompom I'd given her this morning. I tried to gather the wiry edges, smoothed them out without having to untie her pink ribbon. My attempt made it worse. More hairs popped out. I left it alone. Ebony could touch up Nya's hair when she got home.

This was the first time I'd brought my little girl here. She wasn't old enough to understand what I was really doing. Nya opened her mouth wide, yawned in my face.

"Hang in there, baby girl," I told her. "Food is on the way."

Ebony should've been here by now. I texted her, How much longer? Nya is restless.

Wish I had a definitive answer for my daughter on her mother's whereabouts. I told her the truth. "Baby, I don't know where your mommy is. What cha wanna watch on TV? The Disney Channel?"

"Where's Mommy? I want my mommy. I wanna go home, Daddy." Nya rubbed her eyes.

I'd spent more time with our daughter than Dev. The days Nya was at home, she was usually asleep when Dev left for work. The same when Dev came in. But this whining for her mom was new.

Nya yawned again. Good. Hopefully she'd be ready for a nap soon. I turned to the Disney Channel. *Austin and Ally* was on. I leaned my little girl's head on my chest. My mom had let her pick out her clothes this morning. Nya had on pink everything. Sparkling tennis shoes. Shorts. Sleeveless T-shirt.

Nya shook her head. Her eyes slowly closed. She stretched them wide. "I wanna go to Grandma's."

My mom hadn't called me since she'd taken off for her so-called vacation. Bet if I drove by her house she was there.

"Daddy, whose house is this?"

I scratched my head. "My friend. Marvin," I lied.

"Where's Marbin."

"Mar-vin. V, not B, baby."

"I'm hungry."

"Me too. Marvin's wife is bringing us something to eat any minute now."

I texted Ebony, Where are you? Nya and I are starving!

Nya fell asleep in my arms. No response from Ebony. She was starting to piss me off again. Maybe I should take a break from Ebony, deal with my home-front bullshit. I put Nya in the bed downstairs, tucked her in, left the door open so I could hear if she got up. Lying across the sofa, I changed the station to ESPN for the sports ten o'clock news.

Heard Ebony's car enter the driveway. I bit my bottom lip, stayed put on the couch. The jingle of keys at the front door made me flaming hot. She'd best have a justification for making my baby go to bed hungry.

"Hey, my babe," Ebony said all cheery and shit. "I got us takeout from Houston's.

Chicken fingers for Nya. Where is she?"

"She's two. McDonald's would've been better," I said. I didn't look over my shoulder. Did not want to see her face. "And she's asleep in the bedroom down here."

"Well, if that's what she likes, it's time to introduce her to something new. I got you the Hawaiian rib eye medium."

"I prefer medium-well. You know that."

She snapped, "Of course I do. By the time you heat it up it'll be perfect."

This time I stood, followed her into the kitchen. "If you had brought your ass straight home instead of getting here three hours late, I wouldn't have to reheat it."

Lowering her voice, Ebony told me, "I have to get up early. Why don't you and Nya take your meals to your house? I'm sure Devereaux is wondering where you are."

Smart-ass.

Damn, Ebony was fine as hell. I pulled her dress over her hips, picked her up, sat her on the island in the kitchen. Removing her panties, I rummaged through the bag that was on the counter. "Lay back," I told her.

"Phoenix, what if Nya wakes up?"

"She's asleep. Relax," I said, opening what I assumed was my baked potato.

Scooping two fingers away from the peel,

I topped it with sour cream, chives, bacon bits, and shredded cheese. I smeared her clit, then sucked it all off. "I'ma feast on you and eat my dinner at the same time."

I rubbed my teriyaki glazed rib eye between her lips, then ate her sweet pussy until she came on my tongue. As she screamed, I hurried to cover her mouth.

My dick was rock solid. He wanted in. I deserved to release my frustration inside of Ebony. "Stand up and lean on the counter," I said, unzipping my pants.

She squatted between my thighs. Her mouth opened wide. Damn near swallowed all of my dick. I watched my head disappear into her mouth, then my shaft, all the way to my balls. She came up, drooled on my dick, suctioned him in.

I pulled out. "I need to be inside of you, baby. Bend over the counter."

Her white saliva drizzled over my head, down my thighs.

Ebony grabbed my shit tight. One hand around the top of the shaft, the other close to my nuts. All at the same time she bobbed up and down sucking my dick real hard while her hands rotated in opposite directions the way I loved it.

She was determined to make me bust. I was struggling not to.

Up. Down. Round. Round. She started going faster.

"Stop," I insisted.

The sensation was incredible, but I wanted to bang my balls against her ass. Punish her for being disobedient. I pictured her in the lingerie she'd worn for yesterday's shoot.

Slowing her pace, her hands and mouth were still in the same rotation. I exhaled.

Gradually she increased the pace. A little faster. Faster. Before I knew it I was gripping the back of her head ready to cum down her throat this time.

I curled my fingers tighter wanting to pull her hair, but I knew not to do that shit. This was why no matter if Dev found out about my side I couldn't leave Ebony alone. Hell, Dev wrote the script; she knew how sides got down. Watching Ebony made me come close to firing off on her tonsils. Ebony giving oral looked and felt amazing.

Oh, shit!

My back arched. This time I needed something to hold on to. My head and shoulders twisted to the left, then right. Her head moved left, then right.

"Fuck," I whispered. "I'm about to cum. Aw. Fuck." My toes raised higher and higher, then pointed to the floor.

She was in fifth gear. I saw my cum splatter all over her face. She caught some of the whiteness in her mouth. I watched her swallow.

I was ready to collapse. Cuming for me standing up was much more intense than lying down.

Softly she fingered my limp dick. Planted kisses on the head, then stood. "I gotta get up early, my babe."

Nya started crying.

Damn. I pulled up my pants, stuffed my chopper inside my boxer briefs, snatched up my zipper. Ebony stepped out of her thong, straightened her dress, her hair, then went upstairs.

"Come here, sweetheart," I said, picking up my little girl. "You just had a bad dream. That's all. Look, I was fixing you something to eat."

I opened the box of chicken fingers. Put one on a plate with the yellow honey mustard sauce.

Nya shook her head. "I don't want that." She cried loud. "Where's Mommy? Where's Grandma?"

I checked my cell. It was midnight. No text or missed call from Dev. I picked up Nya, carried her to my car, and took my baby home.

CHAPTER 33
SPENCER

"Have you ever had an HIV test, dude?"

LB's whole face squinted. "Nah. What made you ask me that?"

I printed the tabs for my last remaining customers. "Been thinking about all the females I hit it raw with. You know Charlotte was cheating on me and shit. Sure she didn't make ole dude wrap his shit up."

LB's eyes shifted several times. "I stroked a few females without protection, but I think I'm cool. I only get down with the decent ones like Alexis." He stood tall; stuck out his chest. "If I had it, I'd know because whenever my dick doesn't feel right, I can tell."

He was trippin' just like me. I dropped the real on him. "Alexis was the one who asked me to take the test."

My boy stepped away, mixed a lemon drop, placed it at the hell well, came back to me. "You said you didn't hit that."

"No, you said you never hit it raw."

LB's jaws sunk in tight. He left again. Did setups, closed out tabs, started new ones. The next six cocktails he mixed were shaken extra hard. Martini glass filled to the rim, spilled over.

I did the same at the opposite end, except I wasn't over pouring my drinks. The finest feline, badder than Ebony, sat at the bar. Neither one of us Morse code her.

My boy cornered me. My butt was up against the ice drawer.

"So what you sayin', Spence? You did my girl? Thought you said she was your sister."

I hadn't planned on this convo evolving from a simple question, but that was how shit always jumped off. Especially in my relays. One minute Charlotte and I could be having the best time ever. Then she read a text on my cell or ole boy's picture would pop up in her Insta feed. Next thing I'd be cursing her out or she'd be breaking my expensive glasses, plates, and bowls. She didn't care. I should've downgraded to plasticware.

"Nah, man. She just asked me some shit that had me reflecting. Thought I'd ask you, bruh. You seem the type that would get tested on a regular. I was coming to you so you could let me know what to expect."

Overkill was on the border of my tongue. I had to stop there. LB knew me well enough to detect when I overexplained things, I was straight lying.

Hadn't exactly lied to my boy, though. Would never tell him the truth about doing my sister. What difference was his knowing going to make?

LB walked away. I picked up credit cards and cash, closed out all of the requests. I covered LB's too. Wasn't sure where he'd gone. It was almost midnight. I was ready to get out of here.

Looking at the gorgeous chick at the bar made me think about the day I got with Ebony and Buster. Ebony was a straight freak. Called me over earlier. Her husband wasn't home. Soon as I rang her bell she rang mine. The front door was barely closed before she had my dick in her mouth. That was a wild female.

She begged me to make her squirt across the room again. Spraying didn't work all the time unless the feline was a natural. Now I could get any pussy wet once I found and fingered her G-spot the right way. Most dudes were too lazy to put in the work, but they claimed they wanted to make their girl squirt. I wasn't special. That was like a dude claiming he wanted to drive, but he didn't know how to accelerate. I educated myself on several positions and techniques. We had fun with my trying to get Ebony to water faucet. She came at least five times before I pulled out.

Seeing how situations went ham with my sister when Alexis didn't know who the father of her miscarried baby was, I wasn't aiming to have a married woman carry my child. We used condoms. All of them. I had three gold packets in my pocket when I'd showed up at Ebony's front door.

Maybe I should give Fabulous a ring. Nah, it was too late. I'd check on her tomorrow. Hadn't heard from her. Hope we were still cool at a minimum.

"You fucking liar, man!"

Wham!

A blow to the back of my head sent me flying to the hell well. I knocked over what was the last round of drinks. My face was on the wooden counter. Fast as I could, I turned around.

"What the fuck is wrong with you, man?"

LB picked up an open bottle of red wine. Started dousing me like I was a lil bitch. Throwing the bottle in the trash, he swung at me.

I wasn't trying to do this but the choice was, whup his ass or let him whup mine. I squared my boy dead on his chin. Knocked him flat on his back.

He looked up at me. Staring at his ass, I moonwalked, spun around, hiked up my pants, kicked one leg in the air. Chris Tucker style from *Rush Hour,* then pointed at my boy. Since half the people at the bar had their cell phones directed at us, I figured I'd give them a show to play it off before our manager Derrick showed up.

"Alexis wanted you to take an HIV test because she had one. You did her, Spence. All I asked was for you not to do this one and you lied to me. What the fuck were her results, man?"

I extended my hand to help LB up. Didn't matter what she told him. "I didn't lie to you."

"Don't touch me, bruh," LB said, standing up. He brushed off his pants.

Derrick rushed toward us. "What the hell is going on?!"

LB stared at me. "I'm done with that bitch! I'd better not see her anywhere I swear! I'm done with your conniving ass, too, Spence. And I'm done with this job. I quit!"

I watched my only real friend storm out the restaurant. He was justified. If I couldn't be loyal to LB, how was I ever going to commit to a woman?

Derrick said, "Spencer. Leave. Now."

Wasn't sure if I was fired, but I headed for the front door. Chilling on the bench outside, I texted Alexis, Where are you?

She texted back, Leaving Brio. Why?

I hit her with, Stay there. Order me a shot of Avión tequila. Make that a double. I'll be there in less than 5.

Brio was a block away from where we lived. Less than a mile and half from Lenox Square Mall. Didn't want to have a convo with my sis at her place or mine. Needed two doubles. I'd hit LB up in the morning. Boys don't end friendships over vaginas.

Derrick probably wasn't going to fire either of us, but we might get suspended. Maybe not even that. LB and I both had regular customers. Derrick had told us sometimes they leave if neither LB nor I was working the bar. That was because we over poured every cocktail.

The valet attendant at Brio wasn't at the stand. I self-parked up front, strolled toward the entrance. Wasn't expecting to see her coming out. My jaw dropped. Lips parted.

"Hey. Blake. You look nice. How are you?" I asked, opening my arms for a hug.

Blake said, "She's inside." Then she walked past me.

Mercedes commented, "Great job, Mom," without acknowledging me. What had I done to her?

"Stay on your side of the bed," Sandara told me.

I stood there waiting for Devereaux to throw her handful of salt into my open wound. She twisted her lips, rolled her eyes, then followed her mom.

Valet dude pulled up, the doors flew straight up. Blake got in her red Ferrari and drove off.

Guess there was no need to call her ever. But I had to. Even if it was over, I didn't want Blake to be mad at me. She looked edible. Entering the restaurant, Alexis was sitting at a high, round table in the corner near the flat-screen television.

"What's up, Spencer?" she asked. All-white everything. Purse. Halter short dress. Shoes.

"What's the deal on this test situation?"

"Chick, my bad. I left you hangin'. There was so much going on today. As you can see my fam met up."

Interrupting her, I asked, "The results were?"

She laughed. Wasn't shit funny to me. I needed to hear her say it.

"Non-reactive, man."

I exhaled, downed my double tequila in one swallow. "You want something?"

"I'm chill," she said. "We been sipping the last few hours."

Sitting on the stool next to her, I said, "Give me the rundown."

Guess since she was HIV free, I was too. I did hit Charlotte after I'd seen her out with old dude, which was after I'd smashed my sister. Damn. Just to be sure, I had to let 'em draw blood. Had to get my own stats.

"I'ma get tested, too, Sis."

"That's what's up. James pulled one over on me. He wasn't solely concerned about whether I was disease free. What he really wanted to know was, was I pregnant."

"Well, we know what those results were."

"Right. But here's the deal. I told my family tonight that I lost the baby, but now I'm pregnant by James."

I rattled my head.

"James and I fucked all weekend. I'm not sure that I am, but I might be. I don't want a kid by some random. I mentioned the money to my people too."

"You shouldn't have, Sis. Peeps look at you different when you come up overnight. That's why I keep my financial stats on ice with these females."

"Like you shouldn't have told LB about

my HIV test. Got that fool calling *and* texting me like a maniac."

"What did you tell him?" I was curious as to did she tell him that I'd hit it.

She shook her head. "He's irrelevant. Banking the two point five mil is my focus. If I'm not pregnant, you're my plan B."

"Whoa." I told my sis, "That's not going to work under any circumstance."

"You owe me."

"For what?" I asked.

Alexis picked up her purse, stood, stared me in my eyes. "I'm not asking you to get me pregnant, chick. You have to find James's replacement."

She kissed me on the lips, then left.

CHAPTER 34
BLAKE

"What are you wearing?"

I hated when men asked me that over the phone. Prayed he didn't ask me to Face-Time. My intent was to call Bing and tell him good night. It was late. I was tired. My feet ached. My bathtub was filled with warm water and bubbles.

I missed my Yorkie. He was still at Sandara's with the kids. We'd be okay. I'd decided to let Max stay with Sandara for one week provided her work schedule permitted. Mercedes was her backup. Alexis could only take care of herself. Devereaux was too busy. Once I was comfortable with my corporate schedule, I'd set up Max's space in my new place.

I told Bing, "I'm going to put you on speaker if you don't mind."

"Not at all. How'd dinner with Devereaux go?"

Folding a plush white towel, I placed it on

the side of the tub, cradled my cell into the slit with the speaker outward.

"She's got a lot going on. All of my girls do. I'm staying out of their business."

Seeing Spencer show up to meet Alexis, I was over it. Done with him. He didn't seriously expect me to hug him. Quietly, I eased into my big spa tub. There were lots of fond memories of Spencer and me here.

"Smart choice. Glad I don't have those concerns."

Wanted to say me too. Didn't want Bing to think I wouldn't accept his kids and their problems, but he didn't have any.

"Are you sure you don't want kids?"

He laughed. "I'm a bit selfish with my time. No. I don't think men should father children unless they're willing to become a full-time dad. Child support. Fighting for custody. Children didn't deserve that. Being responsible, using protection, that's the easy part."

Didn't want to soak in the bad decisions I'd made. I changed the subject. I asked, "What are you wearing?" I felt his energy. "Let me guess. A smile."

"That, and aqua blue boxer briefs."

"And?"

"Soon as you tell me what you're wearing, I might not have on anything at all."

No he didn't flip it to me. "I have to admit, I'm not good at phone sex." In my sexiest voice, I spoke real soft. "I'm relaxing in my tub big enough for two with my erect nipples poking through the bubbles."

"Oh, really?" he moaned.

"Yes, I wish you were here with us."

"Us?"

"Yes, my pussy is calling . . . Bing."

"You're a good liar, Blake. My manhood is swollen. Circle the tip of your finger around your areola without touching your nipple."

"Okay." I did. It felt good. I moaned a little.

"That's it. Now real slow, slide your other hand down the side of your body, to your thigh, bring your hand to your inner thigh. Pause for me. I'm imagining my bald eagle's head is surfacing to the top of the suds parting the bubbles between your breasts. Kiss it for me."

"Huh?"

"Blake?"

"Oh, I'm sorry. I dozed off. Told you I wasn't good at this."

"I'm going to let you get some rest. To be continued. Give me a call when you have time."

I really was exhausted. I got out of the

tub. My doorbell rang.

It definitely wasn't Bing. Wrapping a towel around my body, I trailed water to my bedroom. I got my gun, went downstairs.

"I can hear you. Blake, it's Spencer. Please. Let me in."

CHAPTER 35
EBONY

#Amped #LoveMe #HateMe #SSCATL #iamebonywaterhouse

"And . . . action!"

I lived for this moment to be back in the #spotlight. I was nervous when I arrived on set. The brand-new studio spread over four hundred acres. The interior of each home was decorated to fit our personalities. As it should be, I had the #mostfabulous #mansion. West-Léon and I were being filmed first for episode one.

I opened my front door. Smiled. Gave West-Léon a juicy kiss, then let him in. My designer black low-rise fitted pants highlighted my big booty and exposed my belly button. The black long-sleeved blouse had a sexy V to show off my cleavage. Diamond pendant necklace sparkled. Six #realblackdiamondstuds, three in each ear, signified I was that #BitchwithBands. Fire-engine red lipstick complemented my long, wavy blond hair. Devereaux had the hair stylist blend a few clips of cotton-candy pink throughout to give me a signature #sweetcandy look.

I loved it!

"Guess what I have for us," West-Léon said, entering as he waved a piece of paper.

Playfully, I tried to grab it. Quickly he pulled it away, kissed me again. "You are going to love me for this, my babe."

Hearing West-Léon call me "my babe" felt natural. Dressed in a pair of relaxed jeans, a tapered cropped sleeved black T-shirt that hugged his abs, and square-toed leather shoes, he wrapped his arms around my waist, picked me up, then swung me in a circle.

"Who's the man?"

Landing on my seven-inch stilets, I gave West-Léon a loving look. "What is it, my babe?" I asked playfully.

"Can't tell you. Grab your purse. Let's go."

"You know how I hate surprises." I picked up my purse, followed him outside.

Trés called, "Cut!" Then said, "From the top."

We ran that scene three more times before moving on to the next. I had my hair and makeup retouched each time. West-Léon had his refreshed too.

The next scene we were standing in front of my place as a white Rolls Royce entered the driveway.

A chauffeur opened the back door on the passenger side. I stared at West-Léon.

"What are you up to?"

"I can't tell you. Get in."

The driver entered onto Interstate 75 south. When he stopped we were in front of ticketing at Hartsfield International.

I was not happy. I scooted away from West-Léon, pressed my back to the door. "You should've checked with me. I can't go out of town, West-Léon. I have an event to attend tomorrow. Where's your main girl?"

"She's in New York," he said, not knowing that was where my event was.

"New York. Doing what?"

"In the studio. Recording." There was a B-roll that would cut to her, then back to us. "We'll be back in the ATL before she gets back here."

Truth was I had plans to meet my married guy Travis in New York for the weekend. He'd planned a private party for my birthday with all of his A-list celebrity friends in Manhattan. Of course Travis's wife would be there, but he'd be spending the night at the Waldorf with me.

"It's for your birthday. I'll have you back

by Monday."

"What time?"

"Eight."

"a.m."

"P," he said.

The camera crew filmed us entering the airport at ticket check-in. Trés called, "Take!"

The viewers would see a studio replica of the inside of the airport. When we arrived at the gate, I'd notice he'd booked us a flight to Puerto Rico. Easing my cell out of my purse, it would show my booking a one-way ticket from Puerto Rico to New York first flight out in the morning.

Devereaux had outdone herself. Memorizing my lines did not compare to bringing my character to life. From my house to the airport completed our part of the shoot for day one.

"You guys did great. Tomorrow is a travel day," Devereaux said.

I told her, "Thanks!" with a huge smile. Almost gave her a hug and a kiss. That would've been inappropriate under the circumstances.

Tomorrow we'd film West-Léon and my arrival into Puerto Rico. I'd stay overnight, we'd celebrate my birthday until sunrise, then (while he was asleep) I'd jet-set escape for my flight to New York and fashionably arrive just in time for my party with Travis . . . and his wife.

Maybe I could have dinner with my real husband while I was in Manhattan. Tonight I wanted celebratory sex. I'd only invited one person to our home one time while Buster was away. This series had me believing I could get over on any man with anything. I felt adventurous and dangerous at the same time.

I texted Spencer, Meet me at my house in an hour. My husband is out of town.

Chapter 36
Alexis

I texted Spencer, Come over right now. I need you.

The odds weren't in my favor to have a child growing inside of me. Not because I'd faked a miscarriage and the odds of being pregnant this soon were slim. My epiphany was I didn't want children at all. When I saw pictures of LA on James's cell, then Chanel seriously ended our relationship, I had no one to rely on to pay my bills. Concocting the pregnancy was to gain sympathy.

Men don't know as much about women as they think. Spencer spoke intelligently on how to please a woman sexually, how to make her squirt. The particulars on miscarriage, abortion, and pregnancy, he wasn't up on calculating why women would lie about those things. There was no way James could check my cervix or medical records to confirm or deny my involuntary termination.

I texted James, I really hate that I lost our baby.

Alexis please spare me your lies!!

I replied, What if I'm pregnant from this weekend?

And when exactly did you stop taking your contraceptives dear liar?

I didn't bother to tell him I'd stopped when I started lying about being pregnant. I'd had sex since then, but not with a man. If I were with child, I'd be one hundred percent sure James was the father. Exhaling, I didn't respond to his last text. I prayed his child was inside of me.

Hit Spencer with the text, Are you on your way? You want me to come over? I need someone to talk to man.

All day I'd chilled at my spot wondering what was wrong with me. Why did I feel the need to manipulate those closest to me? Money wouldn't make me better. I had to want to treat people good. I'd be glad when my college classes resumed next month. Had too much idle time.

The flowers I'd sent my mom were from my heart. She didn't deserve the way I'd disrespected her for too many years to count. She seemed happy last night at dinner. Even offered for me to call her attorney. This inheritance would give me financial freedom for life. Hopefully I'd be kinder.

A more considerate Alexis Crystal, didn't even feel right thinking it. I enjoyed being a bitch.

Three boxes of pregnancy test sticks were on my coffee table. Didn't want to take it without my brother being here so either way somebody would know I was telling the truth. If I weren't expecting, I'd lean on my brother for support.

Spencer didn't need the money my dad left me. Maybe that's why Conner left it all to my baby-to-be and me. I was going to get pregnant. Soon. Real soon. Tonight maybe. James couldn't resist me.

I called my brother. Got his voice mail.

The suspense was killing me. Picking up one of the boxes, I went to the restroom. Peeled away the seal. Peed on the stick, then waited for a $+$ or $-$ sign to appear. The results gradually showed in the window. The information stated the test was 99% accurate. It was a $+$.

"Yes!" I jumped up and down. Danced. "Wow!"

I took a picture. Started to text it to Spencer. Changed my mind. Sat on the toilet.

"Now what, Alexis?"

Well, I had to have the baby. I didn't have to keep it. And I was sure who the father was. Initially I was excited, but now I wasn't. What was going to happen to my gorgeous figure? The added weight, wide nose, big feet, possible morning sickness for real this time. Why was I tripping? I was going to be on the same level with people with money who could afford trainers and nutritionists.

Sitting on my sofa, I picked up the trust. Scanned the pages. I stopped. My eyes stretched wide. "How in the hell did I miss this?"

I read, "The baby must be born on or before December 31st, of the current year." It was July. The only way for that to happen was to let a doctor cut me open three months early.

All I could do was cry and scream, "I hate you, Conner Rogers!"

Chapter 37
Phoenix

"This shit has got to stop before I lose it, man."

Marvin was my boy. He was out there getting his stroke on. Just like me, but he didn't have my problems.

"I finally got the contract from my lawyer. I lowered my fee from ten grand to five a month. I'm going to take it to Goldie tonight. That way I can be on set soon as I find a sitter."

Marvin busted out laughing. "You're killing me, dude, and Devereaux is going to abominate your ass. Let it go and chill this season."

"Man, I've tried to stop fucking with Goldie but I can't." Marvin didn't understand. He'd never fallen in love with one of his sides.

"Try harder, dude," Marvin insisted. "I'm your friend. I wouldn't tell you this if I thought you couldn't handle it, but you're fucking up. Devereaux is a *good* woman. She's rising to the top and you're drowning in two feet of toxic water. Time for you to uplift the woman who's got your back. When this series hits, Goldie is going to drop you, bruh. Then what? I'm not going to tell you again. Leave Goldie alone!" This time he was obviously pissed with me.

"Man, I want to but, I just can't let go."

"Fine," Marvin said, then asked, "What about Sandara keeping Nya?"

"Man, she's trippin'. Said she got a job and she's going back to school." I laughed at that bullshit, went to Nya's bedroom.

Nya had fallen asleep. It was eight. I could leave her here, go to Ebony's, get the contract signed, and make it back before my baby girl got up.

"I know I said fine, man, but I'm your friend. What you need to do is chill," Marvin said. "Devereaux is all that."

"Man, she ain't going nowhere."

Marvin laughed hysterically. "No. She's not, but your black ass is if she finds out. Where are you going to live? How are you going make it, man?"

"And how's she supposed to find out? Ebony is not going to say a word."

"Nya might say something if she's ever around Devereaux while Ebony is there too.

See, you're not thinking this shit through. You're thinking with your dick, dude. Don't blame Goldie or nobody else when you fuck yourself."

I was too on top of my game for that to happen. "I don't take Nya to Ebony's. I take her to Uncle Marvin's house."

"Aw, hell no, man! Don't put me in the middle of your foolery. Devereaux is my girl and I respect her even though you don't have enough sense to. You're dumber than I thought. I'ma talk to you later, bruh."

Anxious to be on my way, I ended the call first. Devereaux would slaughter me if she came home and found Nya here alone. I picked up my baby girl, put her in the car seat, then drove to Ebony's.

Shit was like *Groundhog Day.* I put Nya in the bed downstairs. Went upstairs. No sign that Ebony had been here.

"What the fuck she gave me this key for?" I said, clenching it in my fist.

Tossing the pages to the contract on her bed, I headed downstairs.

I texted her, Where the hell are you!

Scooping up my baby girl, I took my black ass home. Marvin was right. I needed to let Goldie go.

But I couldn't.

CHAPTER 38
DEVEREAUX

"Hey. How's it going?" I asked.

"Can you meet me at Strip in Atlantic Station?"

Answering Dakota's call ended my chat with Trés. I walked away from the Buddha statue in his house, saying, "I'm on my way."

My heart raced with anticipation of the unknown. *Lord, please let her have good news.* The meeting with my family was inspirational. All of us were moving forward. I was most proud of Sandara. Outside of Mercedes telling our baby sister she wasn't qualified to give Alexis advice on having a kid, I was pleased.

Mercedes might want to stop being judgmental, take a long look in a mirror, and admit she was not perfect. None of us was. Not me. Not Phoenix.

"Great. I'm upstairs outside on the patio sitting at a high table overlooking the courtyard. It's a beautiful day. Bring your sunglasses."

Sunglasses? Oh, no. I told myself, don't read into her saying that. Stay optimistic. "Be there in twenty minutes."

Since the day Phoenix mentioned managing Ebony, Trés had become my confidant. I shared intimate details about my feelings for Phoenix that my fiancé was not aware of.

I wanted a man whom I could be proud of. My fiancé was never that guy. I always believed in him more than he did in himself. Paying our bills wasn't a problem. I had to do that regardless. Phoenix's not making enough to provide for our daughter or himself bothered me.

I told Tres, "I can't stay for drinks tonight. Have to meet with my investigator."

"I can go with you, Dev, for support. Never know what bomb she's going to drop," he said, picking up his keys.

That was true, but what if there was no bomb. If I was wrong, and there was no explosion, either way this was my relationship. Perhaps she had good news. I chose to remain hopeful. Regardless of how others felt, I did not want my daughter growing up without her father. I made the decision to have Nya. If I had to, I'd do exactly like my mother had done with me. I'd put my little girl's happiness ahead of mine.

Trés embraced me. I shouldn't get comfortable being at his house after we left the set. With the best of intentions to remain faithful, the unexpected could happen. I found myself here again knowing the peacefulness of his home was what I needed after a hard yet productive day of work.

Inhaling the sweet vanilla scent of burning candles while we were chanting in front of the jade life-size waterfall statue of Buddha made me want to forgive Phoenix no matter what Dakota told me. Relaxation music played at a soothing audible tone that I could hardly hear. I didn't want to leave but I had to go.

"I'll call you later if I need to talk. You've been a real friend. And for that, I can never repay you."

Trés hugged me. "Your indebtedness is no good with me. I love you, Dev. The time of day or night doesn't matter. I'll be waiting for your call."

Getting in my car, I waved good-bye, then turned down my radio. Trés would say loud music could at times be entertaining for the soul. The faint sound of birds chirping, water falling, and wind blowing, feeds the spirit. He was right. There were times when I'd drift into meditation simply embracing the moment with him.

It wasn't necessary to talk all the time. In fact, learning when to sit still and be quiet was more beneficial than my having the last word.

Taking a ticket, I entered the garage at Atlantic Station. I wondered how Trés's wife felt about him. Was he one of those men who masked their true selves while marking their territory?

The grass was always greener from a distance.

I rode the escalator to the upper level, bypassed Z Gallerie furniture store, entered Strip. The security person inside made the guy in front of me remove his baseball cap. I walked around them, went upstairs. Exiting onto the patio, Dakota waved.

"Glad you could make it." Patting the stool next to her, she said, "Sit beside me."

The waiter brought me a glass of iced water and handed me a menu.

Before he could ask what I wanted to drink, I ordered a cabernet. "I haven't eaten. I need to order something. Please come back soon," I told him. I knew alcohol shouldn't be my first consumption of the day but what if Dakota gave me bad news?

Dakota told me, "I haven't eaten dinner. I waited for you. How was your day?"

I stared at the camera on the edge of the table closer to her. Made me think of the video Mercedes showed me with Benjamin and his mistress.

The waiter returned. I was starving but decided on the sushi. Didn't want to throw up if what she was going to show me made me sick. Dakota ordered a steak medium.

"If you don't mind, I'm more concerned about what you have to share with me than recapping my day."

Dakota held my hand. "I want you to take a few deep breaths. What I must show you will probably shock you, but I understand your request to view it now. I'm not going to delay giving you this information. I'm also not leaving you hanging. I have a plan in place. All you have to do is give me permission to proceed."

Felt like my heart stopped, then accelerated. "Is it that bad?" Was I getting ready to crash into a cement wall?

"Let me show you," she said, picking up the camera.

My cab came on time. Focusing on the footage, there was nothing unusual about her trailing Phoenix's car. I took a sip, keeping my eyes on the video.

I said aloud. "Okay, he didn't go that far." It was about a mile from our home. "He's still in Brookhaven. That's our neighborhood." I frowned. "Whose house is he parking in front of?"

"Keep watching," she said.

The waiter placed our food on the table. I held on to my glass of cab. I swear what I saw . . . "Can't be."

Phoenix got out of his car. Took Nya out of her car seat. Carried our baby to the front door, unlocked the door with . . . a key? No one let him in?

"Aw, hell no!" I said.

The waiter fast approached. "Is everything okay?"

Dakota calmly replied, "We're fine."

No, I was not fine. I was very concerned, more so about my child.

"A few more minutes, then I'll explain the details," she said briefly touching my hand.

Wasn't sure if I could take much more. A black Benz drove up. Immediately I recognized the vehicle with the license plate AYMSSIK. She parked next to me at the studio all the time. Ebony got out carrying a bag marked 'Houston's'.

I insisted. "Stop the video. I've seen enough."

"Okay," she said. "I agree that you don't need to see everything. If you change your mind at any time, I can show you the rest."

Not wanting to think the worst, I explained to her. "Phoenix's mother is out of town for a few weeks. You heard Sandara say she's modeling so she can't babysit Nya. Phoenix is managing Ebony, so maybe they had business to discuss."

Dakota nodded. "Did you see Phoenix, your fiancé, let himself into Ebony's house? That was not the only time."

I became quiet. I wanted to nod but I couldn't move.

"Dev, Ebony lives in Conyers with her husband. And she also owns that house in Brookhaven. She has property in Hawaii, New York, and a few other places."

"Who's her husband?"

Dakota shook her head. "You don't know."

"I knew she was married, but I didn't dig into her personal life. That's not my business."

Quietly, Dakota exhaled, glanced toward the courtyard, then looked at me. "Buster Jackson is her husband. He's the primary angel investor for your series."

I froze. Felt like I was going to die. The glass slipped from my hand, crashed to the floor. My empty hand was still in the air. I couldn't breathe.

"You need to inhale. You're going to be okay. It's my job to make sure of it."

I gasped. Started heaving between words. "I wasn't expecting all of this. His company practically owns my production. If he pulls out, I won't have a second season."

"Don't be so sure. Now that you know, what I recommend is you take this one step at a time. Don't do anything irrational. If you feel like yelling, screaming, crying, or swearing, call me immediately. Buster's name is not on the house in Brookhaven. He may or may not be aware of Ebony having that residence. I'm not sure. He probably doesn't know about Ebony's affair with Phoenix or Spencer Domino." Dakota repeated, "Probably."

OMG! "Well, that doesn't surprise me. Spencer seems to be sticking his dick in lots of holes." Disappointed in my man, I asked her, "So what now?"

"Don't show Phoenix your hand. In fact, be a little nicer to him if you can."

"Really? A part of me wants to kill him or at least make him wish he were dead."

Calmly, Dakota said, "Really. Just a little sugar sprinkled on top. Don't check him. That's where some of my clients undo all I've done. I have a locksmith on standby right now a block from your home. When Phoenix gets home, when he's asleep or in the shower, take his keys. Text me when you have them in hand. My locksmith guy will be out front at your place in seconds. Give him Phoenix's key ring. He'll make a copy of everything on the ring, then give it back to you. The set he makes is for me. I'll let you know what's next. Got it?"

I nodded. Tears poured down my face. "Do I get a copy?"

Firmly, Dakota said, "No."

"He had my baby over there. Seriously, I want to kill him."

"No, you're not. He's not going to harm Nya. Neither will Ebony. Look at me, Devereaux. It's fucked up right now, but I got you. Get his keys. Let's have them copied and move on to the next steps. You have to trust me on this."

CHAPTER 39
SPENCER

Pussy often divided men who were boys but rarely divided men who were boyz.

Had to find a way to mend my connect with LB. Didn't want to ignore my sister's request to do a face-to-face but I'd had enough of her schematics. Pregnant. Not. But she was expecting again. I just couldn't pacify her. The money, house, cars were all hers. If she had to cough up a kidney and a lung to keep it all to herself, she'd make that happen. I didn't care. Her lack of consideration created mine. She'd be all right.

I raised my hand, pressed the doorbell, and my beautiful booty call appeared. Actually, I was hers. Either way the results were going to be the same. We were both at her spot fixing to get in the mix.

"You smell edible, Spencer. Get your sexy ass in here," she said, grabbing my tee.

Ebony had platinum pussy, breasts, butt,

lips, hazel-gray eyes, everything including access to me. I would've been on some chill shit waiting to go to work if it weren't for her hitting me up earlier.

She pulled my T-shirt over my head, unfastened my buckle, unzipped my pants, pulled out my dick, then stuck it in her mouth. Good thing my bartending threads were in my car. I'd change when I got to work.

Her hand slid up and down as she wiggled her fingers sucking me between those thick beautiful lips of hers. Ebony did a quick teabag, then got right back on the mic.

Wow! That's what I'm talkin' 'bout. Blake would never just take the dick at the door.

I stood in the foyer. She was on her knees on a pillow. Premeditated fellatio. Yeah. That was what was up!

"Oh, yas. Suck your dick, bitch."

Ebony turnt up. Started using both hands.

Fuck it. I was not holding back or pulling out. I came in her mouth. She didn't stop until my dick and her mouth were both empty.

Passionately, she kissed my ear, then begged, "Make me squirt again."

I looked toward the nearest room. The living room.

"No, not there. The Jacuzzi. That way my

332

husband can't tell."

Buster needed to be gone more often. Having sex in the bed was never my first choice when there was the bathroom, kitchen, family, and theater room. Closet. Not to mention backyards and front yards. Leaving my clothes near the front door, I trailed Ebony outdoors. There was a huge pool. The Jacuzzi was already bubbling. The water was hot. I loved this shit!

Made me want to move out of my apartment and back into my house. I hadn't stayed there because I had too many memories of my mom. Everything was still the same. The only photo I'd taken from the house and hung in my place was the one taken of us one Easter Sunday.

That's when she was still with my — with Conner. We went to church every Sunday. He never went with us. Maybe he would've been a better man if he had. My mom and I were dressed in all white. Her in a pretty dress. Me in my knee-length shorts and a short-sleeved button-up with white shoes and socks. Her hand covered mine. All I saw was my thumb. Had to switch my mental before I messed up the moment with Ebony.

Doggie-style, I massaged her G-spot. Did the running man with my pointing and middle fingers facing down. Teased her clit at the same time. Did that for about ten minutes while she moaned, grunted, squirmed.

Sexing an uninhibited woman kept my dick hard. I had to please her. Didn't want to end up on her socials with the #BadDick #SpencerDomino. This chick had over a million followers and she wanted to fuck me. Yas!

My dick was on swole so I stuck it in her ass. She screamed so loud I thought I'd hurt her until she started laughing.

"I did it again, Spencer! You're my squirt man," she said.

Our lips never touched. Ever. But I wanted to French that tongue of hers. Maybe she was on one of those "I'm a married woman" "kissing was too personal" trips. Didn't matter. If she kept giving me insane brain, whatever she wanted I'd do. Just couldn't do it all day.

"Hey, can I ask you a question?"

She smiled, then said, "Yes."

"You like being choked?"

The smile on her face grew like the Grinch. "Hell, yes!"

I told her, "Next time, I got you. I'd love to chill, but I have to clock in."

"No worries. There's a shower right

there," she said, pointing to an outdoor wall.

I did what I needed, went to the foyer, dressed, then left.

In transit to the job, I hit up LB.

"What up?" he answered.

"Man, listen. I apologize for everything. Let's not dwell on that shit. Cool?"

"If you say so, Spence."

"Dude."

"I'm listening," he said all dry and shit.

"Two point five million dollars," I told him.

LB was quiet. That meant I had that nigga's attention.

"That's what my sister will get if she has a baby. Tag on four luxury cars and a mansion. I'll fill you in on the details, but she might be worth another round."

LB was silent.

A chick with bank made some niggas jump through hoops like a circus dog. That could never be me. Didn't do it for Blake. Would never play myself for Ebony no matter how rich and fine she was.

CHAPTER 40
ALEXIS

I was done with all dicks.

I prayed my baby wasn't a boy. Last night was the loneliest I remembered. The one person I believed would always be there for me hadn't returned any of my calls. Spencer was jealous. His mom left him everything. Our dad willed all of his possessions to me. I didn't see what the problem was long as we made certain our uncle didn't inherit shit. I was down with that.

I'd witness Spencer ignore my mom's texts and calls when I was with him at T.I.'s Scales 925. Maybe being his sister didn't make me special because he first saw me as a piece of ass the way most men did.

My mom might be right. It made me question the sincerity of Conner's trust. What was the point of all the stipulations? I wondered if the trust was valid. Did our dad give me this to retaliate for Spencer's refusing to bond with him? I kind of saw him, although I promised my brother I wouldn't. I didn't dislike Conner as much as I'd pretended. I'd never understand why he'd put his brother in the trust knowing his brother had molested Spencer? Maybe he didn't have any other living relatives. I wasn't cosigning on the fact that Conner didn't believe Spencer was his son. Or that Spencer had shot him. That would make my only brother a murderer.

Shit! What if Conner had other kids? Oh well, too late to worry about it now. If my dad hadn't claimed them, neither was I.

Maybe having this baby was God's way of slowing me down. Sitting at the foot of my bed, I called my mother's attorney.

A woman answered, "Kendall Minter's office. This is Louise."

"Hi, Louise, is Kendall available?"

"Who's calling?"

"Alexis Crystal. Blake Crystal's daughter."

"Hold, please," she said.

The next voice I heard was cheery. "Well, hello, Alexis. This is a first. I would ask if everything is okay, but you wouldn't be calling me if it were. How can I help you?" he asked.

"Yes, and no," I told him, flipping through the pages of the trust.

He repeated, "How can I help you?"

The smile in his voice cheered me up somewhat. "Can you see if this trust that I have from my father is legitimate?"

"Absolutely. Fax, e-mail, or snail mail me a copy. I'll get back to you shortly."

"Thanks, Kendall."

"My pleasure," he said, ending the call.

He could bill my mother. If this was real and I got a check, I'd pay her back.

I dialed my classmate Tréme. Hadn't spoken with her since right before summer break.

"Hey, you! I was just thinking about you," she answered. "You enjoying your summer time off?"

Wanting to say hi, I cried instead.

"Honey, what's wrong?" Tréme asked.

I whimpered, "Everything."

"Stop crying. Where are you?"

"I'm at home."

"I'm on my way."

"No, I need to get out of here. Can you meet me at Legal Sea Food in an hour?"

Tréme didn't hesitate. "See you there. Whatever it is, know that everything is temporary. You'll be okay."

"Thanks." I ended the call feeling better already.

I didn't wish I was more like Tréme. The world would be no fun if everybody was optimistic and bubbly all the time.

Today, I wasn't feeling a halter and heels. Normally, I wouldn't be caught dead in sweats, a men's small tank with no bra, and my tennis shoes, but that was exactly what I put on. I swooped my hair into a ponytail, fastened my Rolex watch, courtesy of James Wilcox. I grabbed my sunglasses, designer bag, then stuffed a few C-notes in my wallet. Opening the door, there was a piece of paper inside of a plastic bag hanging on the knob. A notice to pay rent or vacate my apartment. Moving out of my loft and into my dad's house was happening soon as I was certain the mansion was mine.

The small amount of joy I had vanished. I was so concerned about my inheritance I hadn't made funeral arrangements for Conner. I'd get to that and take care of my rent tomorrow. Wasn't as though my dad or the manager was going anywhere. One more day won't matter. Holding on to the ten grand did. It was all I had right now.

Tréme had sent a message. Lunch is on me. I got you.

A text came from Spencer. Saw the notice on your door when I got off last night. I know you have the cash from your dad, but I stopped by the office, took care of the rent and late fee for you, sis. No worries. Remember, I got you.

Tréme's offer I understood. Spencer's? What was his motivation? He saw me pocket the ten grand.

Just when I wanted to hate all men, I realized that I loved my brother. I put the notice in my purse, then headed to the restaurant to meet my friend.

Maybe she could help me make sense of my situations.

CHAPTER 41
BLAKE

Slamming my door in Spencer's face felt good.

Whatever he came to offer — an apology, a confession, dick — I no longer wanted. When I was in love with him, his dick drove me insane. Spencer had hurt me one time too many.

Reality check. I'd put myself in a position to let him use me. Had to accept my responsibility. What I wasn't going to do was lose the man in front of me trying to hold on to what would never be healthy.

"It's just you and I, Max," I said, looking down at my Yorkie.

Max wagged his tail. Followed me from the closet to the bed as I packed clothes for the week. "We're going to learn to like Charlotte. North Carolina, that is." His nubby tail moved faster. Taking him with me was selfish, but I wasn't comfortable leaving him with Sandara since she could sporadically get booked for a go-see, fashion show, or photo shoot.

My cell rang with a special tone. It was Bing. I smiled, then sang, "Morning."

"You hungry?"

"Yes," I said softly.

"What time are you heading out?"

Checking the time on my phone, it was ten. "We should get on the road by two. No later than three."

"We?"

"Yes, I've decided to take Max with me."

"I don't think that's a good idea. You can't take him to work. What if he gets depressed being home alone all day? Dogs do suffer from depression, you know."

I knew that but . . . "Sandara can't keep him."

"What about Alexis? She might be able to until she starts school. At least that'll give you time to get settled into your new position, Ms. Executive. You can get him when you come home on the weekends."

What Bing had said made complete sense. I smiled. "That's not a bad idea. I'll call her."

"Do that now. We can drop your baby off. Then you can enjoy brunch with me."

This time my heart smiled. He was in an indirect way claiming me as his woman.

Don't get ahead of him. I told Bing, "I'd love that."

"I'm on my way to get you guys," he said, ending the call.

Was this surreal? Was he for real? Did he have a woman or two here in Atlanta? Married, single, bisexual, straight, gay, lesbian? Lots of people had multiple situations. I wasn't going to dwell on Bing possibly not being totally honest. I liked the way Bing expressed interest in me and that was that.

I shouldn't ask this, "But, God, why am I leaving now that you've sent me the one?"

There I went getting ahead again of letting the man take charge. He made me feel good. About him. About myself.

Picking up Max, I gave him a passionate hug. Maybe the love I have for my dog allowed my heart to open up. Definitely couldn't credit Billy for my willingness to be vulnerable this soon after my breakup with Spencer. I hadn't heard from Billy Blackstone since I got Max, but if I ever saw him, I'd thank him.

I called Alexis.

She answered, "Hi, Mom."

"You sound sad. Is everything okay?"

"I'm just grateful, Mom. Not sure what direction my life is going in, but I'm at lunch with Tréme talking things out with someone who, no offense, won't judge or condemn me."

"None taken. I understand. I called because I need a huge favor."

"From me?" my daughter asked.

"Yes. Can you keep Max until I get settled in Charlotte?"

Alexis laughed.

"I'm serious."

"No, Mom. I'm not laughing at you. Tréme just told me I needed to get a dog or a cat. Something to love and care for. So my answer is yes. He's a cool dude. When do you want me to get him?"

"In an hour," I said, crossing my fingers.

"Drop him off."

"I'll give you money to care for him. He's expensive."

"Mom, I'm good," she said.

I frowned. This was not the daughter I was familiar with. Since she was a kid, Alexis never turned down money from any source even when she had her own.

"Okay, sweetie. I'll see you at eleven. Bye."

"Ma."

"Yes."

"I love you," she said. "Bye."

Before my baby girl hung up, I told her, "I love you, too, sweetheart."

Since I was driving, I'd pack enough

clothes for two weeks. Ten business suits. Ten pair of shoes. Enough panties and bras for twenty-eight days. I'd purchase toiletries when I got there. This promotion was a long time coming. Grateful, I had no buts. If Bing were meant for me, things would work out.

Zipping my suits in garment bags, I put my shoes in a suitcase. My underwear inside a leather tote. My Buckhead residence would become my weekend getaway. Every weekend could be a vacation. I'd fly back Friday night or Saturday morning and leave out Sunday afternoon. The company would reimburse me for all relocation expenses and pay the closing cost on the purchase of a home in the Charlotte area.

"Come on, Max," I said, carrying my wardrobe to the garage. Had to make two trips to get everything in the trunk of my Benz.

The doorbell rang. Max barked, looked at me, wagged his tail, barked again. The entire time he stayed at my side. He looked at me again. Stared at the door as if to say, if you're not going, I'm not going.

Opening the door, I thought it was Bing.

Spencer said, "Blake. Please. Can we talk before you leave? I want to apologize to you."

"Apology accepted." I motioned to close the door.

He held it open, stepped inside. Max started barking at him.

"Hey, dude. It's me, Spencer. Chill."

Max wagged his tail. Licked Spencer's hand. I picked my baby up.

A black town car cruised into my driveway. The driver opened the door. A pair of impeccably shined black shoes appeared first. Navy slacks, a light blue button-up with pinstripes, and the face of a man who cared for me beamed in the sunlight. My heart raced with excitement.

Bing leaned against the rear of the car.

Fearing what Bing would think seeing Spencer in my home, I whispered, "You shouldn't have come here. Please, leave."

I wasn't stupid. Spencer wanted to piss on what was once his and I refused to let him give Bing the impression we were still involved. I made sure there was six feet of space between us.

I told Spencer the truth, "You were never good for me."

He shook his head. "I just wanted to see you one last time." His eyes scanned down to my vagina. He licked his lips seductively. "Do you still have feelings for me?"

Spencer wasn't desirable. My pussy didn't

pucker. Eyes didn't shine. There was no smile on my face. He was good to me in the beginning. I was . . . whatever.

"No, I do not." In my professional proper banking tone, I told him, "Spencer, it is over between us. I hurt you. You lied to me." When I said, "Please do not show up at my house unannounced again," Bing headed in our direction. I said loud enough for Bing to hear, "Spencer, we have nothing to discuss."

Bypassing Spencer, Bing said, "Hi, Blake. You ready? We don't want to be late for our reservation."

Max's tiny tail wagged hard against my arm. His body moved side to side. He almost wiggled out of my arms when he saw Bing.

Bing didn't address Spencer. "Hey, little fella," he said, taking Max. "Blake, we have to go. Now."

That was a fair demand. I gestured for Spencer to exit my home. He did without saying another word as if I'd done him wrong.

Getting in the town car, the driver closed the door after we settled in.

"Blake, I'm not going to interfere with whatever relationship you have or no longer have with that very young man. If he shows up again while I'm at your house, I'm done courting you."

Wow. Even if I didn't invite him? I was not going to argue with Bing over Spencer. Courting? That was a word I had never heard a man say directly to me.

I texted Spencer, If you come to my house again, I'm calling the police.

I meant that. I was not going to allow Spencer to do what he was obviously attempting . . . and that was to ruin my new relationship.

CHAPTER 42
PHOENIX

Aw, yeah. The first body stretch of the morning was the best.

Had to get it in before opening my eyes. I extended my arms above my head, pointed my toes to the wall. A wide mouth yawn, rotation of my head, and I relaxed back into the comfort of the mattress.

Opening my eyes, I was surprised to see her watching me. I expected Dev to be in her office consumed with creating her next brilliant show or perfecting her current episodes.

"Morning, babe," I said to my lovely fiancée.

An awkward silence divided us. She stood there. Speechless. Wish I could read that blank expression on her face.

"You okay?" I asked.

"Afternoon, Phoenix."

I snatched my cell from the nightstand. "One ten. Damn." Hadn't planned on sleeping in that long.

"I'ma go shower, babe."

Slowly she pulled the gold satin sheet uncovering my body. The cool air blowing from the vent made my chopper rise. Fluffing a pillow, Dev scanned me head to toe. Felt she was taking still photo shots of my body with each blink of her eyes.

She wasn't upset, didn't appear happy.

"Wash everything real good for me," she said with a lustful smile.

I frowned. Ebony would've awakened me with my dick in her mouth. Taking initiative was out of character for Dev. I liked it, though.

Rubbing the cover against her breasts, she continued, "I want to try something new. You have to be squeaky clean."

I expected her to be a total bitch after my staying out past midnight and having our daughter with me. Damn! The thought of Dev French kissing my asshole made the head of my dick touch my belly button. Hope she'd planned on tossing my salad for lunch. That shit felt amazing every time Ebony had done it. Getting my ass licked right before fellatio always made me cum fast.

Something was off. Didn't want to question her motivation. "You don't have to work on your writing today?"

"I do. But I can get to it after I'm done pleasing you."

"Where's Nya," I asked, hoping I didn't have to babysit on a Saturday.

"Sandara picked her up this morning."

Yes! That was the greatest news. "Oh, okay. Cool."

Dev stared at my dick. "Go wash your ass, Phoenix. Now."

I sprang to my feet. Saluted her as though she were a five-star general, clicked my heels, then did an about-face. I marched into my bathroom, closed the door, and turned the bathwater to warm.

Maybe she sensed she might lose her man if she kept denying me. As the tub filled with water, I flossed, brushed my teeth, then washed my face. I flexed in the mirror.

Biceps, chest, abs, all that. *If I were a woman, I'd definitely want a piece of this rock.* Glancing over my shoulder, my sunken spine divided my back. I had an ass tighter than a running back's. All of this sexy wrapped in the tone of sweet black licorice. Not many dudes were black as me.

As a kid I'd scrub to lighten my color. Classmates called me the tar monster. Got worse with puberty. Huge pimples were all over my face. The forehead was the worst.

My grandmother used to tell me, what the world hates today people love tomorrow. She'd also preach what goes around comes back to you.

Lathering up the washcloth for the third and final round of cleaning my genitals, I unplugged the tub, then turned on the shower.

While I was wet, I massaged myself with baby oil, dried off, dabbed cologne on my neck, under my arms. Ready for whatever Dev had planned, I opened the bathroom door.

"Get in the bed, babe. Lay on your stomach. Close your eyes," she said in the sultriest voice I'd ever heard from her.

I felt her straddle my thighs. Her pussy eased up to my ass. Hot oil drizzled on my back.

"Make love to every part of me, Dev." I needed to be loved right now.

Her hands glided from my ass to my shoulders. She massaged the nape of my neck, the back of my head. Aw, man. Felt like the cells in my body were regenerating me into a new man. I shivered when her lips trailed kisses down my spine.

I whispered, "Babe, this is wonderful. Thanksgiving Eve."

"Don't speak. Enjoy the moment," she said.

The room was quiet. No music. No birds chirping outside our bedroom window. I'd slept through that. My dick was flaccid. I did not care. This was a special connection that I'd better soak in. No telling when this would happen again.

"Our wedding date, Dev. Let's make it official. Thanksgiving Eve." Weddings in the middle of the week were cheaper. Plus, most people were either off from work or unable to attend due to their own family plans. I didn't want anything over the top.

The slickness of her palms pressed firm moving up to my shoulder blades. Her fingers tapped in small circles.

"So you're not going to answer me?" I asked.

She kissed me again. This time her tongue wiggled down to the split in my butt cheeks to my asshole. Instantly my dick got hard. I felt the tip of her tongue circle my rectum. Wanted to ask, What's gotten into you, babe?

"God, that feels so good." With the exception of my man, the chopper, my body was limp.

Dev's cell rang.

I heard a snapping sound. The kind when

a doctor puts on a fresh rubber glove. I was open to whatever.

She picked up her phone.

"Hey, where are you?" She paused. "A block away. Wow, I thought you guys were —" She paused again, then continued. "No worries. I'll meet you at the door," Dev said.

"Who is it?"

"Sandara. She has to do a go-see. She's dropping off Nya."

Just like that, I was shit out of finding out what she was going to do to me. There was no pleading on my behalf. Baby girl's needs always ranked over mine. A thick blue glove with an open set of lips my dick could fit through was on her left hand. A pink latex glove with the fingers cut out was in her left hand. Man I had to find out what was in store. Maybe Nya could nap for an hour.

Dev took off her glove, tossed it on the bed, put on a robe, then left the bedroom. I was dressed by the time she returned. "You seen my keys? I thought I left them on the dresser. I'ma meet up with the boyz."

"Sorry, we couldn't finish babe. But you need to stay here until Nya gets home. Something unexpected came up and I have to go to the studio. I think I saw your keys somewhere downstairs," she said kissing me on the cheek.

My fiancée almost gave me the most pleasure I'd received from her in months, now she was walking out? Dev showered, dressed. She had on a sexy red wrap dress that exposed her inner thighs each time she stepped toward me in those red high heels.

"The studio?" I asked.

"Yes, the studio," she said, kissing me passionately.

"Dressed like that?"

Dev peeped out the bedroom window. She didn't look back as she said, "Sandara and Nya are here. Don't wait up for me, babe. I might have to pull an all-nighter."

CHAPTER 43
EBONY

#celebrityhairstylist #marcusdarlin #imfab #bitchiwasrichb4ibecamefamous #iamebony-waterhouse

I parked my Benz in the lot by the salon. I had been coming to Marcus Darlin since I was nineteen and on the "if you're going to have a man with money you must look the part" grind. So wherever Marcus Darlin went, Goldie followed.

Stepping into his shop, he told me, "Girl, you know I love you to have cleared my calendar on a Saturday afternoon just for you. I'm so proud of you, Mz. Goldie." Marcus Darlin locked the door. "Honey, we can't have your fans coming up in here. I know you're about to tweet it."

He was right. I sat my designer handbag on the sofa in his lounge area by the window so my #fans could snag a pic. They wouldn't see me, though. I followed Marcus into his private room in the back.

While tweeting, #imthatbitch #richfriends #MarcusDarlin and attaching a before selfie, I told Marcus Darlin, "Goldie is dead, bitch. I'm Ebony Waterhouse." I'd started believing that was true.

Marcus Darlin said, "Ya mama named you Goldie. I'ma call you Goldie. Take off those Hollywood shades and sit in my chair. You're not the only one with a life. I have a date tonight with my new wealthy white sponsor, honey."

We both could relate to having sponsors. Didn't matter that we'd both come up and now had our own money. I winked and smiled at him. "Yas, bitch. We still value the system of," Marcus Darlin chimed in as we said together, "getting paid, throwing shade, being laid, and spending others people's bread."

"That's the American dream," I said, sitting in his chair. "I'm going to have to find a way to get you on my show."

"I stay ready," Marcus Darlin said, running his fingers through my hair.

He was right about that. Marcus Darlin worked his #fashion #body better than most women. His hair was bronze today, faded on all sides, spike twists on top. His gray-hazel contacts were the same as mine. One might think he was from Scotland with his long-sleeved wrap dress that stopped right above his ankles. Those deep pockets of his weren't at the hips for nothing.

"I have an idea. I'm going to insist that you be my exclusive stylist on set. That'll get you in front of Devereaux. I know she'll love you. Hell, she might even give you your own series, bitch."

"You're the star of the show, bitch. Don't start acting like it's your show. You know Devereaux Crystal is my client too. All her sisters and her mama have been coming to me for years just like you. What are we doing today?"

His stomach was flat as mine but was cushiony soft. Said the only thing he liked hard on his body was his dick. The juicy-looking red lips tattooed on his neck was #allthat. I didn't have and didn't want any tats.

"Make me sexier. I need to turn up. But Dev wants me to keep these cotton-candy clip-ins."

As Marcus Darlin said, "Honey I'm tossing these." He dropped them in the trash. "I'll dye you some human hair that color and sew it in. That way you can tease as you please."

"For real. All of the Crystals come to you?"

He nodded real slow. "For years."

"Alexis too?"

"Yes, Goldie. All includes Alexis with her on-again/off-again pregnancies."

Staring at Marcus in the mirror, I said, "Say what? By whom?"

"More like whoms, but you didn't hear this from me. First it was for her fiancé, James. That man is so fine. I wish he would cross over. I might sponsor him and have his baby."

We laughed, then I asked, "Who's the next daddy?" I inquired, trying to stay on track.

"Mr. Cheesecake, Spencer Domino."

My jaw dropped.

"Aw, bitch. I recognize that look. Don't tell me you fucked him too? Yup, you did. I can see it all over your face. Did he make you squirt too? Too late bitch. You took too long to answer."

"How do you know all of this? And how do you know any of it's true?"

"Honey, I only know what people tell me. Let's just say, Spencer is Alexis's brother. He boned her mother first. I heard he has a Leaning Tower of Pisa package. I wish he'd cross over too. I'd have fraternal twins. One for him and the other one for James. Back to business. I'm feeling Devereaux on this blend. It looks hot on you."

Tripping in my head, I nodded. "You know I love my red lip, but with this I have to rock my raspberry pink matte lipstick."

"Back to the gossip. I know you've heard that Alexis is about to inherit a few mil. You'd think that bitch already had it rolling around in that Ferrari one day, the Bentley the next. That bitch came up overnight. The same way you did when the ink dried on your marriage license. How's Big Buster? He still on my team?"

Laughing, I said, "Whatever, bitch."

"Oh, your dick is safe with me. I don't like 'em that damn old no matter how much he has." Marcus Darlin leaned to the side, snapped his finger.

A text from Phoenix registered on my cell. I'm at the house with Nya.

I replied, What house?

Ours.

"Can you believe this? I gave Phoenix a key to my house in Brookhaven."

Marcus Darlin interrupted, "Devereaux's fiancé, the one you've been fucking for the last two years, Phoenix, has a key to your house now. You crazy as hell. I know it's the one in Brookhaven. Hell, can't nobody get up in Fort Knox Conyers with all them damn gates. Why now, Goldie?"

"With the show and him wanting to manage me, I just thought it would make it easier for us to see each other."

Marcus Darlin stopped shampooing my hair. "What the hell is wrong with you women? You get your time to shine and you give away the spotlight to a man who doesn't deserve it. When you see him, demand your key back. If you tell him ahead of time, he might make a duplicate."

I texted Phoenix, I'll be home when I'm done.

Where are you? he questioned.

I replied, I'll be there in two hours, three tops.

Didn't really matter when I got home. It was my house, not his.

I texted Spencer, Meet me at my house in two hours.

Spencer didn't have my Brookhaven address yet. Had to keep my two sides and their locations separate. I wasn't a sex addict. Phoenix was the only steady affair I'd had since marrying Buster. Spencer was a crave I wasn't ready to phase out.

Had to get more of that good dick before dealing with Phoenix and Nya. I was no babysitter. I did not want him bringing her to my house on the regular. This was the last time he could come over with his kid.

"Girl, you'd better appreciate that your

husband's dollars keep the film rolling on *Sophisticated Side Chicks ATL,* honey, or you'd still be an unknown."

My jaw dropped.

"Damn, Goldie. You didn't know that shit either? Bitch, I need to lighten the color of your hair."

CHAPTER 44
SPENCER

Ebony's text was right on time after getting Blake's message about calling the police.

Fuck Blake. Ebony was the only one I wanted my baseball bat hittin' raw.

Lusted for her 'cause this celeb feline was drama free. Raising my hand to knock, it fell on the other side of the threshold as she opened her door.

"Wow, I'm feeling the sexy all up in here. Love the fresh cotton-candy blend."

She gave me one of those *Gone with the Wind* fabulous twirls. I could smell the perfume in her hair. For a moment, the scent reminded me of Charlotte. She used to do the same.

"Let's go outside," she said, leading the way.

The sun was shining bright. It was damn near ninety degrees. The Jacuzzi was nice, but I was ready to skinny dip in the pool this time.

Picking up a remote, she clicked a few buttons, naked people popped up on a projection wall. Girl-on-girl action. That was what was up. Instantly, my dick got hard.

"Let me undress you," she said. Not waiting for a response, Ebony removed all my clothes.

"Where's your legal?" I asked.

"He's at home."

My eyes scanned the room. Was dude hiding this time? Was he upstairs?

"Solid?"

"We have a house in Long Island. He's there most of the time."

I exhaled. "Chill. How you wanna do this today?"

"I want you to watch me play with my pussy while you stroke your dick in the shower. I wanna see the water splash off your sexy body. When I'm ready for you, I'll spread my legs. Come to me and I'm going to lick you dry. While you watch me star in my homemade video, you're going to jack-off all over these pretty titties."

Yas, yas, yas, yas, yas! What did I do to deserve this freak?

The breeze was fresh, slightly humid.

Ebony slowly walked to the outdoor wet bar, poured two glasses of cognac, sat hers

364

on a short roundtable beside a lounge chair that was positioned directly in front of the shower. Handing me a glass, she told me, "Drink this."

She refilled me, placed the glass in a cup holder on the wall next to the shower. "For when you're done. But go slow. It's not often that *I* get to watch."

Sitting on the edge of the lounge chair, she snipped the tip of a cigar, dipped it in the cognac. Firing it up, she wrapped her lips around the end.

I stroked my dick wishing it could trade places with that damn stogie. I despised smoking, but her drag was so damn sexy I had to make her the exception. Admiring myself, I faced Ebony. Did a slow grind for her. Turning sideways, I did soft, long, slippery strokes from the head to the base. I wanted her to see all of this dick that she was about to get. Preferably in her ass.

Holding the cigar in one hand, Ebony fingered herself with the other. Real sexy, she said, "That's hot, Spencer. Just like the inside of my wet pussy." She pulled out her finger, eased it in her mouth. "Wanna taste me?"

I nodded. Stroked my shaft faster.

"Get your ass over here then, man."

Downing my drink, then hers, I placed

the glasses on the tile. Moved the wicker round table behind her lounge chair, then I lowered the back of the seat two notches.

"Lay down and place your legs over the top," I told her as I made the wicker table my seat.

She took a long drag on her cigar before she positioned her body. I slid her hips to the very edge, put her ass in my palms, brought her closer to me. I needed full access to this vulva and vagina. Flicking my tongue for her to see, slowly I moved toward her clit.

Ebony puffed on the cigar. When the tip of my tongue lightly touched her clit, I kept it right there. She tossed the cigar aside and spread her lips wide for me.

"Um, hmm," I said. Inserting my middle finger, I gave her that come-hither motion that she'd come to enjoy. "I could eat your sweet peach forever."

My mind flashed to Blake remembering how I made her squirt the first time we had sex. Dude could never be me. Even if she married his ass she'd be back for this Spencer special.

Adding my pointing finger to the mix, I sucked Ebony's clit real slow. Did that running man on her G-spot, massaged right above her pubic bone, pressed gently against her bladder.

Every woman didn't squirt for me in less than twenty minutes. Some thirty. Others ten. I was a patient man. Sitting on this table, I was chilling soaking up sunshine.

Ebony played with her titties. I felt her G-spot swelling. The bubble protruded more and more. I kept the pace. Running with my fingers. Suctioning that precious pearl.

A lot of women didn't gush because they couldn't relax. That, and they didn't mentally stay with the feeling. Some gave up too soon. Others tuned in, but before they released they'd tense up and blow it.

Closing my eyes, I gave her a slight come to me pull on the inside using both fingers while bearing down right above her pubic area.

Felt like I was in the shower all over again when she ejaculated in my face. Fluid seeped into my ears. I rattled my head as Ebony belted a soprano, "Spencer!"

Couldn't lie. Making her scream like that . . . that shit turned me on.

CHAPTER 45
BLAKE

Brunch turned into a late lunch.

The ride from the restaurant to my place to get my car was nice. I rested my head on Bing's shoulder. "I'm a little nervous about my new position."

Bing's fragrance was heavenly. I could inhale his scent and never tire. He told me it was the same cologne President Obama wore, John Varvatos.

His driver parked beside my Benz.

"I'm proud of you, Blake. When you get to corporate, my best advice is to listen more than you speak." He grazed his fingertips over my hair. "Make a mental note of who's in charge and what person thinks they're running the show." The back of his hand stroked my cheek. "Best way to tell, hon, is when you're in a meeting, the person who silences the room where you can hear a pin drop when they say their first word is highly respected. That's the real PIC.

Person in charge."

"That's solid." Soon as I said those two words, I heard Spencer's voice in my head.

"Solid? Hmm."

I was done with Spencer. Hadn't realized his lingo had crept into my psyche. Definitely couldn't use that vernacular at corporate.

"That's sound advice. Thank you," I said, rubbing Bing's thigh. "I wish we could share the rest of this day." I exhaled. "I suppose I've prolonged the inevitable long enough. Better start my four-hour drive."

"When you fly back in on Friday, I'll be waiting for you." Bing traced my lips with his finger. "May I," he asked.

I closed my eyes. His lips glided across mine. His mouth opened. The sweet taste, the minty scent, from his tongue to mine was divine. I could fall in love with this man over and over again.

Getting out of his car, I got into mine. I was cruising Interstate 85 north on all the good memories Bing had given me. From the Lobster Bar at Chops to feeding me lobster at his house to our phone conversation to now, I had to say I was impressed.

It was nice not to be consumed with my past but present with my future. I thought about my girls. The two I'd worried about most were now my least concern. Devereaux had been quiet since the family meeting with Dakota. Overall, I was pleased with how they were concerned for one another.

I talked a text to Alexis, Send me a picture of Max. Truth was, I missed my Yorkie and my man. Living in Charlotte, I'd be closer to a few of my siblings.

Brandon had promised to come visit me in a few weeks. He was temporarily promoted to my old position. Hoped they'd make him the new branch president. If not, he could use the experience and go elsewhere.

Powering on my sound system, I listened to Joe, Kemistry, The Whispers, Angela Winbush, Chrisette Michelle, and Will Downing. Three and a half hours later I was happy to be at my destination thirty minutes early right at the start of sunset.

I'd hoped Bing would've called to check on me. The bellman retrieved my luggage, handed me my keys.

When I opened the door, I couldn't believe what I saw.

CHAPTER 46
ALEXIS

"Sweetheart, remember when things were great between us?"

I sat on my sofa. James lay on his back; his head was on my lap. Admiring how handsome he was, I traced his hairline knowing I'd never be happy with just him. Wondered if I'd ever feel complete with one person.

Familiarity brought us to this moment. "The weekend getaways are what I miss most."

"Yeah, me too," he said. "We can still do that, sweetheart. If you hadn't miscarried, the baby would've been due six months from now. That would've given us an esti-mated due date between Christmas and New Year's. Having a child would've been the best gift ever."

I wanted to say, Nigga, stop lying.

We looked at one another. I should tell him I'm pregnant. This was not the time.

He wanted to give our engagement one more chance and so did I. If I received all of my inheritance, I knew I could trust James not to want me for my money. Some of these Atlanta men were on some real scam bullshit.

"I was hoping it was a boy," I said.

The room was quiet. No television. No music. Just the two of us chilling on a Sunday morning.

"You know I want a little girl."

"You sure about that? We'd have to name her Princess Queen Diva Crystal Wilcox."

He laughed.

The best part of this pregnancy was my certainty on the paternity. James would make a great father. We would be an attractive family. If I could have all of the money without having this baby, that would be my preference. A three-month early delivery usually came with complications for the mother and the child. Bed rest. Low birth weight, possible respiratory problems for the baby.

Was I that selfish that I'd have my labor induced or request a cesarean just to cash in?

My cell chimed indicating a text had come in. I picked up my cell from the arm of the couch.

It was Chanel. You want to do breakfast at Copeland's. My treat.

I replied, Yes. I'd like that. Be there at eleven.

The Cumberland area was twenty minutes away. It was ten thirty. "Babe, I'm hungry. Let's go to Copeland's for brunch."

James sat up. "Cool, I'm starved myself. Haven't been there in a while."

We went upstairs, dressed. I packed my gun in my purse.

James shook his head. "Some things never change. When we do get pregnant, are you going to be fully loaded everywhere you take our baby?"

"Double loaded," I told him.

"That's scary, but I believe you. I'll drive."

We went to visitor's parking on the rooftop to get his car. James opened my door. His gentleman qualities were second nature to him. The sun was bright, sky clear. It was already eighty degrees. We drove past the St. Regis Residences. When I collected my millions, I was selling Conner's mansion and buying a two-bedroom condo at SRR.

They had valet parking, a spa, pool, and maid service. I lived for being in a place with amenities that would spoil me without me having to get in my car. The corner units had covered patios with a fireplace. Chops and The Lobster Bar were next door. Whole Foods was across the street.

Driving north on Interstate 75 was nice. Light traffic on the freeway.

"James, why do you love me so much. I know I'm not always deserving."

"Yes, you are, Alexis. There's just something about you that keeps me coming back to you. You're the one for me."

"What about LA?" I asked.

"Let's not discuss her."

"Yes, let's. I didn't know you were attracted to white women."

He exhaled. Gave me look out of the corners of his eyes, then focused on the freeway. "It's not about color. It wasn't supposed to happen."

"It? What's it?" I questioned.

"Getting with her, Alexis. I didn't see it coming."

That was a lie. Even if he didn't see it coming, he knew what he was doing when he was cuming.

"You love her?"

This exhale was softer. He didn't respond. I asked him again, "Do you love her?"

He nodded. I became quiet.

Getting angry at James for letting another woman into his heart was not right when I knew I cared deeply for Chanel. Love? Not sure if that was what I felt all the time, but there were moments when I thought I had those feelings. My emotions were so guarded I didn't know if I ever truly loved anyone, including myself.

"You mad at me for telling the truth?" he asked.

Softly, I said, "Naw. Actually, I kinda understand how one person can be in love with two people at the same time."

He parked next to Chanel's car. James opened my door. At the same time Chanel opened hers.

"Hey, Alexis. Hi, James."

He turned around. To my surprise, they gave each other a hug.

James asked me, "Are we brunching together?"

Chanel answered, "I'd like that."

This could be the beginning of a three-way relationship. The question I'd have to ask myself would be, If I had James and Chanel, would I be happy and satisfied?

A threesome was definitely in our not-so-distant future.

CHAPTER 47
DEVEREAUX

Unexpectedly, my cell rang. It was Dakota Justice. I hadn't heard from her since the locksmith copied Phoenix's keys.

Unenthused, I asked, "Hey, what's the latest?" not really wanting to know. I was starting to regret hiring her. Should've worked through my problems with Phoenix like normal people. On our own.

"I need you to meet me at the Dunkin' Donuts on Peachtree right now," she said.

I checked my phone, it was ten o'clock at night. I had to get up early. "What's going on?"

"Now, Devereaux," she insisted.

"Okay, I'll be there in ten minutes."

Dunkin's was right up the street in Brookhaven. I put on a pair of pink sweats and a T-shirt, grabbed my purse and keys, then left. The white silk bonnet was still on my head.

I was torn. A part of me wanted to make

love to my man. The flashback of the video footage of Phoenix at Ebony's made me not want him inside of me ever again. Setting him up was easy.

Not wanting to deal with Phoenix, I spent the day at Trés's. We meditated, prayed. Shared creative ideas for future series. Discussed doing an Indiegogo campaign to raise money to finance the next production ourselves. Being with Trés made me feel like I had a business partner and a friend. He didn't try to seduce me, but intellectually he'd stimulated more than my mind.

Parking next to Dakota's car, she leaned over and opened her passenger door. "Get in."

I did.

"Close the door, Devereaux."

I did that too.

"We're going to Ebony's house here in Brookhaven. Phoenix is there with Nya."

Didn't make sense to ask how she knew. I questioned, "How do you know he's still there?"

"I have more than my eyes watching him, darling. I have security posted outside the home. Now, what we're getting ready to do is go there, enter the residence, and confront them."

"That's breaking and entering," I said. "I

won't do that. What if they start shooting?"

"Think about it, Devereaux. With Nya there, they're not going to fire a gun or call the cops? Especially when we announce our names."

She was right. I was looking for a way out. I told Dakota, "Okay. I trust you. But let me get Nya's car seat out of my car."

Dakota pointed behind me. "Already got one. Let's go."

My stomach felt like my intestines were tying knot after knot. Each loop pulled tighter and tighter.

"We have to be extremely quiet," she said. Dakota turned off her headlights. We drove another block before getting out of the car.

I followed her to the door. She slid the key into the lock. This was worse than an episode of *Cheaters,* but I could definitely benefit from the experience when penning a future series. Everything happening in my life was an opportunity to create dramatainment.

Soon as the door cracked, we heard, "Yasss! Yasss!"

Sadly, that was the voice of my fiancé screaming like a bitch. I opened my mouth to call out his name. Dakota covered it. Tiptoeing, she motioned for me to follow her toward the staircase.

My gut told me to check the rooms downstairs. I headed in the opposite direction from Dakota. She followed me. I scanned the living room, a family room, two bathrooms.

Placing my hand on the knob of a closed door, quietly I turned it. The yelling upstairs was now the voice of Ebony's shouting, "Call me a bitch!"

Slowly, I opened the door. A night-light was on. My heart dropped to the floor when I saw my baby sleeping.

Dakota looked at me. I picked up Nya. Phoenix and Ebony could scream all night and fuck each other's brains out. Tears streamed down my face. My heart was numb. Tiptoeing, I didn't stop until my baby was strapped into the back car seat. I got in on the passenger side. Dakota started her engine.

My baby opened her eyes. Sleepily, Nya said, "Mommy, I love you," then dozed off.

"I'ma kill him. It's over." I told Dakota, "If I had gone up those stairs, only Jesus could've saved them." Rocking, I started crying. "After all I've done for Phoenix. Four years." I kept rocking. Crying. Ebony didn't have personal allegiance to me. My fiancé did.

"I have another idea," Dakota said, driving south on Peachtree.

Dakota made a call. Instructed someone to meet us at Dunkin'. A man dressed in black slacks, a nice button-up, and shoes approached Dakota's car.

She told me, "Give me your car keys."

I handed her my purse. Instructed her which pocket my key was in. She handed it to the guy. "Leave your car here. Take hers and follow us. I'll bring you back."

"What are we going to do?" I asked, looking over my shoulder at my precious little girl. "We can't drive around with Nya all night."

"We are going to take Nya to Mercedes's. And you, my dear, are going to act as though you have no idea where your little princess is at. Basically, honey, we're going to let Phoenix sweat this one out."

Suddenly, the knots in my stomach untangled. "Yeah, I like that plan. In fact, I love it."

We parked in Mercedes's driveway. I called her. When she answered, I said, "Open up the door."

Mercedes appeared with a satin scarf on her head and wore a blue silk robe. "What in the world? Is everything okay?"

Dakota said, "We need you."

"Come in," Mercedes said.

Benjamin entered the living room from the kitchen the same time we stepped into the foyer. He was fully dressed. Slacks, shoes, shirt. His phone was in his hand.

I said, "I hope we're not interrupting you guys."

Mercedes answered, "Benjamin stopped by to see the kids. He's leaving."

Benjamin looked at me. "I see Mercedes has pulled you into her foolery with this private investigator shit. You women are never satisfied. When you have a good man, you neglect him. When he finds another woman that appreciates him, you blame your man. The problem with both you and Mercedes, you're hating the wrong people. Try giving us some of that attention you devote to the kids and your businesses." He looked at Mercedes. "I'll be back to pick up my kids in the morning and take them to school like I've always done."

Mercedes said, "Bye, Benjamin."

I chimed in, "Bye, Benjamin."

My sister shut the door, took Nya from me. "I'm going to put this baby in the bed with Brandy. I'll be right back. You know where everything is."

"I'll get us something to drink," I said, heading straight to Mercedes's vintage wine collection.

I filled three glasses, then joined Dakota in the living room.

Mercedes walked in, sipped her wine, and then sat beside me. "Benjamin can try to turn this situation on me, but I did not make him fall in love with another woman. I did not make him stick his dick in another woman. I did not make him buy her a car, a house, or a ring. He chose to do all of that. Do my children need their father? Absolutely. Do I need my husband? Unequivocally, yes. Will I ever trust him with my heart again? Hell. No. Will I take him back? The jury is still out on that one. Enough about Benjamin. Tell me, what happened and what's the plan?"

CHAPTER 48
BLAKE

Sitting on the sofa, I held the card in my hand.

Will you be my lady?
— Bing Sterling

One dozen of the longest stemmed yellow roses I'd ever seen were in a gold vase on the dining table when I arrived yesterday. I must've smelled them a thousand times. I sat on the sofa holding one in my hand.

I'd called Bing to thank him. He was on a business call. Promised to get in touch with me soon as he was done. That was over twenty-seven hours ago.

Spencer had done some memorable things for me. The day we'd met he'd given me two hundred dollars saying, "Buy something for us." I'd bought a sexy nightie and stilettoes that I'd never worn. I'd left everything at his place. Now that I was reflecting, whatever happened to those items?

Spencer had also surprised me with a night's stay in a suite at the Mandarin. That was the time I looked him in his eyes and lied. When he'd asked, "Have you had sex with any other man since we'd met," I told him no. Most women in my position would've done the same.

Maybe his holding the ring in front of me convinced me to lie. Or that I was afraid to lose him convinced me to tell Spencer what I knew he wanted to hear. Regardless of my reasons, I lied like a man . . . with a straight face. I made a vow to myself never to deceive Bing.

I said aloud, "Hey, baby." *No, that didn't sound right.*

"Hello, handsome. You want to explore paradise with me tonight?" I said, then sniffed the rose.

That sounded better. I'd taken a bath. I was ready to initiate phone sex with Bing, but I wanted him to call me.

The tone from my phone made me smile. It was the new love of my life. I answered, "Thank you for the gorgeous flowers."

"You are truly welcome. My apology for not getting back to you sooner. One thing after another came up. How was the drive? You settled in?"

Hearing him acknowledge he'd promised to call me back made me feel better. Why didn't more men do that? To a woman, the little things were important in a relationship.

"It was peaceful. Listened to music. Didn't talk to anyone on the phone. Thought about you. Us. How did you have flowers delivered before I got here?"

"I have my way of doing things. When are you coming back to Atlanta?"

"Saturday," I said, hoping he'd be the first person I'd connect with.

"Can you fly in on Friday?"

Soon as he'd said Friday, I remembered that I'd forgotten to call his assistant to schedule my flight to Paris. Softly, I told him, "I can do that."

"Great. Text me your departure availability. I'll arrange your flight on my jet and I'll have a driver pick you up at your place in Charlotte so you can relax."

I felt myself frowning and smiling at the same time. "Okay. Thank you," I said, hoping he'd mention Paris. I really wanted to go there with him.

"Get some rest, baby. You probably have a long day ahead of you. I'll call you tomorrow night."

"Okay. Good night."

What had I done to attract this man?

CHAPTER 49
ALEXIS

"James, you're a really nice man."

Chanel sat on one end of my sofa, James on the other. I was in the middle. After meeting up earlier, I invited them to my place. They shared two bottles of champagne and were on bottle number three.

It was two in the morning. "I can't believe we're getting ready to watch the last episode of *Love & Hip Hop,*" I said, pressing the button on my remote to "play next."

"For real," James commented. "Y'all got me hooked. Alexis, you know I do not tune in to these types of insane asylums."

Starting with the first hour of this season, we laughed and commented on all the ratchetness. Erica and Cyn reminded me of Chanel and my relationship. I couldn't say any of the men compared to James. Had to give James due respect for not being like Rich or Peter. I always believed that not many situations were meant to last forever.

People lied too much.

Brunch at Copeland's earlier was delicious. The catfish nuggets were the best. I don't usually eat fried but I had two helpings along with the red beans and rice, jambalaya, cheese grits, bacon, sausage, eggs, ham, and bread pudding. I did not need another thing in my mouth unless it was a pussy or a dick.

Touching Chanel's thigh, I slowly moved my fingers up and down. She didn't move my hand. I squeezed James's thigh, working my way up to his balls. They became quiet.

If I requested their permission for a threesome, they probably wouldn't, but I could tell they were okay with my initiating one. Wasn't sure if it were all the liquor they'd consumed, or if the idea was on their mind too.

I teased Chanel's nipple while massaging James's dick. They stared at the television. No one protested.

"Baby, stand up," I said, looking at James.

He did without hesitation. I unfastened his belt. Unzipped his pants. Pushed him onto the sofa. I went to the bathroom, lathered up a towel, soaked another with water only.

When I returned to the living room, Chanel was stroking James's dick. I cleaned him up, took the towels to the bathroom. When I returned this time, Chanel was on her knees, between James's legs, sucking his dick.

I knelt beside her. She pointed his engorged head at me. I eased it in and out of my mouth. Gave it back to her. From the expression on his face to the placement of his arms, James was like a mime.

Chanel placed his hand on her breast. I put his other hand on mine. She stroked his shaft. I sucked his head. I stroked his dick, she licked his head with that wicked tongue of hers.

"You want to fuck my girl?" I asked him.

His eyes widened.

"C, get doggie style on the sofa for James," I told her.

She did. I didn't have to tell James to get behind Chanel or penetrate her. He was already inside. I went to the bathroom, got two fresh towels, cleansed his ass. This time I tossed the towels on the hardwood floor.

Kneeling behind James, I kissed and licked his asshole each time he penetrated Chanel.

"Aw, man. This shit is the best. I don't want to cum yet," he said, slowing his pace.

I massaged his nuts while licking his asshole. Gradually he picked up momentum. I maintained my pace. Right when he yelled, "I'm about to cum," I slowly inserted my pointing finger all the way in his ass.

If it wouldn't have altered the rhythm, I would've strapped on and did my man while he was fucking my gurl. I could do that next time.

James screamed for at least thirty seconds straight before collapsing on top of Chanel. I picked up the towels, went to the bathroom. Got a plastic pan from under the vanity. Got a pregnancy test. Went into the living room.

Chanel stared at me. I open the packet, pissed on the stick, handed it to James, picked up the pan with urine in it, then went back to the bathroom. Flushing the pee down the toilet, I undressed, then got in the shower.

I heard footsteps. Chanel entered the bathroom, got in the shower with me. Washing my back, she said, "What's going on? James already knows you are not expecting."

This woman was so polite. "It's a long story. I had a miscarriage and now I'm pregnant again."

Chanel stopped bathing me. "This is really real?" she asked.

"Yes, you saw the results."

"Are you sure James is the father?"

I nodded. "Positive."

"James?"

I nodded. "Yes, James."

Chanel said, "I want to have his baby too. We can be one big happy family."

I gave her a hug. That shit would never work.

CHAPTER 50
EBONY

#cantsleep #thirsty #getyourmind-outofthegutter #iamebonywater house

I was starting to feel like I was married to Phoenix. Wouldn't want to trade places with Devereaux. It was three o'clock in the morning and her man was in my bed snoring as though he had ten jobs when he didn't have one.

We'd passed out shortly after having sex. Phoenix was still my guy, but I had to admit Spencer was better at sexing me. I bet a getaway with Spencer would be fun. Phoenix was scared to travel outside a thirty-mile radius from Devereaux.

I texted Spencer, Wanna go to Miami or Nassau next weekend? Your treat.

Spencer was supposed to be my boy toy. He didn't know that while my husband was jacking off, Buster was turned on by him, not me. Had to keep that part a secret.

He texted back, I got you. Confirm when

and where and we're there.

I wanted out of my situation with Phoenix. Since his mother went out of town, our going to restaurants had turned into my picking up takeout for him and his daughter. Phoenix was ungrateful. Complained about what Nya didn't like to eat. We needed a break.

Tapping his shoulder, I said, "My babe, wake up."

"Huh," he said, rolling onto his other side. I shoved his back. "Phoenix, wake up."

Facing me, he opened his eyes. "What, Goldie? Give me a few minutes to recover."

"I'm going downstairs to get something to drink. You want anything?"

"Yes, put your pussy on a platter and serve me," he said, then chuckled. "Bring me a glass of crushed ice, my babe."

That meant he wanted me to suck his dick with my mouth filled with ice. I didn't mind but not now. I had to get some rest. He needed to leave. Maybe his plan was to wait until Devereaux left for work so he didn't have to deal with her right away.

Earlier I turnt up to please Phoenix. He was upset that Devereaux had initiated sex, then walked out on him before he came. Phoenix closed his eyes.

Trotting downstairs, I was glad Buster

didn't want children. Passing through the kitchen, I went to check on Nya. The bedroom door was open, the covers were ruffled, but I didn't see the little girl. Turning on the light, I checked the closet, under the bed. I turned on every light downstairs, looked in every room.

Called out, "Nya, sweetheart. Where are you?"

Maybe I misunderstood Phoenix when I came in last night.

I filled his glass with ice only, mine with ice and water, then headed back upstairs. He was flat on his back and snoring.

"Wake up," I said, shaking him.

He took my glass of water. Started drinking it. "Thanks."

I placed his cup of ice on the nightstand. "I thought you told me Nya was here."

"She is. She's downstairs in the bedroom."

Slowly I moved my head side to side. He stared at me for two seconds, dropped his glass in my bed, then rushed down the steps. I followed him.

Frantically he stripped the sheets away from the bed, got on his knees. "Lord, this can't be happening to me," he prayed, searching under the bed.

I pushed back the curtains, tried to lift the window. "No one came through here.

It's locked."

Phoenix ripped clothes from hangers in my closet as he yelled, "Nya! Where are you?! Ny-ya!" He sounded like the Geico gecko in the flat tire commercial.

In my back-in-the-day, loud, high school cheerleading voice, I called her name too. "Maybe she got confused and left out of the wrong door. I'll check out front, you search the garage."

Where would an almost three-year-old hide?

We went from downstairs to upstairs and back down for an hour. Phoenix cried out, "What the fuck! Where is my baby girl?"

Calmly, I tried to reassure him. "We'll find her. Let me get my phone. I'm calling the police."

Phoenix grabbed my hand. "Dev is going to kill me."

"Better for Dev to kill you than for Nya to end up dead. This missing little girl is not about you. Does Nya know her address or your or Devereaux's cell number?"

"Yes, my mother taught her."

"Okay, that's good."

"Ebony! Shut the fuck up! If you had brought your ass home on time, I'd be at home right now! With Nya!"

I stared at him. "You ingrate! Get the fuck out of my house, but give me my key first."

395

"Babe, I'm sorry. I apologize." Phoenix pleaded, "Please give me a moment to clear my head. I'll figure this out." He sat on the sofa staring at the wall.

Conveniently, he ignored my demand for my house key. I didn't want to add to his frustrations at this moment but this relationship was over.

I told him, "Get up. We can't sit here and do nothing. We have to find her. Let's get dressed and drive through the neighborhood."

CHAPTER 51
PHOENIX

This was the worst day of my life and it was all my mom's fault. Driving around my own neighborhood until four in the morning, there were no signs of Nya. Dev hadn't contacted me. She was probably home asleep. How was I going to tell her I couldn't find our daughter?

"Let's go back to your place. If someone finds Nya before I tell Dev Nya is missing, I might have to come stay with you." I yelled, "Fuck!"

Ebony yelled back, "Damn, Phoenix!" She slammed on her brakes. "Don't do that shit. You scared the hell out of me."

Whoop. Whoop. Blue lights twirled behind us. Ebony parked in front of a home a few blocks away from hers.

"Great," I said as an officer approached the driver's side.

Ebony lowered her window and mine. "Just be cool. We didn't do anything wrong," she said to me what I should've told her.

The officer flashed his light in the car. "License, registration, and insurance, ma'am."

"Yes, sir," Ebony said, gathering all three from her glove compartment.

"Where are you guys headed?" the officer questioned.

His light was blinding me. I remained quiet. Didn't want to explain how my child came up missing while I was at my side's home fucking the shit out of her. Publicity would be bad for Ebony, too, if we were caught together at this hour.

"May I ask why you stopped us, Officer?" Ebony questioned, handing him her information.

"There has been several reports of someone repeatedly cruising the area." He asked again, "Where are you guys headed?"

Say something, I thought, staring at Ebony. She was quiet.

In a firm tone, the officer said, "Sir. Ma'am. Step out of the car."

I memorized his badge number. Eyed his name. D. Remick. White guy. Blond hair. Clean shaved.

"Have you been drinking?" he asked me.

What the fuck difference did that make! I was not the one driving. "No," was all I said.

Another patrol car double-parked in the middle of the street next to us. A female officer got out, approached us. She looked at Ebony, then smiled, and then told officer D. Remick, "It's okay. This is Ebony Waterhouse. Gurl, are we going to see this on television? Am I being filmed?" Jokingly, she glanced around. "Is this a *Sophisticated Side Chick ATL* undercover wink-wink moment? He one of your sides? Okay, I am kidding. But seriously, can I get your autograph? I'm loving your pilot previews." Then she asked the other officer, "Did they do anything illegal?"

I should've been glad this female cop was in a jovial mood, but my jaws were tight. It wasn't Ebony's show. It was Dev's. Ebony signed a piece of paper to work for my fiancée.

Remick got in his car. The female officer thanked Ebony, then drove off. I was on mute until Ebony pulled into her driveway.

"I'll call you later," I told her. Getting in my car, I drove to the gas station on Peachtree Street. Sat in my car.

An idea came to mind. I called Dev.

The second she sleepily said, "Hello," frantically, I started lying.

"Dev, I don't want you to panic. I need

you to meet me at the Chevron by our house."

"Phoenix, I have to get up in a few hours. Are you okay?"

What the fuck? I was out until after four in the morning, I was hysterical, and all she cared about was her having to get up early?

"I'm fine. It's Nya, babe."

Dev screamed, "Nya! What about Nya?"

Now I had her attention. "I need you to come now. Chevron station by our house."

Ending the call with Dev, I went into the convenience store. Browsed. Purchased a soda, candy, chips, and handed the attendant my credit card for a fill-up on pump number three.

I took my time, snacked on the corn chips while waiting for the pump to stop. Went back inside the convenience store. Browsed. Closed out my transaction.

I went outside, started crying. Running into the store, I said, "Man, my daughter is missing from her car seat. I was only in here for a few minutes. Did you see anything?"

"I cannot come from behind here. I will call the cops for you."

I ran to my car, dialed 911.

"911 operator, is this an emergency?"

My voice trembled. I cried and sniffled at the same time, "Oh, my, God! Help me,

Jesus! My two-year-old daughter has been kidnapped!"

CHAPTER 52
DEVEREAUX

It felt good to rest in my bed for an hour. I'd left Nya with Mercedes.

When the call came in from Phoenix, Dakota told me to keep on my nightgown, robe, bonnet, and wear my slippers to make my response appear urgent.

Turning onto Peachtree, several police cars were pulling into the gas station. Dakota was a short distance in front of me. She drove into the station's lot, backed into a space in front of the store. I whipped my car into the station, slammed on the brakes, stopped inches behind Phoenix's car, left my engine running, and hurried to him.

Phoenix's eyes were blood red. Tears poured down his cheeks. I screamed, "Where's my baby!"

An officer approached us.

Searching Phoenix's car, frantically I cried, "Where's my baby?" Pounding his chest, I yelled, "Where is Nya!"

The officer told me, "Miss, calm down. We're going to help you. Who called 911?"

"I did," Phoenix said, wiping his snotty nose.

This is the first time I wanted to punch him in the face.

As the policeman said, "Sir, tell me what happened," another cop walked up to us.

Shifting my eyes, I saw Dakota get out of her car. She started speaking with an officer who had just pulled up.

Phoenix sniffled as he explained, "Our daughter was asleep in her car seat. I came here to get gas."

The officer interrupted, "Do you have your receipt?"

Phoenix handed him a piece of paper. The officer looked at it, then at Phoenix.

"Did you fill up, sir?"

"I did, Officer."

"Six dollars filled you up?"

This guy was good. There was a blank expression on Phoenix's face.

I asked, "Baby, the officer questioned if six dollars filled you up?"

Phoenix started sweating as he answered, "Yes."

"So what happened next?" the officer asked.

Phoenix seemed relieved that he could

continue with his lie. "I went inside, picked up a few snacks and a drink, then gave my credit card to the cashier. I came out here, pumped my gas. Went back inside, picked up some chips, paid for everything, then I came outside. Something told me to check on my daughter. That's when I noticed she was missing."

He cried. I cried, then punched him in his chest as hard as I could several times.

"It's all your fault! This is all your fault! You shouldn't have had her out here this late!"

Phoenix held me. I yelled, "Don't touch me! Go find our daughter."

I wasn't faking. My tears and hostility were for the truth I knew. Phoenix was the ultimate liar.

"Ma'am, calm down. I'm going to check with the clerk to see if I can watch the surveillance camera footage," the officer said, then left.

Phoenix stopped breathing. A third patrol car drove into the station. When the officer got out, Phoenix turned his back. "I can't believe anyone would do this to us," he said.

Rolling my eyes at him, I walked over to Dakota.

The officer told me, "Ma'am, we've got the details. I'm going to go inside the store and tell the sergeant. We'll play this out with you." He called out, "Mr. Watson. Can you come here please?"

Phoenix didn't turn around.

This time the officer spoke with authority. "Mr. Watson."

My fiancé faced us. Slowly he moved in our direction.

The last officer who had gotten out of his car spoke low. "Now it makes sense. I stopped him an hour ago. He was a few blocks away from here in a car with Ebony Waterhouse. That's why he didn't say what he was doing. I'm gonna have fun with him."

Dakota mumbled, "Give his ass a hard time, Officer Remick."

Phoenix finally made it to where I was. I stood so close to him, I could feel each time he exhaled. Vehemently, I told him, "Don't come home until you find my child."

I got in my car and drove off.

CHAPTER 53
ALEXIS

I eagerly entered Kendall Minter's office, needed to hear the details of my trust.

He greeted me, "Hi, Alexis. Have a seat. How's your mother?"

Small talk was not what I was here for, man. What was up with my money? I smoothed the hem of my strawberry halter minidress, crossed my pink high heels at my ankles.

"She's good. Got a nice promotion to corporate in Charlotte," I said, being polite.

"I'll have to call and congratulate her. I know you're anxious to hear the details. Here's the big picture. If you are pregnant —"

I interrupted him to confirm, "I am."

Kendall smiled, then continued, "Congratulations. That's great. You inherit everything. The house, cars, yacht —"

"Yacht?" Really? Well, I knew where my birthday bash was going to be come July

28! My theme was going to be swimsuit and stilettoes. Goldie probably wouldn't come, but I had to invite her and Marcus Darlin.

Kendall emphasized, "*If* your baby is born on or before December 31, it's all yours."

Now I was confused. If I wasn't getting it all now, I had to ask, "What happens to the house, cars, yacht, and money between now and then?"

Praying he didn't say something outrageous, I crossed my fingers and my legs. I had $7,500 of the cash left at my apartment.

"You get five hundred thousand immediately. It'll take about two weeks for you to get the check. I've already requested the other attorney, who happens to be my colleague and he was your father's lawyer, start the process. He's a trustworthy, by-the-book guy. Once you have the baby, the remainder is all yours, my dear."

"What happens if the baby is born say, New Year's Day?"

I was certain Bishop was hawking and praying he'd inherit the rest. If I hadn't lied about being pregnant, I probably would've walked out of here with all my daddy's riches.

"The bishop doesn't inherit anything directly, but everything will go to his church if the baby is born one second after midnight on New Year's Eve. I'll arrange for a cashier's check to be delivered to you or you can pick it up at my office. I'll call you when I have it in hand."

He stood, extended his hand. Took me a minute to get up on my feet. I shook his hand.

"Oh, one more thing, Alexis. *If* for any reason, heaven forbid, your baby is stillborn or you have an involuntary abortion, that's a miscarriage, then you split everything equal shares with your brother, Spencer Domino."

Wow. I recalled how Spencer had offered to pay to find my father. That was before we discovered we were related. Would Spencer have inherited it all if my mother hadn't asked Kendall to locate Conner?

"Thanks, Kendall."

"One last thing I recommend is that you hire a financial consultant immediately. Louise can give you the names of a few good ones. If you'd like, ask her on your way out. People who are not accustomed to having a lot can lose it quickly. Everything your father has left you is free and clear."

Wow! Well, at least I'd get a half mil now. So much for my twenty-seventh smash on the yacht. Waiting for Louise to provide the contacts, I text Sandara, I'ma need the

Porsche back. I'll explain later.

Leaving Kendall's, I went to the mortuary and confirmed Conner's arrangements. I hoped everyone would make it to the services. The total cost was $11,000. I only had $7,500. I could have his ashes spread over the ocean for five grand and call it a day. To let Conner go out like that seemed heartless, but where was I going to get the rest? James was my only reliable or I'd have to put Conner's homegoing off for two weeks.

I was going to be rich. I was going to inherit everything. I was having this baby by December 31, if I had to . . .

CHAPTER 54
SPENCER

Knock. Knock. Knock.

Straight up I was taking a chance showing up without hitting her up prior. Underneath all her sexy, she was emotionally unpredictable. Moody. More crazy than sane at times.

"Spencer, what are you doing here? Unannounced," Alexis said, leaving the door open.

"Checking on you, my sis." I invited myself in. Stood at the foot of the stairs.

Solid as usual. She had on a strawberry halter minidress and pink high heels. Her hair was flowing. Makeup flawless. I felt bad for leaving her hanging, but if I explained my conflict, she'd definitely understand. I copped a seat on the opposite end of the sofa from her.

"I'm good. Nya and I are getting ready to meet James for lunch."

"Pause. Nya? You? Babysitting? James? So y'all back together?"

"I'm kinda like the safe house for my niece right now." Flatly, she said, "As for James, something like that since I'm having his baby."

"Are you serious, Sis? How is that feasible?" I mean, she'd just miscarried. Could she get knocked up again that fast?

Sarcastically, she replied, "How else do you make a baby?"

I wasn't trying to piss my sister off, but she was known to tell a lie or two. Or three. "That was nano split quick, though. Didn't know you could get pregnant that fast after losing a baby."

LB and I weren't back to chill yet. Now that Alexis didn't need him to donate seeds, I'd slack up on trying to get my friendship back on track with dude. Let it happen on his terms. The reverse of things usually worked faster, especially when it came to dealing with females. If I were sweating Shorty, Ebony would've probably lost interest in me.

"I didn't know either," she said. "Nya, come let me do your hair, sweetie. We have to go."

I asked, "So what did Kendall say? You'll collect the two mil now or after you have it?"

"I knew you came for a reason other than

just to see me, chick," she said, then called Nya again. "If I have it on or before December thirty-first, everything is mine."

"That's impossible. You're having a March or April baby."

Man, what was Conner's point for real? If Sis was a liar, she didn't deserve his cash flow? If he hadn't disowned me, he might still be live. He was dead and I still hated that man for how he treated me and my mom.

"Kendall didn't mention any stipulations about my having the baby prematurely. I might schedule a C-section," she said, looking at me.

I stared back. Doing that two weeks early wasn't as risky. Three months. The kid might not survive. I couldn't cosign on that.

"Then I'd have to split it with you," she said.

A frown was definitely on my face. I may have been a lot of things but a murderer or an accomplice to, wasn't one of them. "He should've just left you the money without all the cobwebs."

I was hoping she'd offer me something, and I didn't have to inherit shit by default although I didn't need it. I was his child, too. Long as his bitch ass brother didn't get shit. I was cool.

Nya came hopping down the stairs. She was a pretty little girl. My first time seeing her. Max was right behind her.

"No more ponytails," Nya said, skipping to Alexis.

Max repeatedly jumped on me, started gently scratching my leg. Happy to see dude, I picked him up.

I tucked Max under my arm, texted Ebony, Wanna go rock climbing, then have lunch?

"Nya, where's your manners? Say hello. This is your uncle Spencer."

Softly, Nya said, "Hello."

"Hi, Nya. I like your dress. How old are you?"

Nya sat between Alexis's legs. She held up three fingers, then said, "Two."

"She'll be three next week," Alexis said, unclipping Nya's bows.

"Her hair looks fine to me."

"Now that Sandara is modeling, I'm the only one who has time. And since Nya is hanging with me, she has to look like a little Alexis. I hope I have a boy. Girls are a lot of work."

"And you have Max, because?"

"Let's not go there," my sister said staring at me.

I clicked a few photos of Alexis combing

Nya's hair.

Alexis put up her hand. "Do not make those public. Wait until I'm done; then you can take social pics."

A text came in from Ebony, On set until eight.

I had to be at work by then.

She sent another, Rain check? Saturday? What are you doing?

I texted, Chilling with Alexis and Nya and Max. Saturday is cool. You still wanna go to Miami?

Alexis said, "Spencer, you're welcome to join us for lunch."

"Who's going to watch Max?" Nya's hair was cute. "Can I take a pic now?" I asked.

Nya flashed a smile, Alexis rolled her eyes? "Max can watch himself until we get back.

Raising my brows, I told her, "Since James is going to be in the fam, I might as well get to know this dude."

Alexis posed with Nya. Clicking a few pics, I texted Ebony the best shot.

Ebony replied, Is Alexis your sister? Did you fuck her and her mom?

I hit her back real quick, What difference does that make? I fucked you in front of your husband.

My husband is gay.

On that text, I dropped my cell. Picked it

414

up. Hit her with a, You B-i-t-c-h!!!!

That muthafucka was jacking off watching me?

That bitch went from friend to foe in zero point one second.

Chapter 55
Ebony

#canttrustbitches #watchyourback #my-mainside #onset #SSCATL #iamebonywaterhouse

Wow! Now I got it, but I still didn't get it. The three years I've had my place no one had violated my space. Brookhaven was a safe neighborhood. There wasn't an alarm when I bought it. Didn't feel the need to put one on. Rekeying all my locks was happening tonight. I wouldn't dare tell Buster any of what had happened and we talked about almost everything. It was time for me to chill at the Conyers location for a minute.

Devereaux had the balls to come in my house? Had she sent the cops to stop Phoenix and I? I didn't give a #fuckaboutthathoe if her baby was in one of my beds and her baby daddy was in the other. You knock, bitch. You call, ho. You do not cross my threshold without my #permission. That was invasion. She could get time for that

#ish if I could prove it. What I didn't need was consent to #whupherass! Off set.

Soon as Spencer texted me that pic of Nya and Alexis, I took a break, stepped outside, called Phoenix.

He answered, "Thanks for checking on me."

"Nigga, get the fuck outta my house now. You best not be there when I get off or I'm going to pop off on your ass!"

There was a Colombian street side of me no one had or wanted to witness. Underneath all the pretty, I was straight ratchet.

"What the hell are you pissed off about? I'm the one with a missing child," he said defensively.

I texted him the pic Spencer sent me.

"Where did you get this and what does this have to do with the fact that Nya is missing?"

"You can't be that damn stupid. Then again, yes, you are. Devereaux is playing you. But you know what, she's not going to play me. Go get Nya from Alexis's house."

A voice from behind me said, "How do you know where my baby is?"

I turned around. Devereaux was three feet from me. How long had that #kidnapper #ho been listening to my conversation. I ended the call with Phoenix.

"Woman-to-woman, tell me why I shouldn't fire you!" she yelled.

I stared in her mocha face. All of her makeup was the same earthy bland-ass tone, including the gloss on her lips. Her dark brown hair was parted more to the left. She was only two years older than I, looked more like five to ten. Obviously she could write her ass off. She needed to learn how to break off some of that ass to her man.

This was not her set. Banking on what Marcus Darlin told me about Buster financing this production, I fired back.

"Bitch, kiss my ass!" I hadn't forgotten how she got all up on me at the read. I turned around, put my bodacious round behind in front of her, patted it, then turned around. "We both know who has the real power to pull the plug on every damn thing and I'm that #bossbitch. See you inside. Don't be late."

I brushed by her. Just what I thought. She didn't do a damn thing.

When I heard Devereaux say, "How about I call immigration and tell them you're not a United States citizen," I felt like she'd stabbed me in my back. Not giving her the satisfaction, I stared her down. That might have been true #threeyearsago #beforeimarried buster.

Calmly, she said, "I know what you're thinking." She came closer. "Hashtag. Newsflash. Buster married his husband in San Francisco." She smiled, politely continued without raising her voice. "Before he said I do to you."

Sitting in my high chair, I felt like I wasn't in control of anything, not even myself. I had to check the validity of my marriage certificate? I needed to relax and ride a dick after all of this was over.

I texted Spencer, Can you meet me tonight? Assuming he could, I sent him a message to meet me at the Brookhaven location.

Locking my cell, I placed it on the vanity in my dressing room. It was almost time for my next scene with West-Léon. My makeup artist touched up my face. Marcus Darlin made sure all strands were in place.

"You look mad as hell," Marcus Darlin said. "Somebody must be about to get it. Let me take a pic of your mug for social."

Normally, I wouldn't mind. I held my palm up facing him. He lowered his phone.

Getting out of the chair, "Thanks," was all I said. If he knew so damn much, why hadn't he told me Buster made his man legal?

The day dragged along. The second the set was over, I went directly to my home.

Phoenix's car was in my driveway. My heart pounded with anger. I unlocked my door; he was sitting on the sofa watching television.

I snatched the remote, turned that #bitch off. "Why the fuck did you give her a key to my house!"

Phoenix hung his head, then shook it side to side. "You really think I'd do that, Goldie?"

"I gave you access to me and . . . Get the hell out!"

"Don't do me like this. I can't just go home and pretend nothing happened."

"You said, Devereaux said don't come home without Nya. Well, now you know where Nya is, go get her, and take your ass home, too, bitch."

"I am at home."

"No, home with Devereaux is where you belong, Phoenix."

He stood in front of me. Stared down at me. "Is it true that you have a husband?"

I backed up. "What the fuck difference does it make who I have?"

His head moved sideways. "So you just a ho."

"I'll be that ho, but I ain't broke, bitch! I'm only going to ask you one more time. Fuck that." I opened my front door wide as it would go, held the knob, tapped my stiletto to the floor.

He didn't move.

I called the police, put my cell on speaker.

"Brookhaven police, is this an emergency?"

I asked Phoenix, "Is it?"

Bypassing me, he said, "You ain't shit bitch."

Ending the call, I told Phoenix, "Yeah, I'd rather be a bitch than to not have shit, #broke #bitch," then slammed my door.

I hit up Spencer. My call went straight to voice mail. Redialed. Phone rang once, then I heard, "Smooth, you know what to do."

My pussy had to get stroked real good tonight. I took a shower, changed into a sexy sleeveless maxi dress with a split up to my left hip, then headed to the Cheesecake Factory to get my dick.

CHAPTER 56
BLAKE

Good intentions could ruin a productive moment.

Siting in my fourth meeting of the day, I took copious notes on my iPad. Bing had made noteworthy suggestions. Most of what he recommended was what I'd always done. There was no need to express that to him. One thing I knew for sure in negotiations and conversations, men did not like women who challenged them on every little thing.

My supervisor, Jordan McCall, an African-American Harvard cum laude graduate who was fifteen years my junior, asked, "Blake, what's your thoughts on your counterparts' responses to how Obamacare will impact the banking industry?"

Looking up from my iPad, I scanned the faces of the people seated around the rectangular glass-top table. They all stared at me.

My response was, "In a global economy

where we service two-thirds of the world, let's compare universal health coverage in other countries. Governments that provide health care to their citizens at little to no cost have proven those countries do not suffer, but prosper from having a healthier working population. In America, our banking industry will benefit financially from the working class poor when there are insufficient funds in their account to cover their insurance premiums and we charge them a fee. This could be a domino effect for other insufficient transactions. On a different note, more people will be healthier to work; therefore, they can afford to pay for their prescription meds, the pharmaceutical industry is some of our biggest clients. Overall, we will indirectly benefit from Obamacare."

Jordan asked the group, "How do we become more customer-friendly to those who maintain an average daily balance below twenty-five dollars and NSF fees cost them more than they can afford?"

The guy seated across from me spoke. He always had an answer to everything. Usually jumped in with his opinion first. I wasn't sure if he had to prove himself smarter than the rest of us. I resumed taking notes that might come in handy if his opinions ever backfired.

I was happy when the workday ended. Didn't have a chance to respond to Bing's question last night. Hadn't spoken with him all day. Standing in my office, I looked out over the city of Charlotte. My hometown. Never imagined I'd be back here. The skyline was amazing.

A text chimed on my cell, I smiled.

Are you hungry? If you have a moment, I'd love to take you to dinner.

I replied, Famished!

Great, what time should I pick you up?

My condo wasn't far from work, but I needed to shower and change clothes. I texted back, In two hours.

A better idea would be to order in, relax, have great conversation and wine. If I were lucky, we'd make love for the first time. I sent him a message offering to eat at my place. He accepted, then offered to pick up dinner.

Jordan tapped on my open door. "May I come in?"

"Of course," I said, placing my phone on my desk.

"How do you feel about your first day?" she asked.

"Good. Learning a lot about how we operate at the corporate level."

"I fought for you to be here, Blake. I saw how many times they turned you down. Now that you're here, you need to be more assertive. At times aggressive. Or you'll end up back in Atlanta before the end of the week. Have a nice evening. See you tomorrow."

Now I needed his companionship more than I wanted it. I prayed Bing would do more than hold me tonight. I got in my Benz, stopped at the liquor store for a few bottles of red wine. Less than twenty minutes later I was at my place.

The hot water splattering all over my body felt amazing. I shampooed, then lightly conditioned my hair. Decided to let it air-dry.

Choosing a comfortable casual white linen pullover shirt that covered my butt, I slipped into a pair of white lace boy shorts. Brushed my teeth. Applied light makeup and one coat of chocolate lipstick. Dabbed perfume behind each ear.

I poured a glass of wine, turned on jazz, and relaxed on my sofa. I closed my eyes. The music was soft and low, the way Bing liked it.

A ring from my cell awakened me. Sleepily, I answered, "Hey, are you here?"

"At your door, my dear," he said.

Oh, wow. I hurried to the bathroom, rinsed with mouthwash. Didn't want our first kiss of the evening to taste like alcohol. Opening the door, he smiled.

"For you," he said, handing me a bouquet of lilies.

A waiter in a white jacket stood before a table covered with a white cloth. Plates with silver lids, glasses, a bottle of champagne in an ice bucket and a breadbasket were arranged.

"Come in," I said, smiling back at him. I felt like a young woman in love for the first time. "Smells delicious."

"I hope you don't mind my taking the liberty of ordering for us," Bing said.

The guy in black pants and a white jacket rolled the cart inside.

"You can leave everything as is. I'll take it from here," Bing told him.

So excited to see him, I hadn't realized I was half-dressed in front of a stranger. Sitting the flower vase in the center of the sofa table, I told Bing, "These are beautiful." The roses on the dining table were blooming nicely. "Thanks."

I took the initiative, removed Bing's blazer, hung it in the coat closet.

"You deserve to be treated special every day. That's why I hopped a flight hoping to see you tonight."

The least I could do was to offer. "I'll set up everything. Make yourself comfortable."

He opened his arms. "Let's not rush this moment. Reheating food is what ovens are made for."

I wasn't going to question why was I so lucky. Laying my face against the softness of his button-up, I inhaled the masculine scent of his John Varvatos.

"Yes, I'd be honored to be your woman," I said, answering the question on his card.

"Well, now that we're official, I have a special dessert for you." He tapped his wristwatch. "Can't make any assumptions. Always have to be prepared. You have your passport with you?"

"Of course I do," I said, uncovering our food.

Dinner was fabulous. We ate, sipped champagne, and laughed. Bing opened a fresh bottle of wine; then we retreated to my bedroom.

"You mind showering together?" he asked.

I was ready to see this man naked for the first time. I undressed him. Touching his watch, he pulled away.

"It's waterproof."

"Okay."

The black boxer briefs were fitted to his

427

protruding manhood. *That can't be all him.* My body jerked. His dick was huge. I worried if it would fit.

"You can change your mind about my being your man," he said, smiling. "Mr. Tasty is addick-tive. And yes, he's massive."

My eyes stretched wide. I dried him off. He did the same for me.

"We'll take this slow. Don't want to scare you off. Lay down and scoot to the foot of the bed. Now bend your knees and spread your thighs."

The sensation inside my pussy made me moan. Bing kissed my clit, then gave it one long, slow lick. I almost came. He pressed a button on his watch. A red light came on. He wiggled his middle and ring fingers, curved the pointing and pinky fingers outside of my vagina.

"You ready for my spider man special?" he said.

I nodded.

He shook his head.

I felt his fingers penetrate me. He played with my G-Spot. Faster. And faster. And so fast I screamed, "Ah!" and squirted on him in five minutes.

He suctioned my clit. I couldn't stop climaxing.

I grabbed his wrist. "What is this thing?"

"It's a squirt watch. Are you ready for round two?" he said.

Nodding, I only did so to see if he could outnumber Spencer and make me squirt back-to-back.

Five minutes later, I drenched his hairy chest and the foot of the bed.

Bing stared into my eyes, lifted his brows. Holding my breasts, I took a deep breath and nodded. "Yes."

CHAPTER 57
PHOENIX

There was no way I could go home.

I sat in my car outside of Ebony's house hoping she'd open the door.

The sunlight was fading. I'd never called or texted Alexis before. Had her number locked in 'cause Dev gave me her family contacts when I moved in with her. If I wanted to go home, getting Nya from Alexis was my greatest chance of getting in with Dev.

Fifteen minutes turned to thirty, forty-five, an hour. The lights went out in Ebony's living, then bedroom. A faint blanket of light covered the sky. She didn't go to bed that early. She knew I was out here. After two years of being with Ebony, she still turned on me.

I scrolled through the A's, selected Alexis's name, pressed the telephone symbol. It rang three times. My heart pounded. I wanted to end the call. That would be the same as ending my relationship with Dev. Waiting, I took a breath.

"Hey, Phoenix. What's up?"

She knew damn well what was up. "You have Nya?"

"Come say hi to your daddy, Princess Diva."

The voice I heard of my little girl saying, "Hi, Daddy. I love you," brought tears to my eyes.

"You want Daddy to come get you?"

"No."

No was not the response I was expecting. "Let me talk to your aunt."

"Okay," she said.

"Hey, Phoenix. Nya is in good hands. We're about to camp out on my living room floor and watch *Home.* I need to microwave our popcorn. Bye," Alexis said cheerfully.

"Alexis, wait. You know why I'm calling."

"And you know why I'm hanging up," she said, ending the call.

It was time for me to confront my deceptive ways. The infidelity, the betrayal, hit me hard. I'd hate Dev right now if shit were reversed. Maybe Dev plotted to kidnap Nya to make our breakup my fault. She was cozying up to Trés. He probably put this shit in my fiancée's head to push me out. First it was my not having a contract. Kidnapping my baby girl, Trés had taken it too far.

I hit Dev.

My call rang once, then went to voice mail. I hit her right back. Same shit happened. I did it again. She declined my incoming call.

"Fuck." Where was I supposed to sleep?

I went to Atlantic Station's hotel, requested a room for one night.

The receptionist said, "Sorry, sir. Do you have another card you can use?"

Aw, hell no! I handed her a different Visa, an American Express, and the Black Card Dev had given.

The receptionist shook her head. "I've seen this before. You must've fucked up really bad." Then she smiled.

"Bitch, this shit ain't funny."

She whispered, "By the end of the night, you'll see who's the bitch. See that man at the bar. Third seat from the left. He'll put you up if you let him put the head in."

I turned around. A cop was there. Didn't need any more problems. What the hell. What did I have to lose? I went home. I was shocked when my key unlocked the door.

Stepping into the foyer, something hit my nose. Felt like a spider. I swatted the white string dangling in front my face. It pivoted back toward me. I snatched it.

432

Aw, man. This was the worst. At the end of the thread was Dev's engagement ring.

CHAPTER 58
ALEXIS

I laid my check for $500,000 on the coffee table in front of the two people I loved most.

James picked it up.

Chanel asked, "What's that?"

"A new start." My voice was choppy. I looked at James. "I never loved you the way you loved me." I paused.

He wiped my tears. "It's okay, sweetheart. You never knew your father and just when he opened up his heart, you had to lay him to rest."

Conner's services were decent. James had given me five grand. I felt relieved knowing I'd done the right thing for Conner's home-going. Shaking my head, I told James, "Don't patronize me. The inconsiderate things I've done are not okay. I used you for your money. That and you're the freakiest man I've met."

James smiled.

I lied to Chanel, "And you're the wildest

woman I've made love to."

The making love part was true at times. By the time I have my baby, I wasn't sure my lie wouldn't become the truth. Chanel was conservative, but she'd turnt up for James. Her willingness to please me is what kept me interested.

James handed the check to Chanel. She stared at me, then asked, "Where did you get so much money?"

"Inheritance from my father."

"The old dude was loaded?" James asked.

I told him, "Very. That's not all I'm getting."

Chanel asked, "Are you okay?"

She was the consummate giver. Chanel would give her last to me if I were her woman.

"I really didn't know my dad. He was more of a stranger than kin. I'm cool. He actually left me two point five million."

"Damn! He was loaded like that?" James said.

"I can only collect the remaining two mil, house, cars, and yacht if his grandbaby is born by December thirty-first."

"But that's impossible," Chanel said.

"Not exactly," I said.

"I don't care if he left you a billion dollars," James lamented, "you're not going to do anything to jeopardize the health of my child."

Could've lied and told him it wasn't his. Trying to do right was hard.

Chanel countered, "Our child. We all agreed that the three of us will parent Alexis's baby."

James said, "My child is due on April first. My birthday. Alexis, we're good. Maybe not two million good, but I've always provided for you."

During our discussion, Spencer texted, Did you hear the great news?! There is a God! The bishop dropped dead while giving a sermon against men being gay! Irony and justice under one roof! This is cause for celebration, Sis!

I read his message repeatedly.

James and Chanel became quiet.

Another text came from Kendall, Alexis I guess you've heard the bishop is deceased. There were no other provisions or restrictions. You can collect the remaining two million dollars and take possession of everything else now if you're willing to split 50/50 with Spencer. I can start the process. You guys can have your seven-figure check in four weeks tops.

I was speechless. I texted back, What if I don't want to share?

A third text came in from Devereaux, Would you like to join my cast of *Sophisticated Side Chicks ATL*? Yes, I'm serious.

You'll have to wait and have the baby by 12/31, Kendall responded.

Placing my cell on the table, James picked it up, read, then handed it to Chanel.

The three of us sat in silence.

Becoming a millionaire and being offered a career in television, within seconds my future had become uncertain.

Now that money didn't matter, did I want James and Chanel? James or Chanel. Did I want to have this baby? Or get an abortion? Did I want to share my empire with my brother?

Truth was, I wasn't sure if I'd change. I was certain I needed to give my brother a hug.

Excusing myself, I took my phone from James. "There's someone else who needs me right now. I'll call you guys later."

I got in my Lexus and headed to find my brother to give him a hug and, if he needed, a shoulder to cry on.

CHAPTER 59
BLAKE

Focusing on my business and personal relationships, in that order, was refreshing.

Jordan stuck her head into my office. "Busy?"

Yeah, right. She asked as though I was supposed to tell my boss yes. "Come in."

She sat on the arm of the chair directly in front of me. "What are your goals for corporate?"

I knew the answer. In my profession I always had a goal. Once I achieved it, I'd set another. Wasn't sure why she'd asked? Some folk wanted to test you. Find out if your objective was to take their position.

"First, I'd like to learn all I can about my job. I've noticed there isn't an expert consultant in-house who can advise department heads on cross-functional crisis management. I'd like to master the major functions of other positions."

I stopped there. Jordan was frowning like

she'd never considered that.

"Blake, your input over the two weeks you've been here has been refreshing. I'll take your aspirations under consideration. Why don't you wrap up early. Enjoy your weekend. I'll see you Monday morning."

"Thanks," I said, shutting down my computer.

I secured my laptop in my desk drawer. I could check my work e-mail account on my cell. There was nothing I needed from my corporate condo. I didn't wait for Bing's driver. I got in my Benz and headed straight to the airport, to take the next available flight to Atlanta to see my man.

I texted Bing, Got off early. On my way to Hartsfield.

His response, Great! We can depart sooner. Send me your flight information. Make sure you have your passport.

I was getting used to this. Dating this man, my passport stayed packed. I called the airline, forwarded Bing my details.

I was expecting Bing to meet me at baggage claim on the Delta side. He was at the gate with a lavender rose in hand.

"How was your flight?"

"Not nearly as amazing as you."

"You ready for an adventure?" he asked.

Smiling, I thought about the four orgasms

he'd given me. Jokingly, I told him, "The question this time is, are you ready."

"This weekend will really be a surprise," he said. "Hurry, we have to make it through customs so we don't miss our flight."

Excited, I told my guy, "I love you."

I really did. The way he packed my bags, planned our trip; for once in a relationship I always expected good things. Racing to take the train to get to our terminal, we dashed to our gate, I wished I'd worn flats. Next time I'd pack a pair in my purse.

He held my hand the entire time. That was another thing I appreciated about Bing. He never left me behind. Arriving at our gate the sign read, LONDON.

"You're taking me to see the crown jewels?"

"The crown jewels do not compare. I'm taking you to a groundbreaking ceremony and gala. My assistant got you evening attire that even the queen would approve of. Since you are officially my woman, nothing is too good for you. And you may as well see what I truly do for a living."

When first-class passengers were called, we boarded. I group texted my daughters and Brandon, Going to London for the weekend with Bing.

Brandon replied, My gaydar was way off

on that one, honey. Buy me something and bring me back a tall handsome man with an English accent.

Mercedes wanted to know all my flight information.

Devereaux asked, Where are you now?

Alexis responded, I'm happy for you!

Sandara sent lots of those Emoji characters followed by, I'll be there tomorrow. Have a runway show.

I was proud of each of them. They'd continued to be one another's support. Whatever was happening in their relationships, I did not want the details for at least another two weeks, especially Alexis's.

Having basic information was great. I stared out the window.

Mercedes and Benjamin were working on their marriage. Devereaux had put Phoenix out, or should I say hadn't let him back in. I didn't know why and that was okay. Alexis had collected lots of money and material possessions. That should make her ecstatic. Lunch in London with Sandara would be lovely.

I was proud of them all. My girls were grown. I'd done my best.

"The world can wait."

I froze. Slowly, I turned to face him.

Bing repeated, "The world can wait."

Then he kissed me.

Those were the exact words Spencer had spoken to me on our first date. I was in a better space with Bing.

I held the side of my man's cheek, pressed my lips to his. "You're right. This is our time, not my time."

Champagne, caviar, jumbo shrimp, and scallops. I appreciated this meal more than I looked forward to the foie gras Bing raved about in Paris.

Descending from the clouds into Heathrow, I knew I shouldn't have asked, "Why me?"

"Blake, I have more money than I can spend in my lifetime. I want to create memories with you because you make me happy. I love you too."

I felt as though my heart stopped beating. Could I allow myself to be vulnerable?

If ever there was a moment for me to fall in love, this was it. I had no reason to give myself to any other man.

I looked into Bing's eyes and told him the truth.

"I am in love with you."

CHAPTER 60
DEVEREAUX

Nothing Phoenix could say would change my mind. Why was it so damn hard to have it all?

I opted to meet him in a public place. I didn't think he'd get physical. We'd never dealt with that type of abuse.

The host seated me at the table I'd requested off in the corner.

"Please have the waiter bring a bottle of cabernet."

"Certainly, ma'am."

Phoenix approached me looking the best he had in . . . years. He was always presentable, well-groomed. Now that I saw him, I honestly missed him. Wasn't like we weren't together for four years. Wasn't as though Nya was ever missing.

"Hey, Dev," he said, sitting in the chair to my right. Across from me would've been better.

The wine arrived in time for me to redirect

my attention to the waiter.

"Sir," he said, gesturing to fill the second glass.

"Please," Phoenix said.

Sipping my liquid red velvet, this was not the time for me to speak. I stared at him. Tears clouded the love I still had for this man. I remained quiet. I had every reason to hate him, but I didn't. Disgust with what he'd done. That's what I felt.

He was silent. He propped his elbows on the white tablecloth, interlocked his fingers.

"What are we going to do?" Phoenix asked.

Softly, I said, "What would you like to do, Phoenix? Better yet, tell me what you would do if I were in your position and you were in mine?"

"Humph." He bit his knuckle. Exhaled.

He actually went from alluring to pathetic in one blink of my eyes. "Exactly. Until you figure it out, let me know where you'd like to have your belongings delivered."

If I were to forgive him now, he'd never respect me.

"I was put in an uncompromising position when I discovered you cut off all of my credit cards."

"So your coming here is about you? Not me? Not Nya?" My eyes scrolled in disgust toward the ceiling, then shifted to the corners at him. I took a gulp of my wine, wanting to throw the rest in his face. I placed my glass on the table, circled the rim with my fingertip.

"How long?" I asked.

"How long what?"

I screamed, "How long have you been fucking her? That's what?" If he wanted to play games, I could go there!

His eyelids stretched north and south. Agitated, I resumed tracing the rim of my glass with my fingertip. Started twirling a lock of my hair. I was angered on the inside. Doing all I could to suppress my slapping Phoenix's face.

"It doesn't matter. It's over between Goldie and I. I choose my family."

Just like that. "It's over, huh? So now what, Phoenix? Maybe I should ask your dick." I leaned my face in his lap. The tip of my nose touched his zipper. "How long have you been easing your way into Goldie Jackson's pussy?" My teeth clenched his shaft.

I hadn't planned on doing that. I wasn't sure what my intent was.

"Ow!" He pushed back from the table, snatched my hair. "Let go!"

The waiter rushed to us.

I sat up straight, opened my purse, looked

into my compact mirror. I touched up my hair, refreshed my chocolate lipstick.

"Is everything okay?"

"I'd like to have the snapper. Grilled. With asparagus. Please." I turned to Phoenix, then seductively asked, "What would you like, babe?"

"I'm good," he said.

I retorted, "No, you're not. But that's a separate discussion." I whispered, "Call me a bitch."

The waiter said, "Excuse me?"

I told him, "That'll be all for now. Thanks."

Phoenix became quiet.

Slightly below room tone, I hissed, "You took our daughter to her house. What were you thinking?"

"Can we talk about this when we get home?" he pleaded.

"Am I embarrassing you? Because I have to deal with your bitch being in my face every day. But I don't have to accept what you've done to our family."

He made a fist. Covered his mouth. My food arrived. I pushed the plate in front of him. "I ordered this for you."

"Dev, don't," he said, sliding the plate back to me.

At the same time I said, "Phoenix, tell me

what you want," I balled a piece of the filet into my palm, then shoved it in his mouth, smeared it over his lips. "You like eating fish?"

He spat it out. "Babe —"

I interrupted him. "You don't have the right to call me that anymore." My voice escalated. "Just tell me what you want from me!"

Suddenly, meeting publicly was a bad idea. More than half of my wine was in the glass. I was done drinking. I was tempted to douse the rest in his face. Sadly, I told my fiancé, "I hate you."

My mind raced, remembering hearing Ebony's voice, with having to take my little girl out of her house, with having to work with a woman who had probably fucked my fiancé more than I had.

"This isn't all my fault," he said.

So now he was the victim. "Perhaps you're right. I could've done some things differently. I could've sucked your dick more. Rode your dick more. Woke you up every morning sucking your dick? Is that it? My holding us, us, us, down didn't mean anything to you. I'm going to go now. It's too late for us, but I want you to have a healthy relationship with Nya. When the time is right. Give me time to process all of this."

I pushed back my chair. Phoenix grabbed my wrist.

"But, Dev," he said, then whispered, "I'll sleep in the guest room until we work this out. Don't abandon me the way my mother did. I have no place to go."

I placed Ebony's key in front of Phoenix. "Yes, you do. Yes, you do."

Chapter 61
Devereaux

The scent of snapper was heavy on my hand. My steering wheel was coated with seasonings. I parked in a visitor's space at Alexis's building.

Alexis greeted me at the security entrance on her floor. "You okay?"

"I'm good," I said, leading the way to her apartment.

"No, you're not. Ew, what's that smell?"

Ignoring my sister, I asked, "How was Nya?"

"My Princess Diva is all dolled up. Wait until you see her. I'm excited about my role in the series. You'll be proud to know, I enrolled in acting classes with Dwayne Boyd. What am I going to be doing?"

Entering the living room, James and Chanel were on the sofa. Nya was putting eye shadow on Chanel. I was still heated from meeting with Phoenix. I honestly didn't care where he laid his head or stuck his dick tonight.

"Told you she was a Princess Diva," Alexis said.

My family wasn't perfect. Far from it. But I did not know where I'd be without them.

Nya dropped the brush, ran to me. "Mommy!"

I held my arms away from her, gave her a kiss. "Get your things, Nya."

I washed my hands in the kitchen sink. "James. Chanel. How are you guys doing?"

They both answered, "Good," at the same time.

Not wanting to reveal my plan to have Alexis replace Ebony, I had to think things through. Maybe I overreacted by offering my sister a part. Ebony was up to six million followers on social media. Her husband, Buster, told me if I worked it out with Goldie, he'd finance the entire next series. Maybe Ebony had done me a favor. Being honest with myself, Ebony was not my problem. Phoenix was.

"Devereaux Crystal. Snap out of it," Alexis said, popping her finger.

"Yeah, smart decision," I agreed. "Dwayne is one of the best. You'll be a perfect fit for *Sophisticated Side Chicks ATL.*"

With proper coaching, Alexis was going to do well wherever I placed her. It would be interesting to see how money would change Alexis. I knew my sister well. Both James and Chanel, their morals would be compromised by Alexis now.

"Gurl, go home and get some rest," Alexis said, ushering us out the door.

Leaving Alexis's, I didn't want to go home. I texted Mercedes, Cool to stop by? I need to talk.

She replied right away, Sure come by. I was putting the kids to bed.

Nya cheered, "Yay!" from her car seat soon as I parked in Mercedes's driveway.

Welcoming us in, Mercedes said, "Have a seat. I'm going to give this one a quick bath and put her in the bed with Brandy."

"No," Nya protested. "I'm not sleepy."

I had to vent with someone who could relate. Alexis with her perfect trio wouldn't understand my concerns. Sandara was in London on the runway. My mom was traveling the world with Bing.

Happy people were sounding boards with no echo.

I kissed my baby good night. We both knew Nya would be knocked out as soon as Mercedes cleaned her up and tucked her in. I thanked my sister.

"No problem. Help yourself and pour me one, too."

A setup of two wineglasses and my favorite bottle was on the coffee table. I helped myself. Filled Mercedes's glass.

My sister sat close to me. I told her, "After meeting with Phoenix tonight, I can't take him back."

Mercedes asked, "What makes you so sure?"

"There was no love in his eyes for me. He wasn't remorseful. All Phoenix needs is someplace to lay his head. I'm done. What are you going to do?" I asked my sister.

"I can't do to my kids what Mother did to us. Benjamin still picks up the twins every morning. Takes them to school. Brings them home."

"And his other woman. Is he still in love with her?" I asked.

Mercedes looked at me. "What matters most is I'm still in love with my husband. And for my family that love is worth fighting for."

■ ■ ■ ■

A Reading Group Guide: Just Can't Let Go

MARY B. MORRISON

■ ■ ■ ■

About This Guide
The suggested questions that follow are included to enhance your group's reading of this book.

DISCUSSION QUESTIONS

1. Which character is your most favorite and least favorite? Why?

2. How would you feel if your father was listed as "unknown" on your birth certificate?

3. Which sex scene is the freakiest? Which one would you want to try? Which character would you sex and why?

4. Who's to blame for the problems in Devereaux and Phoenix's relationship? What about James and Alexis? Mercedes and Benjamin? Blake and Spencer?

5. Do you think inheriting 2.5 million dollars will change Alexis? If you received that amount of money, would it change you? If so, how?

6. Do you like Bing Sterling? Do you think he's a good partner for Blake? How long do you believe their relationship will last?

7. Would you like me to write a television series for *Sophisticated Side Chicks ATL*? If I do, it'll be scripted. Who do you think the four leading ladies should be?

8. Do you agree or disagree with Mercedes influencing her sister Devereaux to hire a private investigator to spy on Phoenix? Would you have done the same? Why or why not?

9. Do you believe every woman can squirt? Have you squirted before? Is the squirt watch that Bing had on real?

10. Why do you think Conner Rogers left everything to Alexis Crystal and nothing to Spencer Domino?

11. Will Alexis ever stop lying? Do you feel she's a good fit for her sister's show, *Sophisticated Side Chicks ATL*? Why or why not?

12. Is Ebony Waterhouse, aka Goldie Jackson, wise for marrying a seventy-one-year-

old man for his money and for American citizenship? If Goldie has to legally marry someone else to prevent being deported to Colombia, should she marry Phoenix?

13. If you could squeeze in between the pages of *Just Can't Let Go,* where would it be and why?